Reader reviews from the first book in
The Dreamer saga
The Dreamer ~ THE BEGINNING

The Dreamer- the Beginning is a captivating tale, giving a convincing and passionate voice to a young man from humankind's early history. It is well researched and based on scientific study, lending additional credence to a very creative story involving a time in our history that is very much shrouded in mystery and conjecture.~ N. I. Bourdeau

Fascinating saga of the times and life amid a Neanderthal family as seen from the perspective of a man with a special gift and a love of his family. It's just like being there; you become involved with their trials and joys. The dreams give you a glimpse of future dangers and events, leading you through an engrossing journey. ~ C. H. Beusee

This is not the usual type of book that I read but I was fascinated and could not put it down. The author did so much research that it felt like I was reading a true story of a family and how they lived during that time! I wish the author could write faster so I could get my hands on those next ones...keep them coming!~ L. B. Collins

This is a unique and interesting read. I couldn't put it down–almost missed my flight! ~ J. Simmons

I read this book and thoroughly enjoyed it...so exciting that you can't put it down. Kept me on the edge of my seat. Great writing. ~ J. Stuller

The Dreamer III

೧೩

THE PEOPLE OF THE WOLVES

By E. A. Meigs

Dreamer Literary Productions, LLC

2018

For information regarding this novel or permissions
to reproduction selections from this work, please visit
Dreamer Literary Productions at:
www.dreamerliteraryproductions.com

ISBN: 978-0-9981259-6-1

 First Edition

Cover photo by my friend, Paula Krugerud
www.PaulaKrugerudPhotography.com

This book is dedicated with much love
to my daughters.

 Fonts used in this novel

Papyrus was created by Chris Costello in 1982.

Garamond was designed by Claude Garamond in the early 1530's.

The Dreamer III

ɷƷ୧ꙥ

THE PEOPLE
OF THE
WOLVES

 **Introduction**

When the last Ice Age was well underway approximately 40,000 BCE (Before Common Era), nearly one-third of the earth's surface was hidden beneath a thick layer of ice. Since a substantial percentage of the planet's moisture was frozen solid, the world's oceans receded and coastlines were greatly expanded. At that time the Eurasian landscape consisted of vast wind-scoured tundra and small pockets of woodland which were populated by at least three groups of people: the Neanderthals, the Denisovans, and the Cro-Magnons. These populations probably coexisted in parts of Europe and Asia for only a relatively short period of time, geologically speaking. They lived a seasonally nomadic lifestyle, and each hunted the same game. We can only guess at what their lives would have been like: their languages, their social behaviors, their spirituality. Due to the passage of time and the impermanent nature of most materials they would have used in their day-to-day lives, little endures to tell us about their existence besides the tantalizing clues left by their remains, their tools, their art, their burials, and . . . their refuse.

Analyses of fossilized Neanderthal skeletons show that the males averaged five feet, five inches to five feet, six inches; the tallest Neanderthal man found to date was five feet, nine inches, and the females were five feet to five feet, one inch. Their bones were about one-third stouter than ours. They were heavily muscled and had tremendous upper-body strength. The Neanderthals had the largest brain size of any known humans. Initial DNA tests showed that they likely had fair coloring: red to auburn hair, green or hazel eyes, and pale, probably freckled skin. Later genetic research on Neanderthal individuals found in different parts of Eurasia revealed that some had brown hair, brown eyes, and dusky skin.

The Neanderthals roamed the earth for roughly 200,000 years before their trail went cold around 37,000 to 42,000 BCE. That said, the Neanderthals may have persisted to eke out a living for some time after that, but we have no evidence of it at this writing. However, since most modern humans outside of sub-Saharan Africa share between 1 percent and 4 percent Neanderthal DNA, it is almost certain that the Neanderthals are with us even now, albeit in diluted form.

The Cro-Magnons first appeared in the European fossil record around 42,000 to 47,000 BCE. Over a period of tens of thousands of years, they migrated from Africa, gradually making their way into Eurasia. They were anatomically constructed more or less the same as most modern men and women. Cro-Magnon men averaged about five feet, nine inches in height, but it is thought that some taller individuals may have been upwards of six feet, five inches. Like the Neanderthals, their brains were also bigger than those of today's people. They are believed to have had dark coloring: dark brown to black hair, brown eyes, and tan or olive-toned skin. (Blond hair and blue eyes are a relatively new development in modern humans, having first appeared about 6,000 to 12,000 years ago, long after the pinnacle of the Ice Age, but possibly coinciding with the end of that last great glacial period.)

This novel introduces the Denisovans to the book series. Not much is known of these people at this time. What little information we have comes from three teeth and one very tiny finger bone. The physical characteristics of the finger bone suggest that the Denisovans were a sturdy people, perhaps with a build resembling that of the Neanderthals. The teeth, on the other hand, were quite large, about one-third bigger than that of either the average modern human or Neanderthal. We might then surmise that they probably had a heavy jaw to accommodate those teeth. DNA from the finger bone disclosed that it was taken from someone with dark hair, brown eyes, and brown skin.

When we consider the artifacts that have been attributed to the Denisovans, it must be acknowledged that they were an intelligent, skilled folk. Their needles (dated to approximately 60,000 BCE) look much like our needles of today. A bracelet of green stone shows that they had sufficient technology to drill holes and to shape and polish stone. We can only hope that further discoveries bring us more data on these intriguing people.

* * *

This is a work of fiction and not intended to hold up to scientific scrutiny. I merely seek to tell a story set amidst this ancient backdrop and peopled with those whose lives – when broken down to their most basic elements – would not have been so different from ours.

I believe that after so many years existing in a world that often presented extreme challenges, these intelligent beings would have been at the top of their game in leveraging the available resources to ensure their own comfort and the continuation of their species. The evidence suggests that early man was potentially much more advanced than is generally credited and it is my guess that we will continue to be surprised by what is revealed when ongoing and future anthropological studies peel back layers of time as we search for ourselves within our ancestors' past.

Chapter One

We are surrounded. The large furry bodies lope through the forest, their wild cries piercing the balmy spring air...

My life as a Dreamer began well over a year ago. The first Dream came to me as a terrifying vision of my father and uncle as they were charged by an aggressive cave bear. I knew right away that it was not a typical dream. This one was startlingly vivid. It was as though I was there, witnessing the scene for myself. I smelled the grasses as they were crushed underfoot and the fetid odor of the beast. I felt the rush of wind as the bear brushed past me, its roar a deafening bellow that rang painfully in my ears.

This new Dream had been repeating itself off and on for almost a moon now, and it contained the same stark clarity. I was unnerved by the event it seemed to portray: an impending wolf attack. I had survived several wolf attacks, but my younger brother Dak had not. Whenever I saw a wolf, the mental picture of Dak making his lonely stand against the hungry pack was never far from my mind. This Dream was trying to tell me something, but what?

Our dog Raena looked at me attentively. She was seldom far from me while I was home, and she intuitively knew when I was experiencing a Dream. I motioned to her that she could lie down and relax so she knew everything was all right. Raena obediently sank down to the floor, sighing deeply as though to signal her ease.

My mate Morning Star stirred slightly in her sleep. Her tawny skin and glossy black hair appeared lustrous even in the dim firelight. I snuggled closer to her, kissing her forehead softly. The act brought a smile to her lips.

"I thought you were asleep," I whispered to her so as not to awaken our son, who dozed nearby in his bed.

"I was, my dear Tris," Morning Star whispered back. "But then your movements roused me from my slumbers."

"I am sorry to disturb you," I said as I ran my hand along the curves of her face. I was ever-conscious of my good fortune to be paired with this woman, so long desired and so hard won.

The Dreamer III ~ The People of the Wolves

We were of two peoples: my family belonged to the Old Ones clan, those who many considered to be ignoble and primitive, while my beloved was of The People from the East's tribe. When her father had allowed us to be paired, I promised him that I would always do my best by her, and I intended to stand by that vow.

Morning Star's only reply was to kiss me warmly on the lips. She had a way of making my Dreams fade to oblivion.

* * *

Sometime later, our son's waking whimpers brought us out of our blissful state of post-coupling and Morning Star pulled away from me, but not before caressing my bearded cheek and giving me one last kiss. I arose as well, to attend to the dying fire. We donned a few layers of clothing and then tugged on and laced boots around our lower legs. Winter had passed and the season of mild days was upon us, but mornings were still quite cold. The sun had arisen, weak in strength but bright enough to turn the early morning sky fiery shades of pink and orange. We ventured outside to purge our bladders of the night's accumulation. Then I drew water from the little creek that wandered across the landscape near our home. Morning Star returned indoors to gather up our now squalling and squirming infant, who was eager to be fed. He was five moons old, and he was a hale and hardy child.

"Little Fox, you are growing so big," Morning Star cooed to him as he nursed. "I do not think I have ever seen a baby so large!" Fox paused from nursing just long enough to grin at his mother. "He is smiling at me," Morning Star said as she gazed at him fondly, completely entranced by her cherished boy. I hoped she was not disappointed that her son did not resemble her in the least. He owned a stout build and he was red-haired and fair-skinned, just like me. There was no sign of her fine-boned frame, silky black hair, dark eyes, or tan-colored flesh. But Morning Star was already pregnant with our next child. Maybe this one would take after her. I did not really care what our children looked like, as long as they were healthy. My only wish was to spend my days with the woman I treasured more than life itself. She had been my first and only love from the time I was a boy. Yet there was a time when I had given up hope of ever being allowed to take her as my mate. It was only due to my first Dream that the lucky event had come to pass.

"Tris, you are looking thoughtful," Morning Star said. She placed Fox in my lap as she began to assemble our breakfast.

Fox stared into my face, as he often did, touching my beard as though it were some sort of oddity – perchance an animal that had decided to take up residence there. I had to watch his hands carefully, since he was apt to grab fistfuls of whiskers and yank them with an impressive strength for one so small.

"What has you so deep in thought?" Morning Star persisted.

"I was just pondering how lucky I am to have you," I told her. "Every time I set eyes on you, I am overwhelmed by the idea that you are my mate."

Morning Star gave me a dazzling smile. I returned her smile, catching her hand as she walked by and giving it a gentle squeeze.

"Well, my dear Tris," she began. "I believe that I am lucky, too. We have love, we have each other, we have our baby and another on the way, and our families are close by. What more could we want? Except maybe more babies."

"I will do my best to ensure that those babies arrive at regular intervals," I promised her lightheartedly.

"I have no doubt that you will," Morning Star laughed. "I expect to have a big brood, and I will need you to do your part!"

"We were meant to be together, and we were meant to bring our children into the world. I Dream about a group of children sometimes, and they always seem to be on some sort of mission."

Morning Star shrugged. She had heard me speak of this Dream before.

"Most children are up to something at most times," she said, "unless they are dullards. But I do agree that we were meant to be together. How else could such an unlikely pairing have taken place, unless it was fated to happen? I despaired for years that my mother and my Da would ever consider you for my mate. I am grateful that your first Dream led you to approach my Da about going in search of your Puh and your uncle. You and Da not only rescued your Puh, but then you saved my Da and in gratitude, he offered to let you have me. That was the most fortuitous day of my life. Well, that day and the day you won me from Snow Leopard."

"Yes, my life, too," I said as I leaned in to buss her cheek.

Snow Leopard was the famous hunter of The People who had asked for Morning Star while her father and I were venturing after my Puh. Morning Star was promised to him in her father's absence, since the rest of her family did not know that I had already been granted the right to pair with her. The only resolution to this unexpected state of affairs was to fight Snow Leopard in the Challenge Circle. I was younger, stronger, and heavier than Snow Leopard, but he was taller and much more experienced at fighting; up to that time, I had never hit anyone in anger in my entire life. All the same, I won. Not because I was a good fighter, but simply because Snow Leopard did not know how to counter my ineptness and brute strength. The last hurdle to beginning our lives together took place when Snow Leopard, unsatisfied with the results of the bout, stole Morning Star from our pairing ceremony. Puh, Morning Star's father Black Wolf, and

The Dreamer III – The People of the Wolves

I managed to get her back, but only after tracking Snow Leopard and his band of cronies for several days. This time, I did not leave Snow Leopard alive. I was taking no chances that this man would ever come after my mate again.

* * *

Morning Star was now placing sliced dried meats and fish on a birch-bark platter, which she set on the floor mats between us. Raena looked upon the platter with naked hunger apparent on her face. Morning Star had not forgotten the dog. She gave Raena a few slabs of dried seal meat, and Raena retreated from our semicircle around the hearth to a quiet corner where she could gnaw on her breakfast in peace.

Our gnawing on the dried flesh was scarcely less laborious. After a long winter, our stores consisted mostly of dried meats and fish, and very limited amounts of roasted shelled nuts, now somewhat rancid in taste, dried mushrooms and herbs, and well-wrinkled apples that barely resembled the hard round fruits harvested last autumn. These days, our meals were uninteresting occasions that required much tedious chewing.

"I never thought I would miss eating seeds and grains," Morning Star spoke up. "Your dear Aunt Vee took wonderful care of your youngest siblings after your mother passed, but I am afraid that she used up every bit of the family's seeds and grains in making her delicious honey seed cakes for them."

I nodded. This was true. Aunt Vee loved children and she excelled at food preparation, which combined to make for a passel of well-fed and spoiled youngsters while she was here.

"Aunt Vee was so good to us all. I am looking forward to seeing her and my cousins in a moon or so when we make our annual trek to the coast to make our summer harvests of fish, seal meat, and berries, and to gather a new collection of shells. Many of our shell bowls are cracked now," I said between breaking off and chewing bites of meat. Fox avidly watched my hand as it bore food to and from my mouth, his mouth falling slightly agape whenever mine opened, like a little bird expecting to be fed by its mother. I removed a tiny morsel of masticated meat and placed it in his mouth. Fox pushed the tidbit around with his tongue with a curious expression on his face. "Get used to it," I told him. "You will be eating a lot of this in the years to come."

"Let me have him, Tris," Morning Star said, holding out her hands for Fox. But I shook my head.

"Finish eating first."

I had always observed that my Puh kept the family's newest baby in his lap until Muh had a chance to take in nourishment. Puh was my mentor, and I was determined to carry on with his habit. Morning Star knew this, but she was eager to hold her baby again. She hastily finished eating and reached for Fox once more.

"I am ready for my little Fox now." Fox smiled at being restored to his mother's arms. "Tris, you are so much like your Puh. And with luck, Fox will be just like you."

"You do not wish that he will be like you, too?" I asked.

"No," Morning Star said firmly. "I am little. He will need to be big and strong like you to survive to an old age."

"You may be small, but you are definitely a force to be reckoned with." My voice was tinged with a hint of jest. My petite mate was capable of wreaking great havoc when she chose to, and her sweet tongue could fling barbs whenever she was adequately riled. I was grateful that she was unfailingly loving and mild-tempered toward me. Just the same, I took care not to provoke her anger.

"Ha!" Morning Star laughed. "You are mistaking me for your Puh's new mate, Ria. If there was ever a person I would call a *force to be reckoned with*, it is she! The little huntress brought back from the wild!"

As usual, Morning Star was right. After my Muh passed, Puh had eventually become paired with a tiny waif of a woman we discovered living in a collapsed hovel deep in the forest. There she had lived alone following the death of her own mate, almost four years prior. She survived by taking down modest-sized prey with her small bow and arrows. These hunting tools were new to me, and at first and she guarded them jealously. It was only recently that she had allowed us to investigate them and showed us how to make the little spears fly into the air. Ria was now six moons pregnant, but the condition did not seem to slow her down or impair her in the least.

I thought on the state of our food stores. We would need to hunt soon. Our families had been involved in the construction of a home for Morning Star's parents and siblings, which meant that we had not gone after fresh meat for quite some time. But now that the home was completed and newly occupied, we would probably embark on a hunt in the next few days. My thoughts were disrupted by a hallooing outside our domicile.

"Mama!" Morning Star went to the doorway and waved her mother inside. "Come in, Mama. We have just finished eating. Would you like to have something to eat?"

Morning Star's mother, Little Fawn, shook her head awkwardly as she stood stooped in the entryway to our home. Little Fawn, like her mate, Black Wolf, was enormously tall – so tall that she could barely stand fully upright in our little home, even in the places where our ceilings were at their loftiest.

"No thank you, Morning Star. We have had our breakfast already. I have come up to see Fox, if I may."

Morning Star obligingly placed Fox in her mother's arms.

"Of course, Mama. He loves to visit with his dear Grandmama."

* * *

Last winter Little Fawn had requested that Black Wolf move their household from its former location a half-day's hike away so she could be closer to us. But we suspected it was primarily so that she could be nearer her first grandchild. Nevertheless, we were glad to have them living in an annex to our family compound, which had steadily grown over the past year. Up until then, it consisted of the main family domicile where I and many earlier generations of my kin were born and raised. Later, my Great Gran's small dwelling was built and there she had resided until Morning Star and I became paired. Then Great Gran moved in with my parents and siblings, and Morning Star and I took up residence in her old abode. After Muh tragically passed during a miscarriage, Puh could no longer bear to live in his lifelong home. So we built a small one-room earth-bermed house for him, which he now very happily inhabited with Ria. The home of Black Wolf, Little Fawn, and their multitude of children and dogs almost doubled the size of the family compound. It felt a little crowded for those of us who were used to the old configuration, but no one complained. Black Wolf had been Puh's closest friend since boyhood. He and Puh had continued to be steadfast chums, frequently hunting together and often traveling back and forth to each other's homes to socialize and trade goods. Now that Morning Star's kin lived nearby, there was no more need to trek all that way to see each other. This made things easier and more pleasant for all of us.

Little Fawn tenderly stroked the baby's cheek and then began to kiss him, as he gurgled with delight.

"Where is that woman of mine?" Black Wolf's voice boomed from somewhere outside our doorway. I arose from my comfortable seat by the fire and exited our home, with Raena trotting alongside me. Black Wolf was coming up the path from the main compound. Raena barked at him, wagging her tail with happy recognition. Black Wolf's long strides soon covered the distance between us.

"Pleasant day to you, Black Wolf," I welcomed him.

"Pleasant day to you, Tris. Is Little Fawn up here? I was just bringing in firewood and suddenly she was gone. I checked the creek to see if she was fetching water but did not find her there. That confounded woman ..."

"I can hear you!" Little Fawn announced loudly from the inner confines of my dwelling.

Black Wolf groaned.

"That confounded woman may as well have ears like a rabbit ..."

"It is not as though I could possibly *not* hear you!" Little Fawn interrupted again.

Black Wolf groaned once more, his deep rumbling bass sounding almost like a growl. This was a fairly typical conversation for them. Most pairings were not bonded with love. They were merely a way to ensure the continuation of the family line, and in Black Wolf and Little Fawn's case, they had been paired simply because Black Wolf was the only man available who was actually taller than Little Fawn. They bickered and sometimes barely tolerated each other, but I hoped that they also managed to find a contentment of sorts in spite of it all.

"You are settled into your new home?" I inquired, ignoring their contentious words.

"Yes," Black Wolf nodded, "for the most part. What do you think about getting out to hunt? We have not been out in over a moon. Our stores are low. I imagine that yours are, too. And your Puh's."

"Yes," I acknowledged. "We are all low on food. Especially after I found that a large portion of the tubers we had put up for the winter went bad and had to be thrown away. If it were not for the patches of winter leeks, we would have had very few vegetables to eat until spring."

"Let us go and talk with your Puh. Little Fawn will not return home until after she has finished snuggling that infant of yours, so I will leave her undisturbed for now."

Morning Star came out to greet her father. She tiptoed to kiss Black Wolf on the side of his face, simultaneously pulling him down to her height so she could reach him.

"Hello, Da," Morning Star smiled up at him, "did you come to see the baby, too?"

Black Wolf grinned back at her. Morning Star was his eldest child, and she had always been his favorite. Despite the disparity in their sizes, in some ways Morning Star resembled her father more than she did her mother, who was exceedingly plain and had a lumpish matronly figure. Black Wolf, on the other hand, was a strikingly good-looking man. He owned a strong well-formed face and a keen intellect. But unlike Morning Star, he chose to wear his hair in a series of stiff braids that sprouted out of the top of his head, making him appear as though he were wearing a giant spider for a hat. Also unlike Morning Star, he was excessively hairy.

"No," Black Wolf replied, "I came to find your mother! I was stacking firewood and thought I was having a conversation with her, and then I suddenly realized that no one was answering me. So I came to find where she had gone to." He muttered under his breath, *the confounded woman left me talking to myself!* Then he continued, "But now that I am here, I will speak with Tris about our next hunting trip. We will need to bring Tor into this, too … and probably his Ria, as well, since she will hardly let him out of her sight."

"Ria had a rough time for a long while," Morning Star interjected. "She waited and waited for her man to come home, eking out a living as best she could on her own. I do not blame her for wanting to keep Tor close by. Particularly now that she is pregnant. She does not want to lose another mate – especially not the father of her child."

Black Wolf laughed gruffly, shaking his head.

"*Lose Tor?* He is the toughest, most resourceful, and most resilient man I have ever known! He will probably outlive us all!"

I had to agree. My Puh had persevered through many trials in his thirty-three winters of life. His lean, scarred physique was a testament to the vast number of dangers he had faced and surmounted.

"I certainly hope that Puh has many good years ahead," I concurred. I turned to Morning Star. "We are going down to talk to Puh," I told her. "I will soon be back." I brushed her lips with a quick kiss and watched her return indoors to rejoin her mother and our little Fox. I motioned to Raena to follow her in. If I was not home, even if I was only going a little way down the hill to the family compound, I always left the dog with Morning Star. I knew that Raena would guard Morning Star and Fox with her life.

* * *

Black Wolf accompanied me on the short walk downhill to the family compound, where we found that our combined families were starting their day's chores under sunny skies, serenaded by a number of birds that flitted through the trees. Puh was hafting tiny stone points to arrow shafts for Ria as she sat next to him, piecing together a selection of small pelts.

"Those are some very fine furs," Black Wolf said to Ria. "Are you making a coverlet for your baby?" Although Black Wolf had recently mocked Ria's concern for Puh, he was genuinely fond of her and admired her spirit.

Ria looked up at Black Wolf with a grin.

"Yes, I am. I never thought I would have a child, but now that Tor has given me one, I want to be sure it will be well cared for."

Puh beamed at Ria and paused from his labors to gently touch her hand.

"We will be sure of that indeed," he said quietly.

"For now, that means bringing in fresh meat!" Black Wolf stated.

"I have been considering that very thing," Puh said with a nod. "Perhaps we could leave tomorrow for a quick jaunt north. The deer and the elk will be busily feeding now that the leaves are on the trees and the grass is growing. We just may be able to flush a few out of the brush."

"We could always trek out to the grasslands and try to bag some ibex or young wisents. Maybe a horse. A horse would give us plenty of food for the time being," Black Wolf said. "Although, I must say, I would forgo the hike if I could. My feet have never recovered from those days of running after Snow Leopard when he absconded with Morning Star."

I glanced down at Black Wolf's feet, which, like the rest of him, were huge. I could imagine that if the pain was proportionate in size, it would be considerable.

Puh stood, brushing off his hands. He was of average height for a man of the Old Ones, but the top of his head reached only the middle Black Wolf's chest. Puh looked Black Wolf up and down.

"Well, I am not going to carry you, so we will have to stay closer to home," Puh said softly, but he had a twinkle in his eyes. "Besides, I do not want to make Ria walk that far, either. I think we can make do with local hunting and foraging until we leave for the coast. We will have another chance to go after deer during the rutting season."

"*Carry me?*" Black Wolf repeated. "While I have seen you heft a deer that must have been about my weight, I may be a bit more lanky in build. I think my arms and legs would likely drag on the ground." Black Wolf then turned to look at me just as I was thinking that it was also possible Black Wolf was nearly as furry as any deer. "We know that Tris can manage my bulk. You would not like to carry your mate's old Da around would you, Tris?" Black Wolf laughed, but then he suddenly became serious. "You are the only reason I am still walking above ground. I will never forget hanging over the abyss of that spiked bear trap ... what could have happened if you had not held onto me ... I am thankful to you every day, Tris."

I was pleased that Black Wolf still appreciated my rescue of him. He had not mentioned it since it had happened. In truth, I did not think it was a remarkable feat; I had done nothing but keep him from falling into the deep pit, whereas he had given me his favorite child as my mate. The two deeds hardly seemed comparable.

"You have given me much to be grateful for, as well," I replied.

Puh smiled at this exchange.

"We are all glad you are still walking above ground, Black Wolf," Puh said. "I am sorry that your feet pain you, though. But we have a good supply of arrows now. We could start out for the river tomorrow morning and roost in perches to await whatever animal happens by. You would not need to spend much time on your feet."

Ria struggled to rise. Puh grasped Ria's hands to assist her. She still had three moons left to her pregnancy and she was extraordinarily round, even for one in her condition. Ria had carefully listened to our conversation. Puh put an arm around her shoulders as she stood next to him.

"Yes, I can be ready to go early in the day," Ria said, always eager to hunt.

This made sense. Not long after Ria came to us, we discovered that her skill with a bow and arrow made hunting much easier than it was when we were limited to striking prey with our spears. Ria's arrows were too small to take down large animals, but she often managed to wound them badly enough that we could track and kill them, without the need to ambush the beast at close range. And, as Puh said, there would be no need to venture any great distance from home.

Just then, my youngest sisters, four-winters-old Saree and two-winters-old Mi, came out of the old family abode. Saree carried her doll Hork casually tucked under one arm and held Mi by the hand. They approached us and came to a stop in front of me.

"Tris, will you bring Fox down to see us?" Saree asked. "We would like to play with him. Babies are so much fun! That is why I like to pretend that Hork is my baby."

"Fox!" Mi piped up. "Play with Fox!"

Hork was a doll made of baked clay, molded by Saree herself. It was a rather homely creation, with deep-set eyes and a maniacally leering grin. Last summer Saree had persuaded Puh to glue onto Hork's head an assortment of real hair, which was now matted and tangled, only adding to the doll's deranged demeanor.

"Fox is too young to play just yet," I said to Saree, noting her look of disappointment. "But he will be ready to play with his aunt soon enough."

"Can he not play with me, too?" Saree inquired solemnly.

"You *are* his aunt," I informed her. "You and your sisters are all Fox's aunts. And Ty is her uncle.

And Morning Star's sisters and brothers are also Fox's aunts and uncles, too. Do you understand?"

Saree looked perplexed.

"What is Puh-Puh to Fox?" she asked.

"His grandfather," I replied.

"What is Black Wolf to Fox?"

"Also his grandfather," I answered.

"What is Little Fawn to Fox?" "His grandmother," I said.

"Is Hork an aunt to Fox?"

"No. Hork is a doll." I told her gently. "If Hork has any relatives, you must make them from clay, also."

Saree brightened at this idea.

"I will do just that! When we go to the beach this summer, I will dig out lots more clay and I will make a family for Hork! Why did I not think of that before? Many thanks, Tris!" she exclaimed.

Puh lifted up Saree and Mi, each in one arm.

"Well," he said to them, "you know the way this family is growing, you will have lots of new playmates before long."

"Play with Fox!" Mi said again.

"No, Mi-Mi. Fox is too little," Saree shook her head. "Let us go and play with Hork. Hork will be our baby for now."

Puh set them down again, and they ambled off to a pile of small stones that Saree had collected and deposited near the outdoor hearth. The little girls then took turns "feeding" the pebbles to Hork.

"Would not life be easier if people could eat rocks, too?" Ria said thoughtfully. "Then we would not have to hunt or forage any more. Just pick up our food from the ground."

"That might be easier, but they would be tough on the teeth and their taste would probably leave a lot to be desired," Puh observed.

 **Chapter Two**

They were running. Running all around us, all the while making odd whooping sounds.

I was perplexed by this Dream. I had never known wolves to produce such utterances. These wolves were very strange. Some of their cries were almost birdlike, rather than canine. And why were their visits to my Dreams so frequent as of late?

But I had little time to ponder this curiosity. We needed to devote most of our efforts to bringing in fresh foods, whether meat from hunts or foraged greens collected from the nearby landscape. What with the gradual lengthening of each spring day and the availability of newly harvested victuals, we all felt emotionally uplifted as we embraced this new season.

It would not be long before we began our preparations to make our annual journey to the coast.

The Dreamer III – The People of the Wolves

There we would spend a moon or two, or however long it took to garner enough foodstuffs to fill our travois sled. The two-day trek included a stopover at my Aunt Vee's domicile, where we could enjoy a visit with her and my cousins. I always looked forward to spending time with them. On the journey homeward, we would again stay with our kin and trade some of the foods we collected in exchange for the meat my cousins brought in during the spring reindeer migration.

I hoped we would leave soon. I was eager to make our trip to the shore and back before Morning Star's pregnancy became too advanced. She would give birth to this child sometime in the fall of this year and I worried that the long hike would be too strenuous for her. My Muh had passed away during a miscarriage shortly after we returned from the coast and she had been a strong, healthy woman. My Morning Star was dainty in comparison, and I feared that the journey would be hard on her. Under no circumstances did I want to expose her to any unnecessary risks. I considered staying home, but Morning Star insisted that she would be fine. Besides, this year her parents and siblings would accompany us to the seaside for the first time, and Morning Star really wanted all of us to be there together.

All of us, that is, except my Great Gran and my thirteen-winters-old brother Ty, who would stay at the family compound with my family's elderly dog, Rooph.

Both Gran and Rooph were too frail to make the long trip, so Ty would remain with them until our return. We Old Ones reach physical maturity at a younger age than The People from the East do, but Ty was still a few years away from being considered an adult. All the same, he was levelheaded, capable, and quite large for his age. Ty was already as tall as Puh.

This trek weighed heavily on Puh, too. His new mate Ria was further along in her pregnancy than Morning Star, and Ria was both smaller and much older than she. But Ria stubbornly assured Puh that she too would be able to make the journey without enduring any undue hardship.

* * *

The next morning as I ventured out to fill one of our water bags at the stream, I met with Great Gran. She was gathering tender new leaves of watercress that grew on the banks of the gently flowing rivulet. The gurgle of moving water was cheerful, and a multitude of ever-present birds sang from nearby trees.

The subject of our upcoming foray to the beach came up in conversation.

"You must be looking forward to sitting on warm sands and feeling the sun on your skin," Gran said to me.

"Yes," I nodded, "Morning Star is also looking forward to showing her family all the novelties they will experience there. She delighted in being at the shore last summer and she cannot wait to get back there. I just hope the long walk will not be too much for her."

Gran smiled and nodded. Gran was a Dreamer, too. It was said that I had inherited my ability to Dream through her. Gran was a little eccentric, but she was also quite astute. She understood Dreams much better than I; she always seemed to instinctively sense what for most people would be the unknowable.

"You forget that you have foreseen that you and Morning Star will have many children. She will be fine." Great Gran reminded me.

"That is true," I admitted, "but I cannot help feeling concern for her. Puh worries for Ria, too."

Gran nodded once more.

"Yes," she said after a pause, "he has good reason to worry after what happened to your poor Muh. Ria is much older than most first-time mothers, but she is a vigorous little scrap of a thing, and if I guess right, she will bear up and do so without complaint."

I felt much relief at hearing Gran's words.

"Have you Dreamt about this?" I asked.

"Yes, I have," Gran replied. "Have you not seen these visions for yourself? A vision of the future? And of those who will follow us, those who will carry on long after I am gone?"

"Gran, please do not talk that way. I do not want to think about a time when you are no longer with us."

Great Gran suddenly seemed tired. She sank to her knees and knelt by the rushing stream. I stood in the icy ankle-deep waters and watched her carefully, looking for signs of illness.

"Gran, do you feel unwell?" I inquired, stepping nearer to her until I was close enough to put a hand on her shoulder.

Gran looked up at me, her eyes boring into mine. She did not speak for a moment.

"Tris," she finally said, "I know one should not prize one child or grandchild over another ... but you have always been my favorite great-grandchild. You have a kind heart. You see things that many others do not, and I do not refer only to your Dreams. No, I am not ailing. I am simply feeling my age. Now and then the weight of all my years presses down upon me and I feel as though I cannot stand for one moment longer."

"Let me help you make your way home," I offered. "I can carry you, if you cannot walk."

Gran grinned a gap-toothed smile.

"Many thanks, Tris, but I am not yet unable to walk. You may help me to my feet, though, if you please."

I set down my water bag and took both of Great Gran's hands, her skin feeling so cool and dry to the touch, and gently raised her to a standing position.

"Come, Gran. I will carry your bundle of watercress for you and escort you home," I offered as we began the short walk toward the family compound. "Did you know," I continued, "that you have always been my favorite great-grandmother?" She was, in fact, the only grandparent I had ever known. All the others had perished before I could become acquainted with them. Great Gran chuckled silently, as we Old Ones do.

"You are teasing me," she said. "But I love you, anyway."

"And I love you, too, Gran," I responded, giving her hand a squeeze.

* * *

The next day began a little earlier than usual, as Puh, Ria, Black Wolf, and I set out in search of deer. We hiked toward an out-of-the-way pond we seldom visited. Our deer-hunting plans soon changed after we saw signs of a sounder visiting this small swampy body of water. Sounders are groups of boars comprising sows and youngsters of varying ages that often spend the day sleeping as they recover from the previous night's foraging. The boars' eyesight did not seem to be very keen, but their sense of hearing was quite sharp. Whenever possible we liked to use Black Wolf's dogs to help corner these animals, but this time, as we attempted to stealthily creep up on the dozing beasts, we were glad to have left the dogs at home. We hoped to track the animals to their nests and possibly surprise a young sow as she slept.

A light steady rain helped to mask the sounds of our movements as the moisture dripped from the new spring foliage and fell to the earth below. We did not speak, communicating only by reading one another's facial expressions or by hand motions.

Except for the pitter-patter of falling rain, everything was still as we neared the place where the boars slumbered. Suddenly the dense brush seemed to come alive with agitated animals. A small sounder consisting of three sows and a collection of shoats burst from the thicket. We were not unduly alarmed since these creatures paid little heed to our presence and ran off to our left. Then, a series of loud howls came to our ears. We froze in our tracks, briefly exchanging glances before taking up defensive positions. If we were facing an imminent wolf attack, it was best to stand back to back so that we could fend them off. I guessed the wolves had managed to kill one of the sows and were celebrating their success … but something about their cries was not quite right.

At that moment, a wounded sow emerged from the thicket at a limping run, leaving a trail of blood behind her. The wolves were at her heels, but oddly, only one pursued the sow. The rest retreated into the brush at the sight of us, where they continued to call out to one another as they noisily conferred and pushed their way through the protection of the forest's undergrowth. I could just see glimpses of their upright ears and furry bodies as one would dash through a gap in the foliage.

This was a large pack, and its behavior was strange, to say the least. The wolves maintained their cover in the brush as they circled us, as they usually do when they are assessing potential prey. But they did not take steps to close in for an assault. The wolves seemed confused at our presence.

Puh, Black Wolf, and I held our spears at the ready while Ria armed her little bow with an arrow, holding several more arrows within the fingers of her right hand. I noted that Puh's eyes followed the movement of the wolves closely.

"These are not wolves," Puh said in a whisper, but he did not lower his spear.

"What are they, Puh?" I asked.

"Look how they are gathering over there. They are breaking off their attack to talk to one another," Puh replied.

"*Talk?*" Black Wolf repeated. "If they are not wolves, then what are they? I saw their faces … their ears … their tails! Granted, they are peculiar wolves, but what else could they be?"

"Men," Puh said simply.

"Huh?" Black Wolf looked at Puh as though he had lost his mind. I, too, wondered at Puh's answer.

A brief silence descended upon the woodlands. Even the birds had become mute. The slow drizzle became a strong torrent. A moment later, the group of harriers, maybe twelve to fourteen in number, stepped forward until they had fully exposed themselves to us.

The "wolves" stood upright. They were, in fact, men, just as Puh had said. They were built much like us Old Ones, but their skin was swarthy, of a hue similar to that of a tanned hide, and covered with charcoal-colored lines, shapes, and markings. Their fierce eyes were dark brown. I could not see their hair, as it was not visible under their wolfskin head coverings and cloaks, but their closely shorn beards were black. It looked as though their cloaks were made up of a largely intact wolfskin. The wolves' heads sat atop their pates and the front legs draped over their shoulders, the forepaws dangling by their chests. The rest of the wolf bodies rode over the top of their packs, while the tails hung down behind.

"You were right, Tor," Black Wolf admitted. "But now what do we do? They seem very puzzled by us."

"No more so than we are by them," Puh acknowledged. "Ria, do not shoot them."

Puh was wise to give Ria this advice. In the past she had proved to be a fast and accurate archer, but it did not take much to prompt her into action.

"My love, I will not shoot them," Ria promised, "… yet."

Puh gave her a small smile as he eyed her staring down the shaft of her poised arrow. Ria, small and very pregnant, might appear deceptively vulnerable, but she was far from defenseless. She feared nothing except losing my Puh or the child she now carried. If she suspected any of those men might make a move that could harm her man or her baby, I had no doubt they would find themselves to be perforated with as many arrows as she could send aloft within the span of a few moments.

The newcomers were also talking amongst themselves, but their gaze never left us as they spoke their incomprehensible words. I could just imagine the sight we presented as we faced them: the enormously tall Black Wolf with his long, plaited beard and spider-like hair; Ria, so tiny and obviously pregnant; Puh and I with our pale green eyes and our long, bright red hair, coiled and bound tightly as it hung down the lengths of our backs.

"They are wearing ornaments," I pointed out. This was unusual amongst hunters, since necklaces and bracelets were apt to clatter as you moved about and that had the potential to scare away prey. Nevertheless, they had managed to get close enough to the sow to wound her, so they must have figured out a way to keep their ornaments and still stalk game. Each of the men was dressed in typical animal hide clothing, a long-sleeved tunic, loincloth and leggings, but each also had an assortment of polished teeth and claws hanging around his neck and wrist.

We were all startled from our mutual staring when a long howl rent the air from somewhere in the distance. One of the men opposite us howled in return and then made a hand motion to his companions. Not turning away from us, they stepped backward until they were swallowed by the rain-drenched forest.

* * *

We waited several moments before we dared to move.

"That was a bit unnerving," Black Wolf stated. "I do not shy from confrontation, but those men were so odd ... I did not know what to expect."

"Who were they, Tor?" Ria inquired. "Could they have been the Bone Crunchers from the north we have heard about? Their teeth are certainly large enough to crush bone."

"I have never seen the Bone Crunchers. I do not know of anyone who has. I have never really been sure that they actually existed, that they were not just figures in stories to frighten unruly children into good behavior," Puh said with a shrug.

"Could it be that Great Gran might know what the Bone Crunchers look like?" I asked. After all, Gran knew everything. If anyone would know, she would.

"I have never heard her speak of them," Puh shrugged again. "We can ask her after our return home."

"But for now," Black Wolf started, "if we want to return home before dark, we are going to have to get back to the task at hand. I do not want to have trekked all the way out here in the rain and damp for nothing."

"Well, old friend," Puh said, putting a hand on Black Wolf's arm. "Sometimes it happens that way, despite our best efforts. Let us track those sows. They are bound to have regrouped nearby."

The Dreamer III – The People of the Wolves

We found the sounder by midday and, thanks to Ria's swift action, one of the sows was soon brought down and quickly killed. It was a small animal, but she would provide an ample meal for our combined families. However, I could not get the image of those strange Wolf-men out of my mind. What were they doing here? Our long-held lands had already been inundated with The People from the East's tribes. Could it be that the Bone Crunchers were now looking to settle on our lands as well?

* * *

Great Gran was helping to prepare our evening meal when I told her the story of our meeting the Wolf-men. She shook her head.

"I have not seen them in my Dreams, so I do not think they will be part of our future. But one can never tell. Even I am surprised at what fate holds in store for us sometimes," she said.

"But are they Bone Crunchers?" I asked.

"They may crunch bones, or suck their teeth noisily, or chew and talk at the same time ... how would I know?" Great Gran answered shortly.

"No, Gran ... I mean the people, the Bone Cruncher people I have heard about," I persisted.

"Where did you hear about them?" Gran looked up at me from her spot by the fire pit, where the fatty juices from the cooking meats splattered and hissed as they dropped amongst the seething bed of red-hot coals.

"At The People from the East's Gathering last fall. So many of The People were unhappy that Black Wolf brought Old Ones with him to tell the Head Elder about the raids we were suffering, and I remember hearing some of the men say at least we were not those *barking-mad Bone Crunchers*. Later, when the raiders were eventually caught, those men were exiled to the lands north of our borders and they were concerned that they would come into contact with the Bone Crunchers."

Gran took a moment to think before she responded; turning one of the smaller spits of impaled meat so that it would roast more evenly, she pursed her lips with concentration.

"I can only guess that those you call *Bone Crunchers* must be another people I heard about many, many years ago. It was so long ago that it was even before your Puh was born. Only, back then, they were not called the Bone Crunchers. Then they were called The People of the Wolves because they modeled some of their behavior around that of wolves, and they wore wolfskins on their backs." Gran paused to pick up my youngest sister Mi, who was overcome by temptation and hungrily inching toward the cooking food. "Not so close, Mi. Saree! Twie! Come take your sister away!" Saree and her older sister Twie were playing nearby, and they obediently approached. Saree tucked the ever-present Hork under one arm and the sisters led Mi away, each holding one of her hands. Gran went on, "I was told that The People of the Wolves use their molars to crack open cooked bones before they extract the marrow; maybe that is why they are now called Bone Crunchers."

I shuddered at the thought of using my teeth to break open bones, unless they were very small light bones, but bones like those would not contain much marrow. We Old Ones usually used hammer stones for such purposes.

"I hope they are not using their teeth to break very big bones."

"I hope so, too," Gran nodded, "I certainly have no plans to start taking up that practice any time soon! Go and fetch the others, Tris. The food will soon be ready to eat." Gran then turned her attention to my eldest sister, fourteen-winters-old Ru. "Ru, help me with these other spits. The coals are so hot that I am afraid the meat will burn, and some of these spits are too heavy for me to move."

"Yes, Gran." Ru immediately left the pile of greens that she and Morning Star were sorting through. Our younger siblings had picked an assortment of dandelion, purslane, and plantain greens, but they had also pulled clumps of accompanying soil as well. So Ru and Morning Star were laboriously cutting off the roots and attempting to shake the dirt from the fronds.

Morning Star lifted Fox from his resting place on the mat and held him up to me.

"Dear Tris, Fox is becoming restless. Take him with you when you go to gather the others. I believe they are at Mama and Da's house."

"Yes, my sweet," I said to her, taking Fox from her hands and stopping just long enough to kiss her cheek. The expression on her face told me that she had been listening to my conversation with Gran. Morning Star looked worried, but she said nothing. I knew we would talk about it later when we were at home by ourselves.

* * *

When I arrived at the dwelling of Black Wolf and Little Fawn, Puh and Ria were also there, discussing today's unexpected encounter.

"I do not like the thought of those strange men being in the area," Little Fawn was saying as she held her youngest child, a toddler named Dewdrop, in her arms.

"I do not like the thought, either," Black Wolf stated. "I am glad that we now live closer to one another so that we can join forces if need be."

Puh seemed thoughtful.

"They had superior numbers and yet they did not engage us," Puh said. "I do not think they mean us any harm."

Dewdrop was wriggling in an attempt to escape her mother's grasp. Little Fawn set her down and

Dewdrop immediately tottered over to me, holding her arms aloft in hopes I would pick her up. I did so, and now carried both Fox and Dewdrop in my embrace. Fox's expression became more animated at the sight of Dewdrop's familiar face. Dewdrop mugged for him, and Fox grinned and drooled in response.

"Great Gran says that she has not seen them in her Dreams. That could be a sign that they will not linger on our lands," I told the assembled group.

"Have you seen them in your Dreams?" Puh inquired.

I did not like to talk about my Dreams. Not even to Morning Star, from whom I withheld little. If asked I felt obliged to respond honestly, but my Dreams were often disjointed and frightening, and I did not like to cause Morning Star unnecessary concern.

Everyone looked to me as they awaited my response.

"I have Dreamt of wolves," I replied cautiously. "Of wolves crying out and circling us. I do not know if they are visions of past wolf attacks or if they represent something else."

"What do you sense about those Dreams?" Puh asked.

Again, I paused as I thought on Puh's question.

"Because the Dream keeps visiting my sleep, I sense that it is trying to tell me something. But, I am only guessing. I really do not know if those wolves are the same as the Wolf-men we have just met."

"It is true that we have fended off plenty of wolves in the past and can expect to fend off more in the future, so your Dream could mean anything," Puh agreed.

We all nodded. Dewdrop continued to make faces to amuse Fox and she chanted to him, "*Fox-Fox-Fox-Fox!*"

"We should make sure that our families all know about these men and instruct our children to stay close to home," Black Wolf suggested.

"Yes," Little Fawn agreed. "I have heard that some men will steal women from other tribes or clans, too. Maybe we should all stay nearby until those men have moved on."

I could understand the men possibly being interested in absconding with Morning Star, my sister Ru, or even Morning Star's younger sister Petal, but I felt fairly sure that Little Fawn, so matronly and hulking, and a good head and shoulders taller than the tallest of the Wolf-men, was safe from being dragged off. I could see that Puh was fighting to quell a wry smile; he, too, must have been thinking that any man attempting to force his will on Little Fawn would indeed find himself with the prospect of a daunting fight on his hands.

"Yes, we will need to be considerably more wary about leaving home. Also, we will have to take care to make sure our homes are defended at all times," Puh said. "I think we should put off our journey to the coast until we know that it is safe to leave. Although I do not think those men plan to hurt us, we cannot be sure. I would not like to leave Gran and Ty vulnerable to attack while we are away."

Black Wolf and Little Fawn exchanged disappointed glances, but they agreed.

"Yes," Black Wolf said, "that makes sense. We have been so eager to see the ocean for the first time, but we cannot put your Gran and Ty at risk."

"Speaking of Gran," I broke in, "she asked me to tell you all that our evening meal is almost ready."

"Eat food?" Dewdrop piped up.

"Yes, my plump Dewdrop," Little Fawn said, taking the tot from my arms, "it is time to eat. Let us go. Poor Gran … I left her and the girls to prepare this meal by themselves. I should have been there to help them instead of gabbing."

* * *

After Fox was put to bed, Morning Star and I settled on a mat in front of our fire, me with my back against the hide-covered earthen and timber wall, and Morning Star sitting between my legs. There, she nestled up against me, an arm around my neck and resting her head on my shoulder. I smiled as I wrapped her in a warm hug and placed my cheek on the top of her head. We both sighed contentedly. Our dog Raena lay next to us, head on her forefeet, the length of her furry body aligned so that it touched the side of my thigh.

"I heard you speaking to Gran about the strangers," Morning Star said, opening the conversation.

"Yes, these men are of a people who are new to us. I have never seen anyone even remotely like them. They are built like Old Ones, but they are dark like The People," I told her.

"And they dress in wolfskins?" Morning Star asked.

"The wolfskins are draped over them," I said. "It is a most peculiar look. The wolf heads are worn on top of their heads and it gives them the appearance of being Wolf-men … that is, until you see them up close, and you can tell that it is just a wolf pelt and not a live animal."

"How very odd," Morning Star remarked.

"We thought so. And now, Puh says it is best that we postpone our trip to the shore. I hope you are not too sad at this development. I know how much you wanted to go." I watched Morning Star's reaction carefully. Her mouth turned downward for just an instant, but she made an effort to suppress the frown and she soon smiled.

"I do hope that we will not miss spending time at the beach this summer, but I understand why we should not leave for now. I imagine that you are more disappointed at the prospect than I am. Have you ever missed a summer at the coast?"

"No," I admitted. "But, I will not mind if we do not go this year."

Morning Star raised her eyes so she could see my face and she smiled up at me.

"I know. You have been reluctant to have me make the trek. My dear Tris, I keep telling you that the trip is not that different from what I do on a daily basis, what with working and toting our little Fox around."

"It may seem silly on my part," I said to Morning Star, bending down to kiss her lips, "but I cannot help it."

"And you do not want to go because your family members receive your annual haircuts when you go to the beach every summer," Morning Star teased. Last summer she was somewhat amused to see that we were all lined up and each in turn had a few finger-widths trimmed off our long hair. Since times untold we Old Ones have believed that our hair endows us with an extraordinary intuition. It makes us better hunters and allows us to sense potential danger. To cut any great length off our hair was to diminish that insight. The People from the East also wore their hair long, but not as long as ours, and they trimmed it whenever the whim struck them.

"Well you can still cut my hair here, if you like. We do not have to be at the shore for that, and I will gladly give up our seasonal trek if it means keeping everyone safe."

* * *

It was well that we had brought in that sow, since these People of the Wolves, or Bone Crunchers, or whoever they might be, were keeping us close to home for the time being. All the same, we could not afford to stay near the family compound indefinitely. We would need to bring in a significant amount of foodstuffs and firewood to see us through the next winter. The firewood could be harvested within sight of home, but most of our hunting had to be done some distance away.

So Puh, Black Wolf, my brother Ty, and I set to work on some of the nearby trees. We had already removed a large number from the local woodlands as we constructed Puh's little house and Black Wolf and Little Fawn's much larger one. Even though Puh and Ria's home was largely an earth-bermed structure, it still required the support of numerous sections of sturdy tree branches and trunks. Likewise, Black Wolf and Little Fawn's domicile was also created using a substantial quantity of wood amidst the mud, stones, sticks, and grass walls. As we hewed the trees, the sky seemed to open up more around our formerly well-shaded family compound.

I was pleased to find that now that Puh and I had the assistance of Ty and Black Wolf, our tree-chopping labors were much reduced. Ty was a willing and able worker, and Black Wolf's great size made him a valuable asset to the project. We stayed near our respective homes and left the dogs with our families so that we would have ample warning if anyone approached the compound.

However, this did not help to provide warning to us while we were absorbed with the chore of accumulating the vast amount of fuel needed to get through the long winter. As the shadows began to lengthen on a warm early summer's day, I suddenly noticed that Puh had stopped working and he was staring off into the forest. I followed his gaze and was startled to see that we were being watched. The Wolf-men were standing silently amongst the trees, leaning on their spears casually, observing us with open curiosity.

We had stripped off our tunics in the heat of midday, and we were winded and sweating from our work. By now, Black Wolf and Ty had stopped to look at the Wolf-men as well. I ruefully noted that we were unarmed, except for our axes, which could be used to deadly purpose if necessary. But I would have much preferred to have my spear at hand.

After a few moments of collective staring, Puh smiled slightly at the strangers and raised his hand to them. The Wolf-men looked at each other as if to consult with one another about how they should react. Finally, a man from the front of the group took a few steps toward us, also raising his hand. He spoke a string of words, but they did not mean anything to us.

"I am Tor," Puh said, determined to strike up a conversation.

The Wolf-man cocked his head to one side, confused. He shook his head and spoke again.

"Who are you?" Puh asked. Puh pointed to himself, "I am Tor. Who are you?"

"*Woooo?*" The man uttered. He turned to look back at his companions, but they just shrugged at him.

"Who. Who are you?" Puh said again. He waited for a reply but, getting none other than another *Woooo?* from the man, Puh went on to touch me and say, "This is my son, Tris. This is my other son, Ty. This is my friend, Black Wolf. Who are you?" Puh took a few steps closer to the Wolf-man, so that he was now within an arm's reach. I nervously gripped the handle of my axe. The Wolf-man held his spear, and although he was not in a defensive pose, I feared that could change in an instant if he felt threatened.

Puh again placed a hand on his chest and said "Tor." He then put the same hand on the Wolf-man's chest and asked gently "Who are you?"

At last, a look of recognition and a smile flickered across the man's face.

"*Who!*" he repeated, "*Who! Karno!*" He tapped his own chest. "*Who, Karno! Karno!*"

Now that he was close enough to inspect Puh's person, Karno seemed to take a moment to assess Puh in detail. He scanned Puh's scarred face and chest, and his lean, powerfully built frame. I moved to stand closer to Puh, and Karno turned his attention to me.

"*Who!*" Karno said, "*Who, Karno!*" He thumped his chest with a closed fist.

"Tris," I said, touching my own chest.

Karno's gaze traveled back and forth between me and Puh.

"*Tor,*" Karno spoke Puh's name with an accent, "*Tris,*" he added in the same slightly off pronunciation.

Now that I could also see Karno clearly, I could more easily take in the markings that covered his skin. Fine lines decorated his forehead. Some of his markings appeared to resemble the outlines of animals, and others were just lines and shapes. His dark visage was beaded with minute droplets of sweat. He must have been exceedingly hot under his layers of clothing, plus the wolfskin head covering and cloak, but he did not remove them.

Karno seemed to be studying me, as well, his amazement plain on his face. I was aware that my pale freckled skin, now flushed pink from our exertions and begrimed with tree debris, must have been a radical departure from the tan-colored flesh he was accustomed to viewing. Karno stared into my face open-mouthed. He pointed at my eyes and my hair, and then at his own, saying words that were just a jumble of sounds to my ears; but I could guess that he was remarking on the differences between our peoples.

Karno then looked up at Black Wolf, who in turn glared down at him. Black Wolf did not care to be ogled, even if his great height, spider-like hairstyle, and the fact that his naked upper body was nearly as furry as that of any bear, might merit an extended glance or two from those not used to the sight of him.

"*Who?*" Karno asked, pointing to Black Wolf.

"I am Black Wolf," he replied, his voice rumbling deep in his throat. To reinforce his declaration, his tapped his chest and said again, "Black Wolf."

"*Back Woof,*" Karno attempted to reproduce the sounds.

Puh now put an arm around Ty and brought him forward to meet Karno.

"Ty," Puh said, touching Ty to indicate whom he was naming.

"*Ty,*" Karno repeated. Then Karno turned to his comrades and waved them closer. They hesitantly approached.

I was now able to count their numbers. There were thirteen Wolf-men in all. They were very similar in appearance, in that they were dressed almost exactly alike. But their faces and skin markings were quite different, and their ornaments also varied considerably. Karno seemed to be a man of some importance; obviously, he was the leader of the group. Karno spoke rapidly to them. I heard him say *who* and each of our names to the men, but the rest was lost to me. Karno brought each man up to us, identifying everyone. I could not remember all their names, but I did recall that one was named Mino and another called Bewok, because he spoke to those two men more frequently than to the others.

Our meeting was interrupted when Karno froze in place and gasped. I was momentarily surprised at this. I wondered for a brief instant if Ria had spied this impromptu gathering and had shot one of her arrows into the unsuspecting Wolf-man. But then I saw what had so captured Karno's attention.

My sister Ru was standing behind us, water bag and gourd cup in hand. Ru was as transfixed as was Karno. Karno recovered before Ru did. He strode toward her, pointing at Ru and saying, "*Who? Who? Who? Who?*"

Puh did not look pleased at this development. He may have hoped to keep our women out of sight, but it was too late now. Puh walked over to Ru and escorted her forward, an arm around her waist.

"You have brought us water. How thoughtful of you, Ru," Puh said quietly.

"*Who? Who? Who? Who?*" Karno asked again, this time more insistently.

Puh still had his arm around Ru. His demeanor became stern.

"Ru," Puh replied, "This is my daughter, Ru." Puh emphasized the words *my daughter*, and although Karno surely could not understand the terminology, Puh's meaning was clear. This was someone he cherished and protected.

Karno nodded sheepishly. He gently touched Ru's arm with his fingertips and said softly; "*Ru.*" Then he touched his chest. "*Who ... Karno.*" Karno smiled at Ru encouragingly, but she only nodded to him, eyes widened and nose somewhat wrinkled in distaste.

Puh reached to take the water bag and cup from Ru.

"Many thanks for bringing the water to us," he said.

Ru seemed reluctant to let go of the items and to leave us. Puh saw this.

"It is all right, Pretty One. You leave these with us and go home. Everything is all right."

"But Puh," Ru started, "there are so many of them." She indicated the mob of Wolf-men.

"It is all right," Puh assured her. "Go ahead. Go home. We will be all right."

Ru still hesitated, but Puh gave her a kiss on the cheek and led her a few steps up the path toward home before leaving her to finish the short walk back by herself.

When we turned our attention back to the Wolf-men, they were, to a man, gazing longingly down the trail after Ru. Then, they were again looking at us perplexed. What had so mystified them? Did they wonder why Puh sent Ru away? Did they wonder about the water bag and cup? Maybe these bone-crunching Wolf-men lapped their water out of rivers instead of drinking from a vessel, as we most often did.

Karno was speaking with his compatriots once again. They seemed to come to a consensus. Karno once again turned to us. He touched Puh's forearm with his fingertips, as he had with Ru, and nodded to Puh, speaking his incomprehensible words. Then Karno rejoined his friends and they once again disappeared amongst the trees.

"What do you make of that little scene?" Black Wolf asked Puh.

"Which one?" Puh responded. "Let us go back home and make sure that Ru has not unduly alarmed the others. She seemed a bit shaken when she left us."

"I am sure she had a notion that those men wanted to get to know her," Black Wolf stated. "Bror will not like this."

"Yes," Puh agreed, stacking some of the limbed branches we had just removed from a tree to clear our work area before we departed. "Bror has hoped to become paired with her for several years now."

Bror was my cousin. At twenty winters old, he was considered to be at an advanced age for one of our people to be yet unpaired. I had paired somewhat late myself, when at seventeen winters old I had taken Morning Star as my mate. But to be unpaired at twenty or older was nearly unheard of. Bror was a fine man: intelligent, reliable, and a good provider. He had an exaggeratedly stout build, even for a man of the Old Ones. Bror was one of the few men I would not care to tussle with. All the same, Bror had patiently and tenderly wooed Ru for some time with little encouragement, if not receiving an outright *go away* could be considered encouraging.

It was not likely that Ru would lack opportunities to find a mate. Ru closely resembled our beautiful mother, who had been tall for a woman of the Old Ones – as tall as Puh – with striking dark red hair and deep green eyes. Ru did not have Muh's height, but she had her dramatic coloring and lovely face, although it was slightly broader through the cheeks. Also, Ru owned an admirable figure that attracted stares wherever she went.

* * *

We found Ru telling our assembled families about the strange Wolf-men.

"They were dark men, and they wore wolfskins over their clothing!" Ru exclaimed.

"Wolfskin cloaks on such a warm day?" Morning Star's next youngest sister Petal asked incredulously. "Were they not hot?" Petal was fourteen winters old and quite tall for her age. She would probably inherit her parents' great height, and she had Little Fawn's long, horse-like face.

"They were sweating, and they stank," Ru answered Petal.

I thought on Ru's assessment of the Wolf-men. I was pretty sure that Black Wolf, Puh, Ty, and I currently reeked of perspiration and may have carried other odors as well.

"How kind of you to overlook our similar condition," I said, grinning at Ru and indicating myself and my fellow woodcutters, "considering that we are equally sweaty and probably just as aromatic as they Wolf-men."

Ru shook her head.

"No, you may be dirty and sweaty from your work, big brother, but you will at least make an effort to wash it off. I have no doubt that those men have looked and smelled like that for many a moon."

 **Chapter Three**

The next day Puh and I busied ourselves with adding newly hewn wood to the dwindling remains of last year's firewood cache. Before long, we were distracted from this chore by the uproarious commotion of ten furiously barking dogs. Black Wolf's eight dogs and my Raena, and my family's old dog, Rooph, had taken up a protective line at the edge of our compound, keeping the Wolf-men at bay. The Wolf-men, however, seemed to be only mildly affected by their reception. They stood absolutely still, waiting to be recognized and granted entry. Two of the men carried a long branch between them, from which a young red deer doe was suspended by its lashed ankles.

As the rest of our families paused from their tasks to look up at the frantic dogs and the ragtag collection of Wolf-men, Puh, Black Wolf, and I waded through the throng of canines to greet our visitors. The dogs settled down enough to allow the Wolf-men to come nearer, but only grudgingly. They still uttered small growls and turned up their lips in half-snarls while the Wolf-men walked past them.

"Karno," Puh said to the leader with a smiling nod. Ordinarily, a guest would have been wished a pleasant day, but since we did not speak the same language, Puh did not attempt the usual conversation starters.

"Tor," Karno said, returning Puh's friendly greeting, adding, "Back Woof, Tris." Karno then pointed to the dead doe and gestured that he was giving it to us.

"He is giving us a deer?" Black Wolf seemed surprised. "What do we do now?"

"We invite them to eat it with us," Puh said quietly, nodding his thanks to Karno.

I also nodded and smiled my thanks to them.

"Many thanks," I said to Karno, and then I looked over Karno's shoulder to the men behind him and repeated my thanks to them.

Even if the Wolf-men could not understand my words, I hoped that they could grasp my intent. One thing was for sure, there were too many of these men to risk insulting them. Black Wolf, Puh, and I had faced uneven odds before this, but not to this extent, and not with our families at close proximity. While I did not perceive an immediate threat, I did not want anything to happen that might imperil our loved ones.

Karno politely acknowledged my gratitude and then appeared to scan those of us who were in the compound. His eyes lingered over Little Fawn, who appeared larger than ever as she stood amongst the assembly of children. However, Karno showed only slight surprise at the sight of a giantess. He nodded in recognition to my brother Ty and gave Morning Star, holding Fox in her arms, a warm smile before his gaze finally settled on Ru, as she nervously clasped Great Gran's arm. Ru would not look him in the eye, but Gran's scrutiny was keen. I knew from past experience there was little that escaped Gran's notice.

Morning Star came to my side, so I introduced her to Karno.

"This is Karno," I told her. I placed one arm around Morning Star and I placed my other hand over my heart for a moment, before then placing the same hand on Morning Star's shoulder and then on Fox. I hoped to convey that Morning Star was my mate and Fox was my child. "Morning Star," I said, touching her again. "Fox." I touched Fox, too, causing him to grin at me in response.

Karno seemed charmed by Fox and grinned back at him, putting a finger under his chin.

"He seems very gentle," Morning Star observed.

"Yes, so far," I agreed.

Fox grabbed Karno's proffered finger and held on tightly as Karno spoke softly to him. Fox seemed to be as delighted with Karno as Karno was with him.

The Dreamer III – The People of the Wolves

Fox's wondering eyes often traveled up to the wolf's face that was perched mysteriously above the man's head. Karno attempted to speak to Morning Star and me as well, but we could not understand him. Was he telling us about his children at a distant home? We just smiled at him and hoped that we were responding appropriately.

In the meantime, the other Wolf-men had filed into the family compound with the doe and began to hang her from a projecting tree branch we often used for the same purpose. Karno took note of their work and nodded approvingly, talking, but also motioning to us that his men would butcher the deer.

By now, everyone had gathered around the Wolf-men. Introductions were made, but what with so many names being exchanged and so little common language to make use of, I did not think that we would later recall many of the other group's monikers.

One thing was clear, though. The Wolf-men, although so far they had shown polite restraint, were obviously quite interested in the nubile females on our compound.

I was curious about these men. Whether or not they were the legendary Bone Crunchers, they certainly seemed to be far from home. Why had they made the long journey? If they were hoping to settle new lands, where were their women and children? Were they part of a scouting party, sent ahead to look for a convenient place to erect their dwellings?

When the deer was neatly skinned and stripped of its organs and flesh, the cooking fire was already reduced to a bed of coals. The organ meat was put over the fire pit to be cooked first. Puh invited our guests to sit and eat with us, but Karno shook his head and spoke at length to us. Seeing that we did not understand, Karno motioned to our combined families, particularly pointing out all the children, pantomiming the act of eating. He called to his men, waving to them to join him. Then he spoke to us once more as the group backed away. It seemed to me that Karno paused to catch Ru's eye and he smiled broadly at her. As before, she did not deign to acknowledge him.

We nodded our farewells and thanks to them and watched the Wolf-men disappear into the forest, as seemed to be their habit.

* * *

"They appear to be much friendlier than they were at our first meeting," Ria noted.

"Now that they see we have young women," Black Wolf said. "I think the present of the deer is due more to the fact that we have daughters than a desire to be chummy."

"I think so, too," Little Fawn concurred. "There is something odd about those men ... besides that they wear those wolfskins and have those markings all over their skin."

"They are lost," Great Gran stated.

We all turned to look at Gran, somewhat surprised at this notion. It had never occurred to me that the Wolf-men were not here by design. How could they be lost? Even children knew the basic layout of these lands: oceans to the west, mountains to the northeast, vast open plains on either side of the mountains, and a few large rivers, one to the north and one to the south, which discharged themselves at the coast; and although we had numerous small ponds, an area with many lakes was directly north of us. Even if you did not know where you were for a short period of time, you would eventually run into one of these landmarks and then would be able to find your way home.

"How can they be lost?" I asked.

"I did notice that they do not always use our trails," Puh said. "They have a peculiar way of getting around, but I did not get the idea that they did not know where they were going."

"I do not mean that they are lost, in the way you suggesting," Gran started. "I mean they are displaced. They are all young men. They are traveling light and they appear to have been on the trail for a very long time."

"They are dirty," Ru spoke up.

"By the looks of them, they are probably sheltering under earthen or rocky outcrops," Puh said. "It could be they are not habitually dirty. I think that perhaps they do not build lean-tos or huts as we do when we are on the trail, and thus they do not have a clean place to rest at night. It is also possible that they do not have other clothing to change into."

A disturbing thought suddenly occurred to me.

"What if they are exiles from their own lands?" After all, The People's Head Elder, Willow Woman, had exiled the band of raiders from our lands; what if the Bone Crunchers' people were doing the same thing and sending their miscreants here?

"That is a sobering notion," Puh agreed.

"Puh, I do not like them being here," Ru said, clutching his arm. "I am afraid of those men."

"There is one big thing in our favor, and that is there is not enough game in this area for those men to settle here. They will have to move on eventually," Puh pointed out. "We will just have to wait them out. And be wary until they leave." Puh hugged Ru. "Do not worry, Pretty One, we will not let those men be a nuisance to you, or any of the other girls."

"But there are so many of them!" Ru exclaimed. Ru, like the rest of us, well remembered when my mate Morning Star was stolen from our pairing ceremony.

"Yes, but we are not defenseless." Puh assured her.

"I have plenty of arrows," Ria chimed in, patting Ru's arm soothingly. "If any man tries to take unwelcome liberties with you or any of the other girls, well, he will reconsider his plans after he finds he is sporting an arrow or two."

The Dreamer III – The People of the Wolves

"Many thanks," Ru said as she hugged Ria. "I still have nightmares about Snow Leopard and all those evil men. And I recall what Puh, Tris, and Black Wolf looked like when they returned with Morning Star. It must have been a terrible undertaking. I do not want our families to go through that again."

"I understand why you are frightened," Puh said gently to Ru, "but so far, they have only brought us a deer. Let us hope that they merely seek friendship. If worse comes to worst, we have our spears, we have Ria's arrows, and we have a large pack of dogs."

Morning Star's sister Petal had come to stand between her parents, also looking anxious. Little Fawn and Black Wolf each took pains to snuggle her comfortly. Of our many siblings, only Ru and Petal were of age, if a little young, to be taken as a mate. It went unspoken that it was also possible that these men might not come from a culture where couples were formally paired. What if, as Little Fawn had suggested earlier, their mates were acquired by abducting them from other clans?

* * *

We never knew when the Wolf-men would suddenly appear. Our dogs were now accustomed to their scent, and they would begin to bark whenever the Wolf-men came near the family compound. The Wolf-men always brought a gift of game, whether large or small. They were slowly learning a few words of our language and they resolutely attempted to make halting conversation with us whenever they came. We began to pick up some of their words, as well, but this endeavor was particularly trying. They used a broad array of sounds that defied most of our attempts to replicate. Thus, even if we understood the word, we were often helpless to reproduce it. I was thankful that most of our communication took place in my native tongue.

One day the Wolf-men brought us the gift of a fine yearling elk. Karno looked for me amongst the many people in view and waved vigorously as soon as our eyes met. I had noted that Karno seemed to feel at ease in my presence, and I speculated that it might be because he and I were close in age. Karno approached Morning Star, Fox, and me, and he held out an object to Fox.

I had never seen anything like it. Karno had found a knobby section of tree branch and lopped it off at one end, etching a bear cub's eyes, nose, mouth and ears into the knob, while leaving a short section of the branch for a small handle. It looked like a tiny bear's head on a stick. We were amazed at the artistry that went into this creation, even more so when Karno gave the stick a shake and the toy made a rattling sound.

Fox held out a hand for the bear-on-a-branch, and Karno, quite pleased at our awed reception to this present, gave it to him.

"Karno make for Fox," he said with a grin.

"Many thanks," I told Karno, "The toy bear is a marvel! How does it make the rattle-rattle-rattle noise?"

I could see by the expression on Karno's face that he did not understand most of my words, but he seemed to guess that I was thanking him.

"Fox like!" Karno nodded with exaggerated bobs of his head.

"Yes, Fox likes it very much," Morning Star beamed at Karno. "You are very kind to make the little bear for Fox. Thank you for the present."

Again, Karno was left to guess at most of our words. He pointed to a spot on the back of the bear's head, opposite the knobby surface that made up the bear's face. There the wood was softer, and evidently he had made a circular opening and partially hollowed out the head.

Karno scooped several small stones from the ground and shook them in his closed fist so that they clattered against one another. Karno stared into our faces to see if we understood his demonstration. It would seem that he had placed a few tiny pebbles inside the head before resealing the hole with a plug and pine pitch glue. All in all, this toy was one of the cleverest things I had ever seen.

Karno's generosity moved me to want to reciprocate, but I did not know what I could give him that would be most appreciated. Then it dawned on me that none of the Wolf-men had a change of clothing. I took off my long-sleeved tunic and passed it to Karno. It would be a little big for him, but it was relatively clean and new, whereas his was old, stained, and tattered.

"Here, you take my tunic," I said to Karno.

Karno held the garment in his hands, looking at it as though he could not believe I was gifting him with this article. Admittedly, the coolness of morning was nearly past and neither of us really needed to be wearing a tunic at that time of day, but I think his surprise derived from never having considered he might receive something in return.

Karno's men and the members of my family all stood by, wearing smiles at this exchange. All except Ru, that is; even now she had not taken to the Wolf-men in the least.

Then Karno's grin widened and he threw off his wolfskin cloak, pack, and tunic, quickly replacing the old tunic with the new one. He looked down at his new tunic, exceedingly pleased.

"Thank Tris!" Karno exclaimed. "Karno thank Tris!"

I was so shocked at what Karno had revealed when he stripped off his upper clothing and pack that I could not immediately respond. Not only was his almost hairless torso covered with the same markings that decorated his hands, face, and neck, but appallingly, the hair on his head was shorn short. None of us had ever seen an adult with cropped hair.

It was no more than a few finger-widths in length and was lopped off unevenly, sticking out here and there, looking much like a preening duck that had not quite gotten all its feathers back into place again.

Luckily, Karno was too busy admiring his new tunic to notice the gasps and stares from those around him. Fortunately, we recovered our senses quickly and managed to be wearing polite expressions by the time he looked up again.

However, one of Karno's comrades, Mino, took it upon himself to say something to us.

"Karno very pale. Long winter." He seemed to assume that we were taken aback at Karno's somewhat lighter skin where it was customarily hidden underneath his clothing.

"Yes, me too," I said, pointing to my own chest, which was very pale indeed, especially compared with the darker skin of the Wolf-men and The People from the East tribes. I was relieved that Mino had come up with a plausible explanation for our reaction that satisfied everyone.

This time, the Wolf-men stayed and partook of our evening meal.

* * *

The moon had run halfway through its cycle and The People of the Wolves were still with us. We did not know where they were camped, or even if they had a camp or moved from place to place. But they visited frequently, bringing more game with them, and we in turn gifted them with more items of clothing. I noticed that now that they had fresh clothing, they had also bathed. Nevertheless, they still wore their wolfskin cloaks, even in the summer heat.

"Is your wolf pelt not hot to wear on a day such as this?" I asked Karno.

"Keep sun off Karno back and head," Karno shrugged. "Tris say he get more spots in sun. Not want spots like Tris!" Karno indicated my profuse freckles and he laughed at his joke. I was dressed only in a loincloth on this warm day, and I could not imagine how he and his friends were not sweltering in their heavy clothing.

"But look, you are hot. You are sweating. If you remove some of your clothes, you will be cooler. See? My skin is dry. Cooler. Why do you not try it and see if you are not more comfortable." Karno's men listened to our conversation carefully.

"Tris, too many words!" Karno pleaded. "What say? What?"

Mino was more fluent in our tongue, so he quickly interpreted for Karno. Karno seemed undecided.

"Ru like me if I ..." Karno seemed unable to articulate his thoughts in my language. Mino spoke to him again and Karno nodded.

I felt for Karno, as he had been earnestly trying to win Ru's approval, to no avail. I had grown to like Karno and I did not want to see him hurt by Ru's persistent rejection. I still hoped Bror would be the one to win her, but all the same, I did not like to see Karno treated unkindly.

"I do not know," I said, feeling the need to be honest with Karno. "I can only tell you that Ru likes very clean things." I thought that maybe if Karno could manage to be consistently well-washed and relatively odor free, it would at least give Ru one less thing to object to.

Karno took off his wolf pelt and held it in front of him so that he was face to face with the deceased canine. He studied the battered visage with its leering grin, eyeless gaze, and semi-drooping ears. Karno sniffed it cautiously.

"I not smell." He held the pelt toward me and I involuntarily backed away. "It smell?"

"It definitely has an odor," I said. I hated to be so blunt, but there was no denying that the pelt reeked.

"*Gah!*" Karno cried out in frustration, throwing the pelt away from him as his friends looked on, aghast. One of his men retrieved the pelt and handed it to Karno. He reluctantly took it back; but he did not put it on. "Not clean," Karno mumbled dejectedly.

* * *

After that, Karno and his men appeared at our family compound freshly scrubbed. They also dressed more or less as we did during the summer season, which meant that most of the time we men were dressed only in our loincloths. Our women were dressed in a deerskin garment that was sewn into a long rectangular and had a neck hole at the middle. When the head was placed through the neck hole and the deerskin hung down front and back, it was then belted around the waist. We were all barefoot and would be until the cooler weather returned in the fall.

Much to Karno's delight, an amazing thing happened. Ru smiled at him. I think that Ru was as surprised as he was. It had not been over anything unusual. Little Mi was playing with Saree when she tripped and fell to the ground. Karno picked up Mi with a few words of consolation and brushed her off before Ru could come to Mi's rescue. When Karno put Mi into Ru's waiting arms, she gave him a small smile. But for Karno it was a huge, if brief, victory.

"Tris, you see? Ru smile to Karno!" Karno exalted. "Maybe Ru like Karno. Will Tris ask Ru? Ru like Karno?"

My shoulders slumped at the request. It brought back the memories of Bror's futile entreaties to have me pass a message to Ru or ask her something. I really disliked being placed between an ardent suitor and my indifferent if not outright hostile sister.

"Karno," I began, "Do you hope to become paired with Ru?"

"What is *paired*?" Karno asked.

"To take her as your mate," I told him.

"Yes," Karno immediately brightened. "Ru pretty. Like Tor say: Ru is *Pretty One.*"

"Then you should talk to my Puh ... Tor ... if you want to ask for her."

"Why?" Karno questioned, "Karno need to know if Ru likes Karno."

"Our men ask permission from the girl's father and state their intentions. This is an important step a man must take before he is paired," I informed Karno.

Karno shook his head. He did not understand enough of my words to get a sense of what I was trying to say.

"You talk to Tor ... ask my Puh for Ru." I tried once more.

"Oh," Karno nodded. "You funny people. Why ask Tor? Why no ask Ru?"

"Ask Ru, but be sure to ask Tor first," I advised him.

Karno shrugged.

"Tris, you funny people. My people ask woman. Give gift. Woman say *yes* or *no*."

* * *

I felt obliged to forewarn Puh that Karno intended to ask for Ru. I had no idea how Puh would respond. I waited until Puh and I were alone later that day, while we were engaged in dragging more wood back to the family compound.

"Puh," I said, "Karno has been speaking with me about Ru. I believe he intends to ask for her. I told him he needed to talk to you."

Puh nodded somberly.

"I have been wondering when this would come up. Poor Bror. He has waited for Ru for so long. The surprising thing is that Ru actually seems to be warming up to Karno. She never did warm up to Bror."

"Yes," I agreed. "I do feel badly for Bror. He is such a fine man. I do not know why she does not make an effort to be more agreeable to him."

"It is her choice," Puh shrugged.

"Will you give Karno permission if he asks?" I inquired.

"I have to," Puh stated. "It is Ru's choice. I cannot forbid her to be with Karno if she cares for him. I would not like to see that happen, because I fear he will take her somewhere very far away and we may never see Ru again. But especially after what your Muh and I endured when we were young, I would never tell any of my children with whom they can or cannot be paired."

I could see that Puh was truly torn. He faced either the potential loss of his daughter if she were to go away from us, or being the cause of her unhappiness if he did not give his consent.

That evening, I told Morning Star about what had transpired during the day. Her reaction was much the same as Puh's.

"Poor Bror. He will be heartbroken after all these years of pining for Ru. Are you actually encouraging Karno?" she asked.

"I am not encouraging him, but I have told him he needs to speak with Puh. I do not like being in the middle of the negotiations. This is not my place … I do not want to be involved in my sister's personal affairs," I explained.

Morning Star paused long enough to look into my face and caress my bearded cheek.

"Well, look at it this way, my dear Tris. It will be good practice for when our daughters are grown and ready to become paired," she said, grinning at me impishly.

 **Chapter Four**

A man is silhouetted against the moonlight as shooting stars arc across a nighttime sky. The man is completely motionless. I sense an overwhelming feeling of anguish and hopelessness.

After my conversation with Karno, he and his troop of fellow Wolf-men appeared at our family compound every day. While we now felt much more at ease around the men, and we were carefully optimistic that they meant us no harm, there was still an element of caution to our lives. We men did not dare to leave our families alone for fear that they would suffer an attack while we were away. Our lesson with Snow Leopard had been a costly one. There was no chance that we were going to drop our vigilance ever again. We would pack up our families and abandon our homes to move them to a safer locale before we would leave them alone with these strangers still in the vicinity.

* * *

I was becoming bored with this day-after-day routine of doing mundane chores around our compound, staying within sight of home. Puh, as always, endured whatever life threw at him with endless patience, and he did not complain. He set to work slicing and smoking any meat that was not immediately consumed, curing hides, and helping Ria to produce more arrows.

The strain particularly showed on Black Wolf and Little Fawn, who by turn alternated between arguing vociferously and not speaking to each other.

The children, however, thoroughly enjoyed the Wolf-men's visits. The Wolf-men brought not only gifts of meat, but just as Karno had given Fox the bear cub rattle, some of the other men also made small presents for the children, mostly in the form of carved wooden animal figurines.

Morning Star's younger brothers, eleven-winters-old Swift River and nine- winters-old Hawk, idolized the newcomers. The Wolf- men were happy to regale them with great stories of their adventures, often told half in words and half in pantomime, due to their limited understanding of our language.

Karno did his best to impress upon Ru his sincerity as a potential mate, but he was admittedly awkward around women.

"Tris, Karno try. At night, Karno think nice things to speak to Ru. But daytime! Gah! Nice things go away from my head," Karno lamented.

I had witnessed this for myself. Karno would approach Ru and she would look at him expectantly but he would just make odd comments, such as to remark that she had sturdy feet or that her hair reminded him of fire. Nonetheless, Ru tolerated his idle prattle better than expected.

One day, as she and I watched the band of Wolf-men make their farewells, I noticed that Ru's eyes followed Karno and she smiled and waved to him as he departed.

"Karno is certainly taken with you," I stated.

"He looks at me as though he is interested, but his words do not reveal any romantic intentions," Ru shrugged. "I cannot tell what he wants."

I did not mention that Karno intended to ask Puh for her. I did not think that Puh had told her, either.

"Well, I am sure he will let you know whether or not he is interested."

"I would like to think he is," Ru mused aloud. I was startled at this.

"Do you like Karno?" I asked.

"He is a fine figure of a man. He is different," Ru said. "At first, I could not get past the smell of him, or the fact that every time I looked at him was I forced to stare into the face of a dead wolf. Ugh. And that hair! Whatever happened to their hair? It is obvious that they are successful hunters, but how do they do it without the connectedness that we Old Ones achieve through our long hair? Maybe it works only for the Old Ones and the Wolf-men use some other means to sense the goings-on in the natural world. Maybe it is all those lines and animal shapes on their skin that work some sort of magic for them."

"Maybe," I agreed. "But what about Bror?"

"Bror is old. Bror is boring." Ru paused as she saw my look of distress on Bror's behalf. Bror and I had always been close, and I hated to hear him referred to so offhandedly, especially by the woman he loved more than life itself. "I know Bror means well, Tris. He is a nice man. He is just not someone I can ever love."

I nodded with understanding. Love was a fickle thing. Sometimes it came only to one person but not another. I was reminded to be ever-grateful that both Morning Star and I were equally madly in love with each other.

* * *

Even if Karno had Ru's approval, he still faced somewhat of an uphill battle. But it was also true that he did not do himself many favors. He would temporarily win her over with a small offering, such as a needle or a bracelet made up of flowers, the stems woven neatly together and colorful blossoms facing outward. But then he would raise her ire by doing something inappropriate. Such as: one day I saw Ru bend over the fire pit to stir the coals, and Karno's better discretion must have been overwhelmed by the sight. Just for a moment, he placed both hands on her rump. Ru spun around with a wrathful expression on her face and she slapped him with all the force she could muster. The wallop made him momentarily stagger and nearly knocked him off his feet. Ru then stormed off amidst the throng of barking dogs without a backward glance. Luckily for Karno, the dogs and I were the only residents of the family compound to witness this event. Ordinarily, I would have taken it upon myself to protect my sister's virtue and sternly warn Karno never to do such a thing again. But as he stood there holding the side of his cheek and looking stunned, I felt assured that Ru had sufficiently made her point all by herself. Yet I was soon taken with guilt at my laxness. I went over to Karno, who stared after Ru with a hand still pressed to his face.

"Karno …" I began.

Karno turned to me and he shook his head.

"I know, Tris. Karno very bad," he hung his head. "Now Ru angry. She hit very hard."

Karno had my empathy. Although his action had been unseemly, on occasion a similar view of Morning

Star had inspired me to put my hands on her posterior in the same way. But she was my mate, and I never did it in front of other people.

"Tris must think Karno come from very bad people," Karno said sadly, "Do not judge my people by me. Karno away from home very long time. My father Great Man of my people. He know Karno sometimes bad and send me away. Karno not go home until Karno good."

"You cannot go home?" I questioned. Although I had pondered this very thing, I was incredulous at this news – both the fact that he had been sent away and the admission that he was *bad*.

"Karno go home soon. Away almost two years. Maybe now father forgive me. Maybe now father think Karno good man."

I looked at Karno doubtfully, since I had just seen him seize my sister by her bottom and he had conceded to his unacceptable behavior. Karno saw my skepticism.

"Karno try to be very good man. Must learn to be Great Man like father. Ru teach me to be Great Man. Father will be happy," Karno stated.

"Why did he send you away?" I asked.

I did not like to pry, but I felt I owed it to my family to find out more about the situation. If Karno and his fellow Wolf-men were dangerous criminals, we needed to know about it.

"Karno not mean trouble," Karno shrugged. "Father will forgive. He very angry at time. Very angry. But it was accident. House burn. Nothing left."

"*House burn?*" I repeated. If this was true, I could well imagine his father's rage. The loss of an entire household's worth of possessions and stores was truly catastrophic for any family. Even if the family survived the period of deprivation from the lack of shelter and food stores, it would take years to once again accumulate everything that was destroyed in the blaze.

"Yes ... Mino and Karno play with sticks ... fire sticks ... play-fighting. House go *phoom*!" Karno motioned that it was a big fire. "House very old, very dry. People not hurt, but father very, very angry. Father send Karno and Mino away, but send good friend Bewok and other men with us to keep watch on us. He say come back when Karno learn good ways. Ru teach me good ways."

If Ru did in fact accept him, I felt positive that she would make sure he learned to stay out of mischief. Karno was swiftly discovering that Ru, like his "Great Man" father, was capable of great ire. Karno had learned the word *forgive* early on, as he often had to plead for Ru's forgiveness.

"Where is your home?" I said to Karno, "Is it far from here?"

"Yes," Karno nodded. "We travel every day until we come here. No stop make camp or clean hides; just walk and hunt. Very hard winters. But father send good men with me. We live to return home. Karno show father Karno can be Great Man like him. Take his place when he die."

I was confused.

"Take his place?"

"Yes, father Great Man. Karno will take his place as Great Man. Ru will be mate to Great Man. My people do what Karno say, what Ru say."

"Do you mean that your father is an Elder?" I was getting the idea that Karno was not just referring to his father as *great* merely out of a son's admiration for his parent.

"What is *Elder?*"

I searched my mind for a description of the term that Karno could understand.

"An Elder is a person who makes decisions for his people. Where and when to hunt. Where to live. The Elder is obeyed."

"Tris, too many words! But yes, my father say to people where, when to hunt. When he die, Karno tell people what to do. Ru will, too."

I was silent as I absorbed this information. I was relieved that Karno was not a miscreant exiled for crimes. He was an unruly young man who had been sent away to repent for his reckless behavior, with an escort to ensure his safety. But I was disconcerted to know that Karno had come from a very distant place indeed. If Ru were paired with him, it was likely we would never see her again. Puh's worse fears for her would be realized. Plus, even while Muh had been alive, Ru had acted as a second mother to her younger siblings. Now that Muh had passed, Ru and Gran took care of the children. If Ru left us, the children would be heartbroken, and since Gran was too old to manage them by herself, we would have to figure out some alternative arrangement for their sustenance and safekeeping.

Karno was studying my face, trying to read my thoughts.

"No worry, Tris. Karno will be good man to Ru. Karno learn to be man Ru wants, make Ru happy. No angry with Karno anymore."

* * *

That night, the Wolf-men again joined us for our evening meal, having supplied the meat that fed the large group. But this time, they did not wander off as they usually did at sunset.

Karno had made up to Ru with another offering of one of his ornaments, a necklace featuring a pendant of a finely polished green stone. Ru wore the gift with great pride.

Karno invited Ru to sit next to him, and after just a moment's hesitation she sat down at his side.

"What do after eat?" Karno asked Ru when the meal had concluded.

"We talk a little bit and then I help clean up and put the children to bed. The men may stay up and talk until all the adults are ready to settle in for the night," Ru replied.

"Talk and clean? Gah!" Karno exclaimed. "No music?"

"I do not know what you mean," Ru responded. "What is *music*?"

"We show you ... show all you ..." Karno broke off and spoke to his comrades in their own tongue.

The Wolf-men seemed pleased with what he had to say. They all arose and after a brief search, during which they collected various stones and pieces of wood, they returned to their seats and looked to Karno for instruction.

"Ho!" Karno called out, and suddenly the Wolf-men began to rhythmically strike their stones or chunks of wood with hammers of rock, sticks, or bone, while chanting in unison. The effect was enthralling and so pleasant to hear. Prior to now we had listened to Black Wolf belt out his songs when we were on the trail, and I suppose that the Wolf-men's chanting could be considered a song of sorts, but this *music* was very different from anything we had previously heard.

I watched Ru as she gazed upon Karno while he skillfully made his stone sing and vocalized his part of the chant in a strong voice that contrasted starkly with the softly spoken tones of the Old Ones. Ru was aglow in a way I had never seen her before. I looked over at Puh and saw that he too was watching Ru intently. His demeanor was very serious. I knew that

Puh wanted Ru to be happy, but there could be so many repercussions with her choice to either go away with Karno or to stay home.

I had told Puh a little of my conversation with Karno, including the fact that Karno was the son of an Elder, or Great Man, as he termed it. Puh then brought up something I had not considered: regardless of Ru's decision, the location of our compound would then be known to a people other than Black Wolf and his family, for the first time since all the many generations of my family had lived here. And worse, Puh soberly expressed his fear that if Karno returned home without Ru, unhappy at her rejection, Karno eventually might come back with a stronger force and either try to take Ru against her will or wreak his revenge on us, or both.

But the song made these possible threats retreat to the back of my mind. When the *music* ceased, none of us wanted it to end.

"Karno, would you and your friends play more *music* for us?" Ru asked.

Karno reached for Ru's hand and gave it an affectionate squeeze.

"We make more music for Ru," he nodded.

After a consultation with the other Wolf-men, the music began again with a different tune. We all listened appreciatively without speaking. Whenever one song was over, they would soon start another one, broken by only a short interlude filled with the peaceful chorus from the summertime frogs and insects as they filled the air with their gentle chirps and hums.

We were so entranced that it was only after the moon was well-risen when we noticed that most of the younger children had fallen asleep or were in the midst of nodding off.

"Tris, Fox must be put to bed," Morning Star whispered to me.

Now it that was dark, she did not want to walk up the hill to our home by herself.

"Yes, my sweet. We will go home now." I turned to Karno and his men. "Many thanks for playing your *music* for us! I very much enjoyed hearing it."

"Yes, thank you," Morning Star chimed in. "I have never heard such lovely sounds. We must put Fox to bed now. Pleasant evening to you all."

"Pleasant evening," I echoed, raising my hand to bid them all farewell until morning.

* * *

Morning brought with it an unusual sight. After we ate our breakfast and Little Fawn had come up for her daily visit with Fox before beginning her chores, I ventured down the hill to the family compound. There I found Puh scanning the many bodies, both human and canine, that still slept around our outdoor hearth. Evidently, the previous day's gathering had run late into the night and the Wolf-men had opted to make themselves comfortable on the mats that covered the ground around the hearth. The morning air was slightly cool, so the men were lying close to one another for warmth, many snuggled up with one of Black Wolf's dogs. Karno had his arms wrapped around one of the larger dogs, and each of them looked completely contented as they slumbered.

I stopped to observe Karno, who was snoring softly. Or maybe it was the dog that was snoring and the noise only seemed to emanate from Karno. Either way, I noted that, as Ru had said, Karno was a well-built man. It took some time to become accustomed to his appearance, but once one was used to his skin markings and short hair, he really did not look too different from most Old Ones, except for his darker coloring and somewhat larger teeth. Despite that his people might sometimes be called Bone Crunchers, I never saw them use their teeth to crack bones. Maybe, as Puh had said, the stories about the Bone Crunchers were tales told to scare children into obeying their parents.

"How late did they make their music?" I asked Puh.

"I do not know," Puh replied. "They were still awake when Ria and I went to bed. But I stayed up long enough to make sure that Gran and the children, including Ru, were safely ensconced in Black Wolf's house. That was the only place large enough to fit them all. Then Black Wolf cleverly turned out his dogs to keep an eye on the Wolf-men."

"Yes, I can see that the dogs are keeping an eye on them," I said to Puh with a grin.

Puh grinned, too.

"Well, they might not be actually keeping an eye on them, but they will certainly know if any of them move."

At that moment, Ru, Petal, and Ty came up the path from the creek, where they had refilled numerous water bags. They greeted us quietly so as not to disturb the sleeping men.

Ru looked upon Karno with an enamored expression.

"He is a handsome man, is he not?" Ru said to Petal.

Petal nodded vigorously.

"Oh yes," Petal agreed. It seemed Petal had hoped she might attract the attention of one of the Wolf-men, too, but Black Wolf had quickly and quite adamantly made it known to Petal that she was much too young to become paired. Even though Petal was fourteen winters old and tall – taller, in fact, than any of the Wolf-men – neither Black Wolf nor Little Fawn wished to see her paired with any of these men. Children of the Old Ones matured earlier than did The People. At fifteen winters old they were considered to be adults. Ru had attained her full size some time ago, and she would reach her fifteenth winter this year. So there was no such excuse for her. That said, I had trouble reconciling the idea that my little sister would soon be ready for pairing, that she was indeed at an acceptable age for choosing a mate.

Puh and I exchanged glances. He looked grimly resigned but said nothing.

* * *

The morning was still young when we heard the sounds of barking dogs, which roused Black Wolf's canines from their peaceful repose with the Wolf-men. Both dogs and Wolf-men sleepily stirred themselves, the dogs uttering halfhearted woofs. They were not concerned; they recognized the distant voices of the pups, and so did I. I was pleased to know that they belonged to my cousins' new dogs; it could mean only that Bror, Dor, and Lor were not far off.

Puh and I withdrew a bit to give the Wolf-men a few moments in which to compose themselves before they had to be sociable. Likewise, Ty and Petal continued on with their water bags to hang them up in their respective homes. But Ru stopped and knelt by Karno.

"Pleasant day to you, Karno," Ru said to him as he still lay on the matting, propped up on one elbow and massaging the sleep from his face. Ru giggled a little to see that Karno's cheek bore the perfect imprint of the matting on which he had slept. Karno smiled at her in return.

"Pleasant, yes," Karno said, "Karno open eye to pretty Ru. Very pleasant!"

"I hope that Bror is on his way here," Puh whispered to me, "If so, Bror's timing could not be better!"

I nodded and speculated that just because the cousins' dogs were nearby, it did not mean that Bror had necessarily accompanied them. But I fervently hoped that he had.

"You must be hungry and thirsty," Ru said to Karno. "Go down to the stream to wash and I will prepare a breakfast for you and your men."

"Yes, Pretty One," Karno nodded to Ru, looking at her adoringly.

Ru rose to her feet and entered the house with her water bag. Karno briefly watched her walk away to admire the view she presented, and then sat up and rubbed his eyes. But he soon did as Ru bade and left us to make his way down to the creek. A few of the Wolf-men followed him, but some still lounged on the ground, apparently in no hurry to begin their day.

Within a matter of moments, the dogs began to bark in earnest as my three cousins Bror, Dor, and Lor, joined by their mother, my Aunt Vee, emerged from the path with their two nearly full-grown pups.

Puh and I greeted them joyously, and soon most of the family had come out to welcome them as well. The younger children vied to get Vee's attention, holding her hand and talking to her all at once. Bror and his brothers looked around at the strangers who still remained scattered around the outdoor hearth. If they had any thoughts about the unconventional appearance of the Wolf-men, with their short hair and body markings, they did not remark on it.

"Have we arrived at an inopportune time?" Bror inquired, speaking quietly to keep our conversation private. "It would seem that you have company already."

"No, you are here at a very good time," Puh told Bror. "We are very happy to see you."

Bror smiled at this.

"That is good. We were worried when you did not stop in on your way to the coast as you usually do every summer, so we decided to travel here to make sure that all is well," Bror informed us, still eyeing the Wolf-men. "If a troubling situation has come about, I hope we may be of help."

Ru then exited the main family domicile, her hands burdened with a large birch-bark tray.

"Bror!" Ru exclaimed, nearly dropping the tray in surprise. She quickly recovered and tightened her grasp on the tray, but Bror strode over and took it from her.

"Let me help you, Ru," Bror said gently. "It is so good to see you. I was very concerned when you and your family did not arrive last moon to stop over with us as you do each summer on your way to the shore. We were so worried when we spoke of it yesterday that we just packed up and left right away. We did not make it all the way here before dark, of course, but we started out again early this morning. It is such a relief to finally reach our destination and see you looking well."

"Um ... many thanks, Bror." Ru reluctantly relinquished the tray to Bror. "We have guests. I am preparing to feed them something to break their night's fast."

"Of course," Bror walked alongside Ru. "Let me assist you."

Ru stared at her feet and suddenly looked grieved. Did she feel guilty at throwing aside Bror's many moons of kind and patient wooing for the dubious charms of the brash young man who had abruptly entered her life?

Before Ru could respond, Karno reappeared at the head of the path from the stream, his hair and beard still dripping wet. He seemed quite surprised to see Bror walking with Ru. Or maybe it was just Bror's size that had him taken aback. Karno was a very fit man with a strong build, but Bror's bulging muscles, quite noticeable given that he was dressed like the rest of us men, in only a loincloth, were enough to give anyone pause on first sight.

"Who this?" Karno asked, pointing to Bror.

"Karno, this is my cousin, Bror. He and his brothers and my aunt have come to visit us. Bror, this is Karno," Ru said by way of introduction. "Bror has helped me to bring out this food so that you and your men may eat. I will go for water now. I will return in a moment."

"I will help you," Bror volunteered. He quickly turned to follow Ru, giving her no chance to object.

Karno looked after them curiously as he approached me.

"Tris, you people funny. You tall and strong, but you cousin like bear wrestler. All have hair like fire. And you do funny thing with face sometimes." Karno shook his head.

I understood the part about me being tall and Bror being brawny, and the fact that we had red hair, but I did not know what he meant about our faces.

"*Funny thing with face?*" I repeated.

"Yes ... Karno see you smoosh face with mate ... what that?" Karno replied. "You Puh, Tor, smoosh face with funny little mate heavy with baby."

"Do you mean kissing?" I asked, somewhat incredulous that he did not know what it was to kiss.

"Karno not know name. But smooshing faces very not clean. Gah! Food and drink go in mouth ... sometime come out of mouth, too! Gah! Very not clean!" Karno seemed horrified at the idea of *smooshing faces*.

"No, no," I insisted, "kissing is very nice!"

"Gah!" Karno said with revulsion, "Not clean! Ru would not like! Not clean!"

I was not so sure that Ru would not like to be kissed, but I was not going to pursue the subject any further. That was Ru's business, and if she decided that she wanted to *smoosh faces* with Karno, it would be up to her to make a convert of him.

The rest of the Wolf-men had returned from the creek and were already eating their breakfasts when Ru and Bror came out with a water bag and gourd cups. Bror carried the bag over his shoulder and silently poured out a serving of water while Ru held the cups under the spout and passed the gourds to the men. There were not enough cups for everyone, so they had to share. This meant that Bror and Ru had to walk amongst the Wolf-men to repeatedly refill the drinking vessels. Karno's eyes followed them thoughtfully.

"Pretty One," Karno called out to Ru, "Karno very thirsty." Ru wordlessly motioned Bror to follow her to Karno so that she could replenish his cup. Karno scrutinized Bror more closely. "You stay here this night?" Karno inquired.

"If my kin will have me and my family," Bror replied simply.

"We make music tonight," Karno announced. "We play. You listen."

Bror just nodded with a benign smile, moving away to help Ru refill the next man's cup.

* * *

It was a relief to have my three male cousins here now that the Wolf-men were making themselves at home on our family compound. The place was more crowded and far noisier than it had ever been previously, but at least the addition of three adult males helped to even the odds, effectively doubling the number of men we could count on to assist us in keeping the peace, if need be. We did not tell Bror about the situation between Ru and Karno; he was an astute man and he would understand without our explanation. Puh and I had faith that Bror would handle things in his usual calm, patient, and stoic way. To affect the injured, spurned suitor would only make him look pathetic in Ru's eyes and turn her against him even more. Bror's best course of action was to continue to quietly stand by Ru and let the scenario play itself out. At this juncture, I did not believe that Bror had much of a chance, but I very much wished for his success.

That evening, as before, the Wolf-men played their music for us. And again, Ru sat next to Karno, smiling at him effusively and allowing him to touch her arm or hand on occasion. Karno was on his best behavior, and the music he and his companions provided was well-received by their audience. Bror was seated with Morning Star and me, his mother also near us so that she could hold Fox, whom she had not seen since a moon or so after he was born. I noted that Bror put on a good front, but I also saw that he had evidently perceived the depth of the developing relationship between Ru and Karno. He said nothing, but I thought I detected a great sadness in his bearing. It must have been devastating for him to at long last see the spark of love in Ru's eyes, only to find it was directed toward someone else.

"Bror," I began, speaking in a low voice so that only he could hear me. "I have not had a chance to go hunting in quite some time ... we have been reluctant to leave our families alone, what with the Wolf-men in the area. Would you and your brothers be willing to stay here so that Puh, Ria, and I could get away for at least part of a day?"

"Of course," Bror nodded. "I would be happy to do so, and I am sure my brothers would be willing, as well. Maybe Black Wolf would like to join you. Perhaps Karno and some of his men would care to go, too."

I nodded. I was positive that Black Wolf would consider even a brief outing an agreeable respite from his perpetual state of discord with Little Fawn. And, as far as hunting with Karno and his fellows was concerned, I would relish the opportunity to watch their hunting tactics. Maybe it would clear up the mystery of how the Wolf-men managed to hunt without the benefit of having long hair.

"That is a very good idea, Bror," I said. "I feel there may be rain on the incoming wind, but it will be warm enough that it will still be pleasant to get away for a bit on the morrow."

"I feel it, too," Bror concurred. "While I do not mind a little rain on a summer's day, I also do not mind staying here with your family while you, Tor, Ria, and Black Wolf venture out on a foray with the Wolf-men." Bror smiled as he said this. I knew what he was thinking. Karno would be gone and he would have Ru to himself ... well, himself and his brothers, who also shared an interest in Ru; but they were not as keenly infatuated as was Bror. Plus, Bror had the comfort of knowing that Ru was even less impressed with Dor and Lor than she was with him, so he had little competition to fear from his siblings.

"I will speak to Puh, Ria, and Black Wolf," I said as I arose, and touched Morning Star's shoulder for a moment as I told her, "I will soon return."

Puh was across the clearing that was situated between the main family domicile and Black Wolf and Little Fawn's new home. I walked around the half-circle of people who sat before the performing Wolf-men, to where Puh and Ria were seated.

"Puh," I said, leaning in close so Puh could hear me over the measured beats and the loud harmonized chanting of the Wolf-men, "Bror says that he and his brothers will stay here with our families so that you, Ria, Black Wolf, and I can get out hunting. He suggests that we take Karno and some if his men with us. What do you think of this notion?"

Puh smiled as he and Ria exchanged pleased glances. Ria was now only two moons from delivering her baby, but she was still eager to go with us.

"Yes!" Ria grinned in response. "Let us go tomorrow morning!"

"Go where tomorrow morning?" Black Wolf had overheard Ria's exuberant reply.

"Hunting," Puh replied. "Of course, you do not need to accompany us, if you do not wish to go."

"Of course I want to go!" Black Wolf exclaimed.

Karno held up his hand and the music came to a stop. He seemed somewhat annoyed that some of the assemblage's attention had wandered.

"What? What?" Karno asked impatiently.

"We were just discussing plans to embark on a hunt tomorrow," I explained. "Maybe you and some of your men would like to join us."

Karno grinned broadly at this idea.

"Yes! We hunt! Must be away with sun. Must sleep now." Karno spoke to his men in their tongue and they immediately broke up their performance to prepare for a night's rest. Karno turned to Ru, resting his dark hand over her fair one. "Karno wish pleasant sleep to Ru."

Ru stared intently into Karno's face and he returned her gaze, smiling softly.

"Pleasant sleep to you, Karno," Ru nodded to him.

Karno arose and left Ru sitting there alone, but Bror was soon at her side and he helped Ru to her feet.

"My mother is already herding the children together to put them to bed," Bror said gently, "but if we hurry, we may get to help her."

Ru twisted her neck so that she might look for Karno, but he had already disappeared into the shadows outside the circle of firelight.

"Yes, the children do need to go to sleep," Ru agreed.

Saree and Twie came up to Bror, looking up at him expectantly.

"Bror," Twie started, "Will you tell us a story tonight?"

Bror's father had been a Keeper of Stories, and although Bror had not officially taken over the role, he did know all of his father's tales by rote. When called upon, he obliged requests for a yarn or anecdote. Bror looked down at Twie and Saree affectionately, and then stooped to lift them both into his arms. Both girls eagerly embraced his thick neck and nestled up to his bearded face.

"Of course I will tell you some stories," Bror promised, kissing each girl on the cheek as they giggled. "But you will have to tell me what kind of story you want to hear so I know which ones to pick. And they must not be scary stories or you will not want to sleep tonight."

* * *

We met at the family compound shortly after sunrise. The skies were a murky gray, but the rain had not yet begun. Despite the promise of a sodden day, I was elated at the thought of getting away from home for a while. This was the first summer I had ever spent in its entirety at our woodland home, and I was enjoying the lush green of the midsummer foliage and the colorful profusion of flowers. By the time of our usual return from the coast, the greenery had dulled to a tired shade of green, and many of the leaves showed evidence of overgrazing by both animals and insects. Additionally, many of the blooms had gone by or were well past their peak. Until now, I did not realize how much verdant beauty we missed by going away for the early summer moons.

Our families and most of the Wolf-men were gathered to see us off. Puh, Ria, Black Wolf, and I waited for Karno to finish speaking at length with his comrades. He seemed to be leaving them with detailed instructions, although his tone also indicated that he was admonishing them, too. Finally, Karno turned to us, at last ready to depart.

"Karno bring Mino and Bewok with me," Karno said.

I nodded in response his statement. I had actually hoped that he would bring more of his men with us, since that still left ten Wolf-men at home with our families.

"You would not like to bring more of your friends with us?" I asked.

"No." Karno shook his head. "Karno leave men to do what Ru say."

Puh, Black Wolf, and I traded confused glances. Even Ru looked surprised.

"Karno tell them," he went on, "do what Ru say! Ru say *wash in stream*, you wash in stream! Ru say *get meat*, you get meat! Ru say *make fire*, you make fire! Karno make sure his men take care of Ru and you families while we hunt. Everyone safe. Cousins, too." Karno pointed at Bror, Dor, and Lor.

"Many thanks," Bror said, quietly acknowledging that Karno intended to keep him safe from harm, as well. It seemed rather ridiculous, particularly as Bror stood there looking so massive next to the Wolf-men, his powerful arms folded across his muscular chest. But the irony was lost on Karno.

Now that it was time to go I kissed Morning Star and Fox as I said my farewells to them. Out of the corner of my eye I saw Karno and his fellow Wolf-men grimace. Not very discreetly, Karno uttered *Gah!* in disgust. I smiled to myself. They did not know what they were missing. I found it hard to believe that any man would not like to kiss his loved ones. Especially his mate.

A few stray raindrops fell from the sky as we walked down the trail leading away from the family compound.

"Tris, we make stop over there," Karno pointed into the forest.

We did not know why Karno requested this detour, but we silently followed the Wolf-men as they broke from the trail until we reached the place where the Wolf-men must have camped before settling in with us a few days ago. It was disconcertingly close to our homes, no more than a short trek away. The Wolf-men had found a large uprooted tree that had torn up a sizable chunk of earth with its roots when it toppled. This had created a large cavern in the ground that the Wolf-men had then turned into a shelter by placing tree branches within the tangled roots to create a roof of sorts. It must have been a tight squeeze to pack them all within the enclosure, but at least it offered some protection from both the weather and predators.

The Wolf-men also made use of the nearby trees' lower limbs to store some of their personal belongings. All around their campsite the branches were festooned with the men's wolf pelts. The hanging wolfskins looked much like an overripe crop of thoroughly exhausted canines. I noted that various other items that were similarly hung there for safekeeping: packs, water bags of various sizes, and other odd bits of impedimenta. Karno, Mino, and Bewok each selected his pack, water bag and pelt. Situating the wolfskins on their heads, the men seemed satisfied to have their old friends restored to their former place. We set out down the path once more.

I wondered at the wisdom of donning those odiferous pelts for this excursion. The strong scent would surely alert every animal in the area to the Wolf-men's presence. I smiled to see the Wolf-men interweaving the wolf pelts' forelegs amongst their clattering necklaces, effectively silencing their ornaments as we hiked down the trail. Now if they could only do something about the pungent smell of their wolfskins. But that did not seem likely.

As usual, we did not speak as we hunted. We pointed at tracks, animal droppings, tufts of shed fur that adhered to the brush, places where some creature had scraped up a section of bark on a tree or the turf at our feet. These signs helped us to formulate a strategy against our potential prey.

At last, we came upon fresh signs indicating that a number of deer had recently passed this way. They were likely fallow deer, since they were larger than roe deer, but not as big as red deer or elk. The hoofprints included the tracks of several does, their yearling offspring, a smattering of new fawns and one very large buck, which appeared to be traveling separately from the rest of the herd, just a little way off. All except the buck were following the path in single file. The buck's tracks crisscrossed the trail at several junctions; it must have been a cagey old stag that was diligently canvassing the locality for possible threats.

These deer were near enough to enable us to catch up with them, but we needed to close in on them without scaring them off. If they took to running, we did not have a chance – that is, unless we could get ahead of them and drive them back toward waiting hunters.

We were all of the same mind. We stopped and looked at one another. Karno tapped Mino and Bewok on their shoulders and motioned that they were to accompany him ahead. He then motioned to Ria, Puh, Black Wolf, and me to lie in wait until they ran the deer at us. We all nodded in agreement. The Wolf-men broke from the trail and departed at a swift trot. Puh glanced up at a nearby tree, touched Ria's arm and pointed in the direction of his gaze. She merely blinked her eyes at him to signal that she understood. Puh boosted her up into the tree, where her arrows would have a clear shot at the incoming deer. Then the rest of us withdrew from view behind clumps of brush, patiently expectant that the panicked deer would eventually arrive.

The dreary gray day progressed from occasional raindrops to a steady drizzle. A gentle breeze rustled the foliage as insects buzzed and birds sang. It had been a dry summer, and the birds particularly seemed to enjoy the refreshing liquid bounty that fell from the sky. I, too, gratefully lifted my face upward and let the rain wash down my parched skin. I was thirsty as well, but I did not want to take a swig from my small water bag and thus call attention to myself. I licked my rain-wet lips to moisten my tongue. As the time passed and the rain continued to fall, I pondered why it was that my nose or my back or some other body part seemed to be persistently itchy just when it was imperative that I stay absolutely still.

Then a flash of motion caught my attention. Shifting only my eyes, I looked at Puh. A bird had perched on his spear, which was poised for the anticipated ambush. Puh did not divert his gaze. He remained focused on the trail. The steady rain slowed until it became a heavy mist.

Suddenly, distant howls reached our ears. I heard Ria adjust her position in the tree overhead and select several arrows, but she did not yet draw back on her bow.

More howling, followed by the sounds of animals crashing through the brush. The frightened deer had left the path and were coming at us in a confused, terror-stricken throng.

In a moment the brush before us parted, exposing the russet white-freckled bodies of the deer. Ria's arrows quickly flew, hitting numerous targets. In the meantime, Puh and I each struck the same large doe with our spears, instinctively twisting the spear as we drove it in to widen the wound. Black Wolf managed to lance a yearling doe.

The howling had kept up during our assault, but now it turned into an assortment of sharps barks and cries. The Wolf-men rejoined us, panting for breath as they emerged from the dewy forest. They grinned at the sight of the fallen deer.

Puh helped Ria down from the tree, finally breaking our silence.

"You managed to shoot at least three deer!" Puh said to Ria, as she grinned triumphantly. "These two are down; let us track the others. They were well hit; they could not have gone far."

We followed the bloody trails to find two deer that were clearly nearing exsanguination. The throats were quickly slashed to hurry their departure from life. However, there was one more deer to be located and dispatched. Karno soon found signs left by the injured animal. It was the big buck.

We stealthily crept through the undergrowth. Karno, who was at our lead, held up his hand and we all stopped in place. Keeping his hand aloft to hold us where we stood, he proceeded forward, step by watchful step, spear at the ready. Then Karno, too, halted his progress. He was completely still, but his gaze was intent on something. Karno's head tilted to one side and then the other.

"Buck stuck!" Karno announced.

"What?" Black Wolf asked. "How could it be stuck?"

"Karno think it dead," Karno said. "It stumble between fallen trees and stay there. Stuck. Much blood."

We cautiously worked our way forward until we could see for ourselves. The big buck had indeed come down between the trunks of two fallen trees. It lay motionless, but still resplendent with its glossy speckled coat and impressive velvet-covered antlers.

Karno passed his spear to Mino and pulled his knife from its sheath.

"Karno cut beast throat … be sure dead," he told us.

It would be an awkward reach over the tree trunks and profusion of tangled branches to access the buck's neck, so Karno stepped over one of the trunks and straddled the buck's body. He then sat on the deer's back, bending forward at the waist and wrapping his left arm around the buck's neck so that he could use it as leverage to make a good, strong, clean cut with his right.

Just as Karno thrust his knife into the buck, it screamed loudly as it seemingly returned from the other side of death to spring into the air with a mighty leap before our startled eyes. Karno's knife flew from his grip, and I could see he was using both hands to desperately grasp the base of the stag's antlers and legs to cling to the animal's spotted back as it plunged wildly between stands of trees.

We soon recovered from our collective stupor and broke out into a run as we pursued Karno and the sorrowfully bellowing buck. Did the deer know this was its last day of life? In any case, the buck did not get far. Between Karno's additional weight and its grievous injuries, the buck soon collapsed again. This time, the stag was really and truly dead.

 **Chapter Five**

Karno calmly dismounted from the stag's back as though this happenstance was an everyday occurrence. And I had to acknowledge that for all I knew of the Wolf-men's hunting methods, it was possible that for him, it was.

Karno looked down at the beast and shook his head. His wolfskin had slipped off the top of his head, but the pelt's forelegs were still interwoven with his necklaces and tied around his neck, leaving the wolf's face peering over his right shoulder like a child on a piggyback ride. Karno adjusted the wayward pelt until the wolf's head was once again properly situated on top of his own.

"Big buck," Karno stated. "Tris, we need cousin, Bear Wrestler Man, to help carry buck home."

"I am sure that Bror would be glad to assist us," I said.

Karno waved my remark aside. "My friends help. We carry what can. Bring friends back get big buck."

"The other deer are relatively small," Puh agreed. "I think we can manage the two does and the two yearlings between the six of us men." Puh then looked at Ria, who had been standing by him, very quiet. "Are you all right, Ria?"

"Yes, my love," Ria nodded. "The baby is kicking. I do not think it likes me to run anymore, and it is showing its displeasure by prodding me."

Puh touched the side of Ria's face, studying her carefully.

"Are you sure you are well enough for the walk home?" he asked.

"Yes," Ria said with a nod; but she did indeed look uncomfortable as she rubbed her bloated abdomen.

We gutted the buck and hung it from a tree so that it could continue to bleed out in our absence. We then returned to the other deer and repeated the process on them before finally lashing their ankles to lengths of deadwood. We carried them homeward, the two yearlings tied together and suspended from a branch between Black Wolf and me, and Puh and the three Wolf-men paired up to similarly transport the does back to the family compound.

* * *

We had been hiking for some time, occasionally pausing to switch our loads from one shoulder to the other, when Puh requested that we halt our procession. We each set down our burdens and gratefully drank a gulp or two of water. All except Ria. Puh went to her.

"Sit a moment," Puh said to her.

"I want to keep walking," she insisted.

"Funny little woman not look good," Karno piped up.

Black Wolf frowned at Karno and disapprovingly elbowed him. But it was true. Ria was pale, and she appeared to be pained.

"I think you should sit," Puh persisted gently.

Puh had no sooner said this when there was splash of water at Ria's bare feet.

Poor Ria was mortified. Karno and his fellow Wolf-men did not hide their revulsion and said *Gah!* multiple times. Both Puh and Black Wolf were well-acquainted with birthing, so they took the scene in stride; but the Wolf-men did not appear to be familiar with what was happening. I myself knew only what little I had been told by Morning Star.

"Are you having contractions?" Puh inquired, easing Ria into a sitting position until she was leaning back against the base of a tree trunk.

"I think so. I started feeling cramps after we chased the buck, but I did not think the baby was ready to come yet, so I was not concerned," Ria explained. "Now I think that the baby is thoroughly fed up at its rough treatment and it has decided to evacuate itself as quickly as possible."

I was worried for the infant. I wondered if it would be born too soon to survive. I fervently wished for this little one to be strong and healthy. Not only for its own sake, but for Puh and Ria. Most premature babies did not live long, but occasionally some overcame the perils of their fragile state and went to live good lives. At that moment I desired that above all else.

"We are not far from the family compound," Black Wolf said as he knelt by Ria, patting her hand sympathetically. "We can carry you home, where you can have your baby in privacy and in more comfort than you would have out here in the damp forest."

"Many thanks, Black Wolf," Ria managed a wan smile at him, putting her small hand atop of his very large one. "But I am not sure there is time to bring me home. This baby is very impatient. Tor, would you please help me to sit up straighter …"

"Yes, my love." Puh put his arm behind Ria's shoulders and carefully propped her torso a little higher. Then Puh looked up at me, "Tris, I need you to run home and bring back some of the blankets from our house. Maybe some extra water … Ria will be thirsty and we will need to wash away the blood from Ria and the baby. Take the Wolf-men with you, if they will go."

"Yes, Puh …" I was cut off by Ria's sudden cry. It was a strangled sort of croak, as though she were trying to stifle the sound.

The Dreamer III – The People of the Wolves

"The baby is coming!" Ria gasped, grimacing as she strained to push out the infant.

"Black Wolf, get behind Ria and support her back so that I can come around and catch the infant." Puh spoke softly, but with urgency.

Black Wolf did as instructed. I stood by, mesmerized. I had never been present at the birth of a child. Luckily, Puh had often helped to deliver many of the children that he and my Muh had conceived. He knew just what to do.

Ria held her clothing out of the way so that the expanding pool of watery blood could flow freely onto the ground, and she continued to gasp every few moments.

"I can see the top of the baby's head," Puh announced, in a tone just above a whisper.

In unison, the Wolf-men said *Gah!*

"It may be easier if you are squatting," Puh told Ria. "Do you want me to help you move?"

Ria nodded, and between Puh and Black Wolf, they gingerly lifted her until she was in position. Ria groaned. We could see that the baby's head was now completely outside of her body. It was gray and covered in blood. The Wolf-men shouted *Gah!* in alarm and turned away, unable to view the rest of the birthing process. I thought they were rather squeamish for men who butchered animals almost daily. One more groan from Ria and the baby came out in a final gush of bloody liquid, followed a moment later by the afterbirth.

I was so enthralled by this amazing spectacle that I had forgotten I was supposed to be running for home. Puh then looked up at me.

"Tris, *run*!" Puh commanded.

"We go, too!" Karno needed no encouragement to accompany me.

* * *

The Wolf-men and I ran in the gradually lengthening shadows until we reached the family compound. The calm and well-ordered peace of the place was disrupted by our breathless entrance. Ru had indeed put the remaining Wolf-men to work. Each one was busily involved in some task, most notably cleaning the hides from recent kills. This was one of Ru's least-favorite chores, and she was quite pleased to have these cheerful laborers do the work for her. Not that she herself had been idle.

I purposefully strode past Ru as she stitched a boot, heading straight for Puh and Ria's home. Ru gaped at me as I passed by her.

"Tris, what has happened? Where are the others?"

"I am going back to them," I said shortly as I entered Puh and Ria's house. I quickly located an armload of blankets and their largest water bag. These items easily filled my arms. I exited the domicile and was met by Ru's anxious face.

The Dreamer III ~ The People of the Wolves

"Tris! Answer me! What has happened?"

"Ria has birthed her baby!" I replied.

After a brief greeting to Ru, Karno spoke to his fellow Wolf-men, chattering to them with great animation. From the horrified expressions on their faces, it appeared that he was describing the child's arrival. When Karno crouched down and affected a suitably pained look for the edification of his fellow Wolf-men, they all exclaimed *Gah!* That confirmed my suspicions. Then Karno, Mino, and Bewok hastened to join me. Karno took the water bag and Mino and Bewok each took a blanket. Ru still wanted more answers, but we needed to hurry away again.

"What was it?" Ru demanded.

"A baby!" I absently called over my shoulder and then we were running down the trail once more.

* * *

It was awkward to run with the water bag and heavy blankets and our spears, but we managed to make our way back before long. Puh and Black Wolf were on either side of Ria, each with one arm around her, and in their other hands they held their spears. They had been left in a dangerous situation, what with the dead deer and the blood and afterbirth nearby, all of which would attract predators. They had moved Ria and the baby some distance away, settling on a grassy plot within sight of the trail so we would not miss them on our return.

"Is everything all right?" I questioned Puh, searching his face for some clue to how they had fared since our departure.

Puh smiled and gazed down fondly at Ria, who was asleep. The baby was inside her garment, where it was nestled against her skin. I could see a bit of its small face and its blaze of red hair.

"Yes," Puh nodded. "We had to move away from the deer. A sow bear and her three cubs came along. They were very interested in the carcasses, so we left before they could take an interest in us. It is a shame to lose the deer, but so be it."

"Deer gone?" Karno asked, crestfallen.

"I do not know if they are gone," Puh said with a shrug. "We were not going to stay and try to persuade the bears to move off. We slunk away as inconspicuously as possible and left them to do as they will."

"Which was tearing into the deer," Black Wolf said – rather lightheartedly – considering that our day's work was probably lost.

"You pack funny little woman for walk home," Karno suggested. "We go look to deer."

The Wolf-men slipped away into the woods, leaving us to prepare for the last leg of our trip home.

"How is the baby?" I asked Puh.

"He is fine. Very tiny, but he seems well enough. And Ria seems well, too." Puh smiled, clearly thrilled that both Ria and the child had come through the delivery in good shape.

"That is wonderful news," I said, smiling too. "Have you and Ria decided on a name for the baby yet?"

"Yes," Puh said, nodding, "we thought we might name him for my brother Mror."

"Uncle Mror would have liked that." I approved of their choice. Uncle Mror had been Puh's next oldest brother, and ultimately Uncle Mror had sacrificed his own life to safe Puh when they were attacked by a rogue cave bear. Uncle Mror was an extremely robust man, like his eldest son, Bror. This mite of an infant seemed a far cry from his namesake. However, Uncle Mror was also an intelligent, warmhearted, and jovial being who was universally loved by all. Even if little Mror could not hope to achieve Uncle Mror's bulky physique, he could at least aspire to emulate his fine character.

* * *

The Wolf-men reappeared with Karno at the lead, and Mino and Bewok carrying one doe between them.

"More bear come. Six there now. Bear still eat. Take one doe. Bear not happy, but not want to leave food to drive us away. So we take one deer they not eat," Karno told us.

"Good!" Black Wolf said. "Let us start for home. We have little daylight left and we need to get Ria and the baby settled, and get that doe butchered before the meat spoils."

"Yes," Karno said with a knowing nod. "Warm wet day … bad for meat!" He shook his head. "We forget big buck … we so hurry to get things for funny little woman we forget to tell friends to come after it!"

"That is a shame," Black Wolf said, "but like the bears gorging on the doe and the yearlings, that buck will feed plenty of other animals, as well."

Puh was gently trying to rouse Ria from her slumbers.

"Ria, my love, we are going home now."

"Yes," Ria said, nodding sleepily. She wrapped her arms around the baby a little tighter and moved to stand, but Puh stopped her.

"No getting up," Puh ordered. "You will not be walking."

"We find stick … carry funny little woman like deer," Karno suggested.

"I think not," Ria said dryly.

"Indeed not." Puh wore a wry grin and lifted Ria and the baby into his arms. "We will take turns carrying you. I get the first turn."

Puh kissed Ria's cheek. The Wolf-man said *Gah!* at the sight.

"Why do they always say that?" Ria questioned. "I

do not know," Puh replied. "It could be their reaction to our ways. Maybe we are strange to them, just as their ways are strange to us."

* * *

The sun was nearing the western horizon by the time we entered the family compound. Ria and little Mror had a festive homecoming. Ria must have been in some discomfort after the birth, but she smiled broadly and allowed us to peek at the puny infant who slept throughout his introduction to his relatives and friends.

Upon our arrival I immediately went up the hill to my home to retrieve Morning Star and Fox so that they could join the merrymaking. Morning Star was shocked at the sight of little Mror. When we had a moment to speak amongst ourselves, she leaned in close to whisper.

"He is so very small," Morning Star said to me as she held Fox on one hip; our child looked huge compared with his new half-uncle. "But I am so happy for Ria. She never thought she would have children, and now, even at her advanced age, she has finally managed to have one. I very much hope that the baby survives, the poor little thing. Ria has had such a hard life; it would be so unfair if she were to lose this long-awaited child."

"Both Puh and Ria are as tough as anything or anyone I have ever known," I said to Morning Star. "If Baby Mror takes after his parents, he will be, too."

"Let us hope so," Morning Star said as she snuggled Fox a little closer.

It was likely that most of those in attendance were thinking the same thing. Even the Wolf-men, who evidently were unaccustomed to being around child-bearing women and had so long been away from family life, seemed to sense that this frail being had a tenuous hold on life, at best. All the same, it was a happy event.

It was late in the day and most of the compound's inhabitants were very hungry by now. Many hands pitched in to skin the doe and carve her into slabs of meat, which were then roasted over the fire pit. As we waited for our meal to cook, Karno gave an account of his novel adventure with the big buck. Ru sat at his side eyeing him with open admiration.

"Karno track big buck," Karno started his story, "find buck stuck in tree!"

"In tree?" Morning Star's younger brother Hawk questioned. "How did the buck climb up a tree?"

"No," Karno chuckled, "no climb! *Fall!* Fall between tree trunk on ground. *Stuck!* Karno think buck dead and want cut buck throat, and when Karno climb over tree and sit on buck, it move little. But sometime dead beast still move until last little bit life gone." Karno shrugged. "I put knife to neck and buck make sound … like … *eeeeeeee*! Buck jump like step on hot coal! And *run-run-run*! Say *eeeeeeee*! *Eeeeeeee*! Karno hold like this" – he demonstrated how he had gripped the antlers — "and wrestle buck to ground! No more life in buck."

"Where is the buck?" Hawk asked again. "I would like to see it."

"No time bring big buck home," Karno said regretfully. "Karno was to take friends to get buck, but funny little woman say she have baby *now*. Then we forget buck." Karno shrugged and sighed. "No matter … we get more deer soon."

"Of course you will," Ru assured him. "You can bring down any animal you choose!"

Karno's chest seemed to swell at her praise.

"Karno show you," he said to Ru. "Karno will bring you biggest animal you ever see."

"What kind of big animal?" Ru seemed a little concerned. "I do not want you to be injured. Please do not take unnecessary risks."

"No." Karno touched Ru's hand. "No risk. Karno strong hunter. Karno will show Ru that he great hunter."

"Yes, I know," Ru said, beaming at him, "you are a *very* great hunter."

Their conversation was heard by all present. The Wolf-men were immensely proud of Karno and they nodded approvingly. The rest of us exchanged glances. Karno had many fine qualities, but we wondered if he might overestimate his own prowess.

Chapter Six

The mammoth is coming at me. The earth trembles with each of her steps. She is the matriarch of her herd. She stares at me balefully, as though she knows that I have hunted her kind in the past.

I awakened from the Dream confused. The feeling of puzzlement stayed with me for a long time. We usually take great pains to stay at a distance from mammoths, especially a large cow mammoth like the one that mysteriously appeared in my Dream. These great beasts are immensely powerful and, when one considered their tremendous size, the creatures are also deceptively fast. Although adult male mammoths can be bigger than even this huge matriarch, it was the males that were usually pursued in a hunt. This was because they typically spent most of the year in a relatively solitary bachelorhood, away from the herds that were made up of cows, infants, and juvenile mammoths. That was an important factor, because mammoths within a herd protect one another, and any perceived threat was liable to be mowed down if unable to escape the long, bow-shaped tusks and heavy feet of these beings. A single male, therefore, was a much more approachable target, if it could be thought a target at all. So why did my Dream show that I was within close range of this clearly anxious behemoth?

I did not want to worry Morning Star by mentioning this Dream to her, but I was moved to mention it to Bror when he and I walked to the creek together to draw water.

"Karno talked of embarking on a hunt again tomorrow," Bror spoke thoughtfully as we arrived at the banks of the stream. "This time he would like to bring a much larger group of men."

"Yes, I heard him speak of it to Ru last night." I nodded to Bror as I bent over the running water to fill the bag.

Bror looked both earnestly troubled and grim.

"Somehow Ru has slipped away from me," Bror said with teardrops glittering at the corners of his eyes. "I once thought that all I needed to do was to be patient and to wait for her to come to care for me. Now I find she has become completely captivated by this man."

I put a hand on Bror's shoulder to comfort him.

"Bror, I am so sorry you are unhappy. I do not know what she sees in him."

"She says that he is handsome and brave, and a fine hunter," Bror supplied.

"Well, Cousin, the same things could be said of you. And Karno has not your great strength."

"Ru is kind to me ... kinder than she has ever been previously." Bror shook his head miserably. "It is as though she pities me. I do not know which is worse ... the loss of her or receiving her pity."

"Again, Cousin," I began, "I am so sorry you have reason to be sad." I did not know what else to say to Bror, except to listen to his words and offer my sympathy. Part of me was angry with Ru for being so foolish over Karno when she had the opportunity to be paired with a man, who was – at least in my opinion – superior to Karno in every way. That said, I could not help but like Karno; he was cocky, impetuous, and sometimes a bit boorish, but he was also good-natured, generous, and always willing to help those in need.

Bror shrugged off my remark and returned to his original subject.

"It sounds as though Karno would like to go after bigger game tomorrow. A woolly rhino, possibly. That would be a first for me." Bror seemed intrigued at the idea of hunting one of those formidable animals.

"Me, as well," I agreed. "You know, I had a peculiar Dream last night. I Dreamt that a woolly mammoth cow was coming at me. She had a funny look in her eye."

"*Funny?*" Bror repeated. "That is a term I frequently hear from the Wolf-men. They say we are funny. Funny because we are soft-spoken. Funny because we Old Ones make no sound when we laugh or cry. Funny because we have red hair. But I do not suppose you meant that the mammoth was looking askance at you because of your bright hair."

"Um … no. I do not know why she was so focused on me." But then a humorous thought suddenly did come to me. "And I also do not think she was looking at me funny because we Old Ones kiss."

"What?" Bror's eyebrows rose high on his forehead. "What does that have to do with anything?"

I silently chuckled.

"The Wolf-men are appalled to no end at our habit of kissing," I told Bror.

"I would be appalled at the notion of kissing one of them, myself," Bror said, shuddering.

"No, I mean our habit of kissing our mates … our loved ones," I went on. "Karno informed me in no uncertain terms that it is *very not clean*. He calls it *smooshing faces*."

"I have never thought about whether or not kissing is clean. Who cares? It is kissing!" Bror clearly shared my opinion. I, for one, could not imagine a life in which I would never kiss Morning Star again. "But I have taken you away from the topic of your mammoth Dream. What does she do?"

"She does not do anything at that time. She is walking up to me and she is staring at me. I can look into her eye as she approaches and I can see that she is alarmed," I said to Bror.

"That sounds rather unnerving." Bror gazed at me with concern. "What do you think it means?"

"I do not know," I admitted. "I just hope that the mammoth is representative of some other being. Perchance it is a vision of Willow Woman represented in mammoth form."

Willow Woman was Head Elder of The People of the East's tribes, and she was the largest women any of us had ever seen. She was not as tall as Black Wolf's mate Little Fawn, but she was still taller than most, and her weight must have been the equivalent of any two sizable men. And Willow Woman was capable of affecting the same sort of intimidating stare the mammoth cow had used.

"I hope she is not still looking for a candidate to father a child." Bror brought up something I had not thought of since we had last seen Willow Woman. "She seemed very taken with you, the *Big Red Buck*, before she settled on Black Wolf as the chosen one."

"It is true we have not heard anything from Willow Woman since we last saw her during the winter," I said, "although I am sure that we will hear something when Black Wolf returns from this year's event. It is feasible he will even see the evidence of his – um – services. If so, I do hope that Willow Woman has given birth or soon will give birth to the son and heir she so keenly desired."

"If not, that means that Black Wolf will be put upon to try again," Bror said thoughtfully. "Unless she decides to replace old Black Wolf with a younger man." Bror gave me a sidelong glance, mischief glinting in his eyes.

"The Big Red Buck will not be attending this Gathering," I assured Bror.

* * *

The next day dawned bright and clear. There was a sharpness to the air, as though fall was not too far away. Most of the men now living at the family compound – Bror and his youngest brother Lor, Black Wolf and I, and all the Wolf-men – set out for the prairie outside of our woodlands. This vast grassland spanned the great distances between the forests and the magnificent snow-capped mountains to the north, and it was home to a broad array of animals, both predator and prey.

This was the first time I could recall that Puh did not join us on a hunting expedition. Ria was doing well after the birth of their child, but she was somewhat weakened from loss of blood. We would not be able to tell how the baby would fare until many days had passed and Puh was not about to leave them. It seemed so unnatural to leave Puh behind. And when I considered all the experience and wisdom he contributed to our hunting parties, it made me realize how much we depended on him. Nevertheless, we were a large group of seasoned hunters, and I was sure we could manage quite well on our own.

As I prepared to leave Great Gran suddenly came to stand next to me, and she touched my hand.

"Tris," Gran said, "keep your wits about you on this journey."

"But I always do, Gran," I assured her with a smile. "Are you worried because Puh is not joining us on this venture?"

"Maybe a little." Gran looked up at me solemnly. "I know Tor is concerned for Ria and for the infant; little Mror will need careful tending to survive the next few moons. I understand why Tor wants to be with them, but yes, I worry for you. I know that Tor has given you thorough instruction from the time you were a boy, but your Puh's presence is just one more factor that helps to protect your well-being. I just want you to be safe."

"Have you seen something in a night vision?" I inquired, wondering at the gravity of Great Gran's apparent distress.

"I have seen nothing I can identify as a definite threat to you or the other men, but I have been experiencing strange Dreams. Although I do not see you, I sense you. And I see much raging water," Gran answered.

"But there are no raging waters where we will go." I hoped that this would comfort her.

"I know," Great Gran nodded. "Sometimes Dreams are difficult to read. Sometimes they show me something that has happened many moons ago; sometimes they show me something that will occur in the near or distant future. And sometimes they show me something from long past ... an ancient memory."

"That sounds a bit like a riddle, Gran," I said, smiling at her. "What do you mean by *an ancient memory*?"

"Someday, Tris, when we have more time," Gran began, "I will tell you of those ancient memories."

"You are going to send me off with such a mystery? Well, try not to worry, Gran," I said as I touched her shoulder soothingly. "I will watch out for the raging waters. What with a loving mate at home, a fine son, and another child on the way, I have no intention of being careless."

"Yes, I know," Great Gran nodded; but I could see a hint of worry in her eyes.

* * *

We would be traveling fast. We expected to arrive at the plains within three days and stay there for a day or two, or however long it would take to bring down our prey. Then we would promptly head for home again. Part of me was excited to be going on this trip, both to experience the hunt and to have yet another opportunity to observe the Wolf-men in action. But another part of me hated being away from Morning Star and Fox. I would miss them, and I was afraid that they would need me while I was gone and I would not be there for them. Morning Star did not like for me to go away from her and Fox. However, she knew that there were times when I had to take part in distant hunts that would involve leaving home for some days. On these occasions, Morning Star and Fox would stay at the main house at the family compound, where she and Fox would have the protective presence of our families.

* * *

Although the day's temperatures were warm, the nights could be quite cool. We were still dressed in loincloths during the day, but we carried our heavy cloaks bundled over our left shoulders for the cold nights, when they would act as both garment and blanket.

The Wolf-men once again made a detour to their old camp and picked up the rancid-smelling wolf pelts. These malodorous skins seemed to perform some important function for the Wolf-men. Perhaps it was because they identified so closely with those canines; maybe they believed that the pelts transformed them into wolves and endowed them with the ability to hunt with lupine skill. The idea seemed ridiculous to me. But after a little thought I realized it might seem just as silly to think we Old Ones would have more success as hunters because of our long hair.

The Dreamer III – The People of the Wolves

I wondered if they would continue their nightly custom of making music while we were on the trail. Regardless, Black Wolf, as was his habit, regaled us with song as we hiked. His theory was that the sound would scare away any potential predators. That might well have been true, because for as long as he was in full-throated song, the only animals we ever saw presented hind-views as they removed themselves from the area as quickly as possible. Black Wolf did not have a disagreeable voice, but it was indeed quite a loud voice.

We were not long on the trail when Black Wolf belted out in his thundering bass:

The mighty hunter is bold and brave
The mighty hunter, fresh meat does he crave
The mighty hunter does not easily scare
Even if he falls into a lion's lair…

I had heard different versions of this song before. Black Wolf often sang traditional songs of the people, but sometimes he took liberties with lyrics or made up his own songs as he went along.

The Wolf-men looked at Black Wolf as though his mind had become suddenly and inexplicably compromised.

"Tris," Karno whispered to me. "What Black Wolf do? He make big noise!"

"Well, he is a big man, so I guess that is natural for him," I replied lightheartedly.

"Gah!" Karno shook his head. "He bellow like giant deer buck at mating time. Black Wolf attract mate this way?"

"No," I said, grinning at the thought. "At least I would not think so."

Karno appeared to think on this.

"Black Wolf funny man," Karno said. "Funny hair. Furry man, too. But Karno not tell him so. Karno no want Black Wolf to be angry with him. He much big. Tall like tree."

"I believe that Black Wolf already knows he is big and hairy," I told Karno. "Black Wolf is a good man, and he has a fine sense of humor. A truer friend you will never find."

"That good," Karno acknowledged. "Not want Black Wolf to be unfriendly to Karno."

"I do not know of anyone who would care to pique Black Wolf's ire."

Karno gave me a bewildered glance.

"What mean, Tris?" He asked.

"I mean that it would not be wise to provoke him."

"Make very angry?" Karno seemed to catch on.

"Yes," I replied.

"You funny," Karno shook his head, "just say *make very angry*! Too many words, Tris! And funny, too … Tor stay home with funny little woman. Why no leave her with other women? They take care her. We lose good hunter."

The Dreamer III – The People of the Wolves

I had to agree with Karno. Puh's decision to stay home was rather unusual. In fact, I had never heard of a man opting to stay with his mate after childbirth when he had a chance to go hunting instead. As much as I adored Morning Star, unless I was concerned that she would be left in a perilous position, I would have trusted my family to care for her in my absence.

"It is not usual for our men to forgo a hunting trip after the birth of a child," I said. "But Ria is very old, and the baby is very small."

"Maybe Ru have baby I stay home with her, too," Karno shrugged. "I feel for Ru as I feel for no another. But man old like Tor and funny little woman … Gah! They beyond that by now."

"Beyond love?" I questioned. "I do not think so. I do not think I will ever be beyond loving my mate. But I do not think that Puh stays with Ria just because he loves her. I think that it is something he feels he has to do."

"Yes," Karno agreed, "just do."

* * *

The weather was clear and calm while we trekked. Every night we set up lean-tos made of hide tarpaulins and fallen tree limbs for shelter, placing them in a rough circle around our evening fire. As it happened, the Wolf-men performed their chanting music for us before we went to sleep. They also busied themselves with crafting wooden objects. Most often they carved likenesses of animals for the children residing at the family compound. The Wolf-men could produce the little works of art remarkably quickly. In their hands an unassuming section of dead wood was magically transformed into a horse, wisent, bear, or any other creature. Bewok was particularly adept at making these things. Clearly, he was an exceptionally bright individual, but his skill with wood surpassed anything I had ever seen. When I once asked Bewok how he brought forth a recognizable animal from a mere stick, he seemed surprised at my question.

"I just look at the wood and I see something in it. I whittle a bit here and there to bring it out." Bewok held out his latest efforts for my inspection. "See? If the stick branches out in a way that can be turned into legs, I make an animal that has legs, or if it has knobby knots in the right places, I will use that part for the head. This one has nothing I can use for legs, and although I can carve the legs separately and attach them with pine pitch glue, I am simply using the curve in the wood to turn this piece into a running wolf."

With this explanation, I could see that he was carefully shaping the front and back legs so that the wolf's body appeared to be stretched out in a long bound, head over the forelegs and tail straight out over the rear legs. I shook my head with admiration.

"This piece is a wonder," I told Bewok as I turned it over in my hands by the light of the fire. "The children delight in your work. You are very kind to make these presents for them."

"I very much enjoy carving the animals, and I am pleased to see how happy the children are to receive them," Bewok said with a broad grin. "I would like to think that one day I will be making more to entertain my own children."

"I hope you will," I said with a nod.

* * *

On the morning of the fourth day, we finally arrived at the plains.

The end of summer was nearing. The tall, sun-bleached grasses barely rippled in the faint breeze. After being in the shade of the forest, the open blue skies were almost painfully bright. Distant mountains appeared to shimmer in the heat. The broad expanse between the woodlands and the rocky ridges teemed with animals. We would have our choice of quarry here. We gathered to discuss our options.

"I see a lone aurochs just over there," Black Wolf said, pointing to the beast. "It is a young cow. She would make fine eating, and there are enough of us to easily take her down. It would mean much meat for everyone."

"I like that idea!" Bror's brother Lor said as he licked his lips. He appeared to be eagerly anticipating sitting down to a fine meal of fresh aurochs meat.

"We can set up an ambush," Black Wolf went on. "Let some of us retreat to the woods, and others can lie in wait over there. We may be able to make our kill and hit the trail again by the end of the day."

"I like that idea, too," I seconded.

"Gah!" Karno snorted. "Too small! Karno want big! Make Ru happy with big kill!"

Too small? This animal might be somewhat small for an aurochs, but she was still a sizable beast.

Bror exchanged glances with me. Although I had never known Bror to do anything even remotely rash, I wondered if he, too, hoped to impress Ru with a big kill. Bror scanned the grasslands for other prey.

"Karno, you said you wanted a woolly rhino," Bror began. "We do not often find them here, but if you truly want one, that large male over there is the finest rhino I have ever seen."

Karno squinted as he followed the direction of Bror's pointing arm. I could barely discern the woolly rhino that was somewhat obscured by the deep the shadows at the edge of the woodlands, some distance from where we stood.

"That fine beast," Karno agreed. "We hunt aurochs any day. Woolly rhino rare! Karno want rhino … big fine rhino like that!"

Without bothering to see if anyone was following him, Karno began to stride confidently toward the woolly rhino. His men faithfully trailed along behind their leader. Black Wolf, Bror, Lor, and I paused to see if we could come to a quick consensus. Bror seemed ready to go along with Karno's wishes, even though Karno had not yet voiced any sort of plans about how we would bring down the animal. No one said a word. Finally, Black Wolf shrugged.

"Let us go and see what Karno has in mind," Black Wolf suggested. "This could be interesting."

"Indeed," I agreed. "I would like to see what methods they employ to kill a creature such as this."

Black Wolf smiled and seemed to consider this idea.

"Yes," he said, grinning. "I want to see if Karno is as keen to hop on the back of a woolly rhino as he was that deer."

* * *

We fell in step behind the Wolf-men, soon catching up to them. I noted that they had pulled their wolfskin pelts forward so the wolves' snouts projected over their faces, effectively obscuring their features in the resulting shadows. The Wolf-men slowed their pace, slipping stealthily between the trees and brush until at length we neared the place where the woolly rhino browsed on the grasses' full seed heads.

I could clearly view the huge animal from my vantage point by a large tree. It was snuffling and snorting as it noisily grazed, its tail in constant motion, swishing back and forth in a fruitless attempt to keep the ever-present flies from alighting on its rump. Given that audible signs of the rhino's digestion process were occasionally clearly heard by all, I did not envy the flies their proximity to the creature's hind end. Black Wolf seemed to be thinking along the same lines.

"Listen to that!" he quietly exclaimed at yet another burst of flatulence. "I will not be standing at the rear of our intended victim during this hunt! That rhino sounds as though he will be ready to let loose his bowels at any moment!"

We could not restrain small grins at the memory of last winter's woolly mammoth kill, when poor Black Wolf had been knocked off his feet by a heavy blast of mammoth excrement. Just then, the rhino turned its head and faced in our direction, its enormous forehorn much in evidence.

"By all means, Black Wolf," Bror whispered, "you are most welcome to the front if you so choose."

Woolly rhinos have rather poor eyesight, but their hearing and sense of smell are acute. We could see it was cognizant that something was not quite right, but it could not decide whether or not the strange sounds that met its ears and the odors invading its nose might pose a threat. It did not appear to be in any hurry to assess the situation. After all, there are not many animals that could afflict serious harm on a being as massive and invulnerable as this one.

The rhino shifted its stance as it stared into the brush that concealed us, its ears swiveling and nose twitching inquisitively. Karno and his comrades were stationed a short distance from us. Now that the rhino had turned to face Black Wolf, my cousins, and me, the Wolf-men moved into position at the rhino's blind side – that is to say, its backside.

The Dreamer III – The People of the Wolves

In a flash, they were upon the woolly rhino: Karno sprinted out first, plunging his spear into the rhino's flank with a mighty thrust. Mino struck the rhino on its opposite flank, just as the animal turned to see Karno duck down and dart under its belly. The rhino swung its ponderous head to face Karno and Mino as the rest of Karno's friends descended upon it, thrusting their spears into the great hairy body, just behind the forelegs where they could hope to hit the heart or lungs. We took this to be our cue to join in, and we likewise sprang from our cover to inflict additional wounds as best we could.

Although we were a large group of hunters – the largest I had ever known to be used in a single foray – bringing a woolly rhino down in this way was no easy task. The rhino had suffered numerous grievous injuries, but it was still quite alive and quite dangerous. Even though it bristled with deeply embedded spears, it charged with impressive vigor toward us, sending us dashing for the protection of nearby trees.

I then noticed that Karno, Bewok, and Mino were setting up spears propped on sticks, the spears' butts firmly planted against the remains of a sturdy tree trunk. All were concealed by the tall grasses. Karno ran out to the rhino, knowing that it would rush madly at anything in its path. As soon as the rhino gave chase, Karno sped back toward the waiting weapons.

When the enraged rhino collided with the carefully positioned spears it cried out in shock and pain and then reared back, the weapons protruding from its neck. We could see that at least one of the spears had impaled its throat, causing blood to run from both the wounds, and its mouth and nose. The rhino continued to cry out pitifully. I cringed inwardly at the sounds. I wanted to end this poor brute's suffering. My hand was on my knife as I considered slashing the rhino's throat, but Karno and Bewok were already approaching the animal as it dropped to the ground with a resounding thud, its head thrashing, sides heaving, and legs still in motion.

Just as Karno and Bewok reached the rhino and poised their spears for a final assault, the tall grasses that surrounded the now well-trampled clearing came alive with the tawny bodies of cave lions. I then realized that the lions must have been watching the hunt with great interest. I had not had much interaction with cave lions before now, but I did know this much: they were the most lethal predators on these lands. All the same, even lions were not usually successful in killing an adult male woolly rhino. However, they were not above stealing the bounty procured by others, be it a rabbit or a woolly mammoth. Or a woolly rhino.

Karno and Bewok, soon joined by Mino, flew into action, their concentration now focused on the lions, which wisely kept out of reach of their spears. The cave lions now began to circle the three men, feigning charges and roaring with agitation. The rest of us sped to our friends' aid, causing the lions to briefly retreat a few paces; but they were undeterred. This prize was too valuable for either side to easily give up.

The group of cave lions was mostly comprised of young males, but their leader appeared to be much older: its face was battle scarred, and one of its ears had been lopped off raggedly near its base. But old or not, it was huge, and every time it opened his mouth to roar yet again, the sight of those impressive teeth, and the power behind its vocalizations, sent shivers running up and down my spine.

The woolly rhino now lay still. Black Wolf had the presence of mind to begin to yank some of the spears from the rhino's inert body, and the rest of us followed suit. We had spent almost all our weapons in bringing down this creature, and we now had little left with which to defend ourselves. It was no easy task to free the spears from the rhino's thick hide, especially since the lions kept charging into our midst, sending us leaping over the rhino's legs and head as we tried to put its bulk between us and the lions' outstretched paws.

"I do not like this," I said to Black Wolf, who stood at my side by the rhino's hind legs. "There are too many of them. I do not think they will be driven off."

"I do not like this, either," Black Wolf agreed. "I was fairly sure that the seventeen of us could slay the rhino, but I did not count on defending the kill from a large congregation of lions! I have never seen so many males all together. I have not been able to count them, since they are in constant motion, but I would guess that there are at least twelve ... maybe many more!"

I barely had time to nod in acknowledgment of Black Wolf's statement before several lions lunged forward, causing us to vault over the rhino's back end, where we joined Bror and Lor. Karno and his friends were at the rhino's head, where they were having some luck in keeping the other lions at bay. The sound of a heavy body landing on the woolly rhino's side made us turn, spears pointed toward this new threat. First one lion, then another and another leapt up onto the rhino and stood over us, growling fiercely. My cousins, Black Wolf, and I further retreated to rejoin the Wolf-men at the head of the rhino, but the lions followed.

"There are too many," Black Wolf said to Karno. "We must abandon the rhino to the lions. It is not worth risking our lives. There is plenty of meat on the hoof grazing these grasslands. Let us go."

I could see that Karno was weighing his options.

"We kill big old lion, other lions go away," Karno replied.

"Or the other lions might not even notice and go about the business of ripping you apart!" Black Wolf countered.

Karno did not spare much thought on Black Wolf's words.

"Great Man's son no shy from lions!" Karno shouted.

Karno lunged toward the lead cave lion, spear at the ready, the ever-loyal Mino and Bewok flanking him. The formidable creature sidestepped them gracefully, and then came in closer, lashing out with one of its huge forepaws. The lion's claws connected with Mino's outer thigh, causing him to cry out in pain. Karno and Bewok drove their spears into the lion, which then closed its massive jaws on Bewok's right shoulder.

The other lions became emboldened by the lead lion's attack, and we were powerless to help Karno, Mino, and Bewok, as we were thoroughly focused on our own efforts to stay alive. Black Wolf and I were targeted by two of the beasts.

"Let us both strike the one on the right," Black Wolf said to me.

"Yes," I agreed. We stood a better chance of killing the lions if we could concentrate inflicting injuries on them in an organized fashion. We did not need to slay all of them; just enough to make them realize that they were not going to gain possession of the rhino.

Bror overheard Black Wolf and immediately understood.

"Lor! Let us strike the lion on the left!"

In a flash, we thrust our spears into the two lions, lancing their chests and necks, and then we withdrew the weapons just as quickly. Lions, particularly male lions, often sustain similar physical damage when they fight one another. Their long fangs and claws, driven in with almost unbelievable force, were as deadly as our spears. This meant that their bodies were built to engage in this type of head-on combat.

Even so, they did not appear to anticipate this degree of trouble from paltry beings such as ourselves, and the two lions backed away, limping and bleeding from their wounds. We now moved on to another small group of lions positioned between us and Karno, Bewok, and Mino. Karno's other men had managed to kill one of the lions; they, too, were doing their best to work their way toward their friends, who were still at the mercy of the big lion. Karno and the injured Mino fought off the lion as best they could; the beast finally dropped Bewok, who fell to the ground and lay motionless.

"How do you like the taste of my flint?" Black Wolf bellowed to the lion coming at us open-mouthed. Black Wolf jabbed his spear into the gaping maw, while my spear deeply pierced the charging lion's chest. The beast did not appreciate neither Black Wolf's novel approach to personal defense nor the apparent hole I had left in its body. It slunk off, drooling blood.

The lions were beginning to fall away, but the lead cave lion still maintained its stance over Bewok. It was probably my imagination, but I thought it looked annoyed that we insignificant humans were still trifling it with our campaign to preserve ourselves and our rhino. It suddenly stiffened and looked straight at

Karno. It may have rightly concluded that Karno was the main source of its aggravation, as it was Karno's refusal to give up that had brought us to this juncture.

Karno raised his spear once again, but the cagey old lion grasped the weapon in its jaws and easily broke the spear in two. Karno reached for Bewok's abandoned spear, only to have the lion counter the move as it stepped forward and placed its sizable paws over the spear's shaft.

Before anyone else could react, Bror darted forward and placed himself between Karno and the determined lion. Bror stabbed his spear into the lion's neck and the creature abruptly went limp as the spearhead severed its vertebra. The lion's weighty body collapsed, but it was not lifeless. The open mouth gasped for air and the blinking eyes stared, but there was no other movement. Bror unsheathed his knife and knelt to cut the old lion's throat.

We were so transfixed by this drama that we did not notice the other lions slink away. All at once we were alone as we panted for breath in the long shadow cast by the dead woolly rhino, standing amongst the bloody carcasses of the remaining lions.

* * *

That night there was no music around our shared fire. We hastily erected a camp where we could tend to our wounded friends and recover from the day's exertions. Mino's left leg was grievously lacerated, but a firm binding helped to stop the bleeding. He was in pain and somewhat enfeebled from blood loss, but he was otherwise unhurt. Bewok, on the other hand, was battered and suffering from severe bite wounds. He barely clung to life. The rest of us had escaped relatively unscathed. Lor had a gash on his hand where one of the lions had caught it with a claw, and one of the Wolf-men had lost several of his front teeth when a comrade in arms pulled back on his spear at an inopportune time, and accidentally elbowed the unfortunate man in the mouth. Yet another Wolf-man had scraped his lower leg on the downed rhino's forehorn when he tripped over it during the clash.

We lit a series of fires around the dead rhino so that we could harvest its meat without fear of harassment from the lions. We managed to process a significant amount of flesh despite the loss of time spent building and settling into the camp and tending to our injured. We roasted some of the meat for our evening meal and placed some on racks where it could be cured over a smoldering fire. Karno also instructed that the rhino's huge forehorn be removed from the skull. He did not say why he wanted the horn, but I wondered if he planned to give it to Ru as proof of his accomplishment and the depth of his esteem for her.

The moon was perched near the zenith of the night sky when at last we had completed our day's work. We listlessly ate the cooked meat and fell into an exhausted sleep.

* * *

The Dreamer III ~ The People of the Wolves

The cow mammoth's long fur is ruffled by occasional gusts of wind. She has caught sight of me. As she nears, I can see that her eyelashes are long and wispy, and her eyes are brown, almost the same shade as her fur. She plods toward me with a determined step, her enormous feet crunching audibly in the gravel. Crunch. Crunch. Crunch...

"Tris! Tris!" Bror called to me.

I broke from my Dream and groggily rolled over to face Bror.

"What? What is it?" I asked.

"You were thrashing around in your sleep," Bror told me. "Were you having a Dream?"

"Yes, I was," I admitted, "that same Dream about the mammoth."

"Last night I dreamt of lions," Bror said. "I think I fought lions until dawn."

"I am not surprised," I responded as I rubbed the sleep from my eyes. "You were very brave yesterday. I hope that Karno realizes that he owes his life to you."

Bror's mouth twisted into an ironic smile.

"There are moments when I wonder if I should have stayed back. But then I ... no matter what, I could not have stood by and watched a man be slaughtered. And I could not have looked Ru in the eye without guilt, knowing that I could have saved her beloved. Knowing that my inaction would have caused her great pain." Bror sighed. "Besides, it might have been easy to let an animal eliminate my romantic competition; but if Ru is to choose me, I want her to choose me because she wants me. Not because I survived a lion attack and her first choice did not."

* * *

After we arose for the day, our work resumed. We continued to smoke and pack the rhino meat. Once the all meat was ready to be transported back home, we would lash sacks of the smoked flesh to poles that would be shouldered between two men and carried back to the family compound. In the meantime, we gorged ourselves on slabs of roasted rhino to fuel the long trek.

Mino would not be able to do more than hobble a short distance for some while. Bewok had still not regained total consciousness. The holes left by the lion's fangs were frightening to behold. Bewok's breathing was shallow and he was strikingly pale. We did our best to nurse his wounds, but his chances of survival did not look promising. It soon became apparent that we would have to leave in two groups: one group to take the meat home, and another to accompany the injured home.

Karno was heartbroken over Bewok.

"Bewok one of my oldest friend," Karno stated with tears in his eyes as he sat at Bewok's side. "He need good healer. But we far from healer now."

Black Wolf suddenly perked up.

"I know where we can find a healer!" Black Wolf assured Karno. "We will have to carry Bewok on a litter for a day or so, but if he can endure the trip, there is help for him."

Karno appeared cautiously hopeful.

"Where this help?" Karno asked.

"We go to Willow Woman's summer camp," Black Wolf said, beginning in his excitement to talk in Karno's vernacular. "I mean, Willow Woman's summer camp is not too distant. Her healer is well-known for his medicinal talents. We can take Bewok and Mino there; that is our best option … and theirs, too."

"Karno not know what is *Willow Woman*, but we go," Karno said with a grateful nod.

Chapter Seven

Black Wolf had never spoken of any particular knowledge of Willow Woman's whereabouts, but apparently he knew the location of her seasonal home sites. I had only a vague idea of the place Black Wolf named: The Fen of Falling Water. I once heard that it was an area of very old trees and that it was best known for a spectacular waterfall that in winter was transformed from a thundering cascade to an eerily silent wall of ice. For now, however, it was likely to be a cool if somewhat noisy place for Willow Woman to spend the summer.

On the day Karno, Black Wolf, Bror, and I took to the trail with Mino and Bewok, Karno sent most of his men, guided by Lor, on their way to our home. Lor and the Wolf-men were burdened with an immense amount of smoked rhino meat. We would have to transport our loads, as well. Bewok was borne on a litter, which we took turns carrying. We were also encumbered by our packs, now brimming with dried meat, and our cloaks and spears. Mino was obviously in considerable pain, but he was able to walk as long as he did not have to move too quickly. We tried to let him rest as often as possible, but he was stoically resolved not to slow us down and he trudged forward, brows furrowed and mouth turned downward into a grimace. Nonetheless, when asked how he fared, he invariably forced a smile and assured us he was fine.

* * *

I heard the roar of the falls and smelled dampness in the air well before we came to see the rushing waters. Willow Woman's encampment was a relatively peaceful place, if you could ignore the din from the nearby cascade. The house appeared to be a large and comfortable domicile, sheltered and shaded by the enormous trees that surrounded it. It was a long, low structure, and it appeared to be devoid of life, except for a few tell-tale columns of smoke that ascended skyward. As we approached the clearing that encircled the building, we were met by the man who managed her household. Slow Bear was quick to recognize Black Wolf, Bror, and me, and he greeted us in a friendly fashion.

"Black Wolf," Slow Bear said, grinning with pleasure. "How good to see you! Willow Woman will be so pleased that you are here!" Then Slow Bear peered around us and saw Karno, Mino, and the litter Bror and I carried, on which lay Bewok. Slow Bear seemed somewhat alarmed at the presence of these strangers, but upon coming closer to inspect the injured in our group he added, "I will alert Willow Woman to your arrival and then I will fetch Gray Owl."

"Thank you, Slow Bear," Black Wolf said, and he placed a hand on the man's forearm to emphasize his appreciation. "We will wait here."

I nodded my thanks to Slow Bear, too. As always, he had an air of unflappable competence about him, and it was a relief to know that Bewok and Mino would soon be looked after.

"You no tell man that I am Karno, Great Man's son," Karno mumbled dejectedly.

"There will be time for introductions soon enough," Black Wolf said flatly.

A moment later, a high-pitched squeal met our ears and the tanned hide that covered the building's doorway fluttered open, revealing the person of Willow Woman. She was very tall and quite round; her black, braided hair wound artfully around her head. Unlike any other female I had ever met, most of her visible skin, except her face, was adorned with tattooed lines and markings. Willow Woman cried out again at the sight of Black Wolf and she trotted to him with surprisingly light bouncing steps.

Black Wolf and Willow Woman eagerly threw their arms around each other. Then Black Wolf actually lifted Willow Woman up off her feet and joyfully swung her around. Karno, already startled by Willow Woman's unconventional outward characteristics, was clearly impressed by this feat.

"That like pick up bear!" Karno said with eyebrows raised.

Fortunately, Willow Woman did not seem to understand Karno's words through his thick accent, but she eyed Karno suspiciously while still locked in Black Wolf's embrace.

"What did he say?" she asked, pointing at Karno.

"He said he likes your hair," Black Wolf spoke, thinking quickly. "A few of his friends were injured while we were hunting. I brought them here in hopes Gray Owl could help them."

"It is true they do not look well," Willow Woman agreed. "Bring the men inside."

* * *

I had never been inside Willow Woman's lodgings until the previous fall, when we attended The People from the East's Gathering. There was nothing in my life up until that time that could have prepared me for the sight of the enormous building, filled with so many men. It was lighted by a great number of torches which emitted a certain amount of acrid smoke, giving the atmosphere a rather rancid murky air. Willow Woman's personal rooms were less fuggy, and they were luxuriously appointed with thick matting and numerous lavish fur pelts. This place, although much smaller, appeared equally well-furnished. Although we were initially shown to an entry room that was utilitarian in nature and filled with spears, cloaks, a wide assortment of baskets, and other sundry items, I could see through an opening into the next chamber. This room had several layers of woven matting on the floor and contained lounging platforms on which a person could sit or lie down.

When I had first met Willow Woman I was both astounded and bewildered by her. Willow Woman was the daughter of the recently deceased Head Elder, and she was his only surviving offspring. She was brash, forceful, and undoubtedly intelligent. Willow Woman was also childless, and she had lost her mate the previous year. When we attended The People's Gathering the previous fall, Willow Woman was seeking a man to assist her in producing an heir who would one day succeed her as Head Elder. Upon our meeting, she dubbed me the *Big Red Buck*, and I was amongst those briefly considered. But then, much to my relief, Black Wolf was tapped to perform the honors, so to speak.

With life being such an uncertainty, strict monogamy is rare, and rarer still for a man like Black Wolf – who did not seem to require anything from his partners other than they be female – but he was initially disconcerted by the request. All the same, over time Willow Woman and Black Wolf had become quite attached to each other.

"Are you well?" Black Wolf inquired.

Willow Woman nodded, seeming to grasp that he was also questioning the condition of their presumed child. I could not see any sure evidence of her pregnancy, but it could be that it was simply difficult to ascertain gravidity in a woman of her size.

"Yes, dear Black Wolf, all is well," she answered, leaning back for a moment to rub her stomach. "He kicks like a wisent! I hope you are in good health, too?"

"Better than ever, now that I am with you!" Black Wolf said as he hugged her again.

Karno edged up to the amorous pair and looked them up and down curiously. Karno then adopted a rigidly formal pose.

"Me, Karno, son of Great Man, Emokki," he said proudly to Willow Woman.

Willow Woman stared at him, her face betraying a mixture of puzzlement and annoyance at having her reverie with Black Wolf disrupted.

"I cannot understand a word he says." She looked to Black Wolf for an interpretation.

Black Wolf released Willow Woman from his embrace and gestured toward Karno.

"He says that he is Karno, son of Great Man, Emokki," Black Wolf explained, and then he added, "Karno, this is Willow Woman, Chief Elder of The People from the East."

"Welcome," Willow Woman said, addressing Karno. "The wounded men belong to you? Ah, here is

Gray Owl. Gray Owl, please see what you can do to ease their suffering and make these men whole again."

Gray Owl was a short, slender man with a serious demeanor. He carried a large bag, which he set on the floor's matting as he knelt by Bewok. The sack presumably contained the various trappings required by a man of his calling. Gray Owl gently touched Bewok's forehead.

"Not too hot," Gray Owl pronounced. "It is dark in here. I need more light."

Willow Woman then called for Slow Bear and relayed to him Gray Owl's request for more light. Slow Bear turned to the wall behind him and he moved several panels so that an opening was revealed, through which shone the bright light of day. The powerful rays of the sun hit Bewok squarely in the face, causing him to flinch ever so slightly.

"Thank you, Slow Bear," Willow Woman said to him.

Slow Bear nodded in response and left us.

"That is much better," Gray Owl began. "How long has he been like this? Semicomatose, that is."

"Since lion bite him," Karno informed him.

Gray Owl looked up at Karno sharply. He frowned and returned his attention to Bewok.

"This is most unusual. I do not see anything that would cause him to be in this state. Has he spoken at all?"

"Bewok has had brief moments of moderate lucidity," Black Wolf informed Gray Owl. "He has asked for water, food, assistance with calls of nature, and such."

"*Be-wok?*" Gray Owl repeated.

"That man name. Bewok." Karno informed him.

Next, Gray Owl gingerly lifted Bewok's cloak and the wraps that covered the gaping holes in Bewok's chest where the old lion had seized him. Gray Owl carefully assessed the wounds, then slowly lowered his head and put his ear against Bewok's ribs.

"These are severe injuries," Gray Owl stated.

I spoke for the first time since our arrival. "We were hunting and a group of male cave lions wanted to take our kill from us. One of them grabbed Bewok by the shoulder and dragged him a little distance."

"We kill rhino!" Karno interjected.

"Well, I would guess that in addition to the punctures, this young man may have some broken ribs. Possibly a broken clavicle, too. He is lucky; I think his lungs are still intact. I will treat the wounds and bind his ribs. As long as there is no infection, he should survive, but he will have a lengthy recovery." Gray Owl sniffed at the punctures. "There is no sign of infection. Yet."

Gray Owl soon turned his attention to Mino and started to unwind the strips of hide that bound Mino's thigh.

"Do you understand my words?" he asked Mino.

"Yes. I am Mino," Mino responded. All Karno's men spoke our language fairly well. Only Karno still struggled with it.

"I am afraid that lion made a mess of the animal tattoos on this section of your leg, Mino," Gray Owl said. "Did these slashes bleed out a great deal?"

"Yes," Mino responded, "but that is good, is it not? The flowing blood cleans the wound?"

"Indeed, it does. It is good as long as you do not lose too much blood," Gray Owl replied. "Was it a long journey to get here?"

Mino shook his head.

"Just over a day's walk."

"Did you walk the entire trek?" Gray Owl asked incredulously.

"Yes," Mino said, nodding. "It was not a long walk at all. Very short compared with the length of our journey to reach these lands."

"You must tell me of your homeland sometime," Gray Owl said with the only smile he had surrendered since our meeting. "For now, I will treat the slashes and rebind your leg. You are a very strong young man. I predict you will heal just fine."

* * *

After Gray Owl had tended to his two newest patients and we had settled Bewok into a quiet corner of the room where he could rest undisturbed, Willow Woman escorted us from the front entryway of her home into the main room, where she invited us to find a seat on one of the lounging platforms while we awaited the midday meal.

Slow Bear soon returned with several men who bore birch-bark trays of food, a bulging water bag, and an assortment of gourd cups. Willow Woman asked Gray Owl to join us, but he politely declined, saying he had much work to do.

Willow Woman was always a generous hostess, eager to see her guests well supped. She was full of her usual stories and humorous banter, but although she made a point to engage each of us in conversation, it was obvious that she had eyes for only one person. And Black Wolf gave his full attention to Willow Woman as well.

Karno was noticeably confused. As the meal progressed and the room filled with noisy talk and laughter, Karno leaned toward me.

"Tris," he whispered, "why Black Wolf have two mate in two house?"

I was not sure how to reply.

"I suppose it does seem very odd ..." I trailed off.

"Yes. At least he not do that smoosh-face with her." Karno winced at the thought.

I had seen them kiss in the past, so I knew that they did in fact occasionally *smoosh-face*, just not in front of people who were not very close friends. Even if monogamy was not generally rigorously exercised, relationships outside of one's pairing were not flaunted.

I had mixed feelings about Black Wolf and Willow Woman's liaison. Black Wolf was my Puh's oldest and closest friend. He was also my friend and the father of my mate. I desired his happiness, and I knew that he and Little Fawn had seen little of it what with the long periods of frequent strife they had suffered throughout their seventeen years together. But every time I saw Black Wolf with Willow Woman, my pleasure for him was offset by an image of the hurt and disruption their association would cause for Little Fawn, Morning Star, and the rest of Black Wolf's family.

Black Wolf's rapport with Willow Woman was completely different from the one he shared with Little Fawn. Black Wolf's manner toward Willow Woman reminded me much of my feelings for Morning Star. She was my mate and she was my life; I adored her; I breathed for her; I felt that she and Fox, and any other children we might have together, were my reason for being. I was happy to see Black Wolf finally find real contentment, but I wished he could have found it with Little Fawn. I sensed that Black Wolf and Little Fawn did indeed love each other despite their incompatibility. But there were no easy answers. There was nothing I could do but hope that in the end no one would be grieved by Black Wolf and Willow Woman's entanglement.

On the other hand, Karno's remarks about the situation left me heartened. He seemed surprised and even shocked that Black Wolf had *two mates* and *two houses*. If Karno and Ru did eventually become paired, it boded well that he would not be likely to seek a similar situation.

* * *

Willow Woman made sure that we had comfortable accommodations for the night. Karno, Bror, and I shared a room. It had a door that accessed the clearing outside the structure, and one wall had the same intriguing movable panels we had seen Slow Bear operate. We set about experimenting with opening and closing the panels to see how they worked.

"This good! Cool air come in!" Karno said, smiling approvingly.

"And they also let out odors!" Bror agreed.

"What odor? What smell?" Karno queried.

"We do!" Bror replied with a grin. "Each time I get a whiff of myself all I can smell is smoked rhino meat, and it surely is not carrying all this way from our former campsite."

Karno's only answer was a noncommittal grunt.

It seemed likely that we would stay here for some days before Mino and Bewok would be well enough to make the trip home, so I examined this little room in the fading light. There was plenty of space for the three of us, more so than we would have had if we had been sleeping in either a lean-to or one of the small trailside huts we often built for shelter when we were trekking. The two wall openings let in ample air, but not too many insects, which were probably somewhat reluctant to sample the blood of three men bearing the pungent perfume of a well-smoked woolly rhino.

As I lay down to sleep on my cloak, I listened to the rumble of the nearby tumbling waters. Suddenly I felt my blood run cold. What had Great Gran said about potential danger lurking in raging waters?

* * *

The next morning dawned bright and cheery. The waters continued their headlong rush to the sea, but today I regarded them with a new appreciation. I would be sure to heed Gran's warning to be particularly cautious while I was around these rough waters. I tried to remember her words. She said she could not see me, but she sensed me. What did that mean?

I had little time to ponder this conundrum, however. We men felt that we could not stay in Willow Woman's household without contributing to its stores, so Bror, Karno, and I left to go hunting as soon as we had broken our nightly fast.

We expected that the task might be made easier by the roar of the falls, which we hoped would mask the sounds of our movements through the forest. After all, our bodies now bore a considerable amount of scent, and we needed every advantage to catch game animals unawares. If the volume of sound was not enough to hide our presence, we might need to bathe not only ourselves, but our clothing.

The Dreamer III – The People of the Wolves

Black Wolf did not join us, which was a tad paradoxical. Soon after our arrival Willow Woman had insisted that he remove any and all remnants of the ill-fated rhino from his person, thus he was the only one of us who had bothered to wash. Besides, hunting was the last thing on Black Wolf's mind. Black Wolf and Willow Woman wanted to make the most of their time together, and they did not often emerge from Willow Woman's private rooms.

Normally I did not mind the idea of bathing, even in very cold waters, but the thought of Great Gran's warning certainly gave me pause. However, following a day's fruitless hunt, we realized that even if we stood upwind from our quarry, our ambush-style hunting methods required that we be within an arm's reach to make a kill. So far, no animal had come that close without bolting away in terror. Then it occurred to me that there might be other sources of water in which I could scrub away the offending odors.

I went in search of Slow Bear and found him outside, near the rear of the building. Slow Bear was splitting wood. He started in surprise when he caught sight of me.

"Tris!" Slow Bear said as he put a hand over his heart. "I did not hear you coming! You startled me!"

"Apologies, Slow Bear. I came to find you in hopes you could tell me if there is some pond or lake in which we could clean ourselves." I spoke louder than was usual for an Old One. We were a soft-spoken people, and I knew that there was no way anyone could hear our conversation unless we raised our voices over the tumult of the waterfall.

Slow Bear was a stout man with kind features. Like everyone in Willow Woman's entourage, he had the appearance of being well-fed. He smiled at me, making the lines at the corners of his eyes deepen.

"These waters are rather daunting. I do not blame you for wanting to bathe elsewhere." Slow Bear went on, "If you do not mind waiting a short while, I can take you to a lake where you and your friends, if they wish, can wash to your heart's content."

"Many thanks, Slow Bear," I said. "I will tell the others."

"I will find you when I have finished splitting this kindling."

"Many thanks," I said again. "Would you like me to assist you?"

"No," Slow Bear said, shaking his head and still smiling. "I will soon be done."

I smiled gratefully and left Slow Bear to return to Bror and Karno. As I neared the main entrance to the building, Gray Owl was just exiting the door. He looked grim.

I nodded my greeting to Gray Owl as he gazed up at me, his countenance conveying openness and acceptance. Many People from the East did not like us Old Ones, and when meeting with one of The People I always scanned their features for signs as to whether they would reject or welcome my presence. I was glad to know that Gray Owl was not one of The People who scorned Old Ones.

"You are Tris, are you not?" Gray Owl asked.

"Yes," I answered simply.

"Black Wolf speaks most highly of you. He has mentioned that you are paired with his eldest daughter and you two are expecting your second child sometime this fall. I wish to extend my congratulations!" Gray Owl's lips turned upward slightly at the happy words, but then they dropped to a deadpan expression once more.

"Many thanks," I responded.

Gray Owl hesitated before speaking again.

"I am concerned about your friend Bewok. Is there anything else you can tell me about what happened when he was attacked? I do not understand why he is so unresponsive most times," Gray Owl said as he shook his head. "I did hear him speak today. I asked him how he felt, and he just said that he was sleepy. He asked for a little water and then his eyes closed, and I heard no more from him. He did not move."

I searched my mind for any details we had not yet divulged to Gray Owl.

"I can think of nothing," I finally told him. "The lion bit down on his shoulder and pulled Bewok off his feet. He dragged Bewok by his shoulder around the head of the rhino and stood there, with Bewok dangling from his mouth." I shuddered at the thought. It had been a horrible sight. Then I went on, "Even after the lion released him, it took us some while to rescue him."

"Do you know anything about Bewok as a man?" Gray Owl queried.

"He is a good man," I promptly replied. "Bewok is a good hunter. He is very kind and cheerful. He loves children and making things for them. Bewok has spoken of looking forward to having a family of his own someday."

As I heard myself speak of Bewok in this way, I was saddened to think that he might not live to see another hunt, to find a mate and beget a family, or to delight more children with his creations.

"Do not be too distressed yet." Gray Owl must have read my sorrowful countenance. "I will do all I can to see that he makes a good recovery. He is young and he is strong. I only ask these questions to get a sense of whether or not he has spirit, whether or not he is a fighter. Sometimes those who are seriously ill or injured not only have to overcome their physical malady, but they must also conquer it here," Gray Owl said, putting a hand on his heart, "and here," he added, tapping his temple.

* * *

Slow Bear soon collected Karno, Bror, and me and guided us down a footworn path until we came to a small lake. I might have called it a pond, but the waters appeared to be clear and deep. It was just as well that we reached this place after midday, when the air temperature was at its warmest, because we found the blue waters to be quite cold. We three bathers stuck the butts of our spear shafts into the soft soil that surrounded the lake and propped the spearheads against one another. Then we scrubbed for as long as we could stand our bracing ablutions. When we could take no more, we waded to a grassy bank and sat in the full sun to dry and warm ourselves while we waited for our newly rinsed loincloths to dry as well. It was necessary to occasionally roll and reroll the loincloths in different directions as they gradually dried or else they would have become as stiff as sticks. We roused ourselves now and then from our idleness to perform this chore. We did not often get to enjoy the pleasure of just sitting and basking in the sun. It felt odd, as though we should have been doing something else to productively occupy our time.

Slow Bear waited patiently until we were ready to leave. He sometimes leaned on his spear, sometimes sat with us on the grass, trading bits of gossip and news with us, but always scrutinizing the surrounding woodland, ever watchful for potential danger.

Karno eyed Bror and me, or, more specifically, he eyed our backs.

"Tris, most times you and Cousin keep hair in binding," Karno began. "Now it loose. What great mass of hair you and Cousin have!"

We must have presented quite a sight to both Karno and Slow Bear. Karno's black hair was still shorn very close to his head, and Slow Bear's graying hair was worn in neat braids that hung just past his shoulders. Bror and I had the dense, curling, bright red hair of the Old Ones, and, as is our custom, it flowed well past our waists. Now that our hair was freed from its usual twisted and bound coils to dry in the open air, it blew around us as though it were a living thing. With the sun behind us, I could see by the shadows Bror and I cast that our long, curly locks moved freely on the breeze like the storm-tossed limbs of a tree.

"I will braid my hair when it has dried a little more," Bror stated, nonplused.

"Me as well," I said. "Morning Star can twist our hair into coils and lash them tightly after we have returned home."

"Your return home may be delayed if you must wait for your companions to be healed sufficiently to endure the journey," Slow Bear said gravely. "I am sure that Willow Woman will be glad for your company, but you may want to consider making alternative plans; especially if you wish to be back with your families any time soon."

This was something that had nagged at the back of my mind for some days now. Lor and the rest of the Karno's men should have arrived at the family compound by now. Morning Star probably worried for me, even though Lor surely would have explained the reason I had not accompanied the other hunters home. I did not like to be away from her, but I particularly did not like to give any reason to cause her uneasiness while she was heavily pregnant.

* * *

The afternoon was almost spent when we ventured down the trail to Willow Woman's house. We had not really needed someone to escort us, but I had the sense that Slow Bear enjoyed any excuse to embark on an adventure, however briefly. The chilling bath had left me feeling revitalized. I walked with a purposeful step, eager to speak with my fellow travelers about how long we could reasonably expect to stay here. I was so preoccupied with these thoughts that it was not until Bror put a hand on my shoulder to stop me in my tracks that I took note of several young bucks. They were standing on their hind legs and nibbling at the low-hanging leaves of a nearby tree. They shifted from side to side with small mincing steps as they tried to follow the wind-blown foliage.

We paused to exchange glances. Karno jerked his head toward the right and then he left us, slowly melting into the forest. Bror and I nodded to each other and backed away into the bushes, taking Slow Bear with us. Slow Bear understood what was going on. Karno would position himself behind the deer and jump out to surprise them. Then he would drive the frightened bucks toward us.

There was only few moments' wait before Karno barked and howled like a wolf, and we heard the sounds of deer crashing through the brush. My heart pounded with excitement as they approached.

Only one of the bucks passed within range, and we moved to intercept the creature, driving our spears into its front quarter and chest. The buck was down, but still alive. Karno was not far behind. He came leaping over bushes, rocks, and fallen tree trucks. Upon rejoining us, he struck his weapon into the injured deer with a fatal blow to its heart.

We stood grinning at one another for a short time while Karno recovered his breath. This deer would feed many people for a number of days.

"I have not hunted in some years," Slow Bear admitted to us. "I had forgotten how exhilarating it is! How gratifying the knowledge that success means your family and friends will eat well! Thank you for this!"

"Why no hunt?" Karno questioned, perplexed at the unthinkable idea.

"I used to hunt almost daily," Slow Bear said with a shrug. "But not since the day Willow Woman's mate was killed. As he lay dying, he made me promise to look after her. And I have. Willow Woman's father, who always doted on his only child, took pity on her in her grief and assigned a great many of us to keep her household. He had known for many years that Willow Woman would be the one to take his seat as Head Elder. He groomed her for the role and set her up with enough staff that she could easily assume her duties when the time came. But it was not as though Willow Woman needed his help. She is a powerful person. She gets whatever it is she wants, one way or another."

* * *

We arrived back at Willow Woman's home just as the sun descended below the treetops. We were no longer quite so clean after butchering the deer, but at least a little blood and gore were easily washed off.

While we waited to join the others for our evening meal and Willow Woman had temporarily adjourned to attend to some pressing task, I took the opportunity to talk to Black Wolf, Bror, and Karno.

"Both Gray Owl and Slow Bear have spoken of Bewok and Mino's lengthy recovery periods," I said. "I am glad to know that they are happy to facilitate their healing and play host to us, but I am concerned about staying away from home for so long." I could see by the looks on my companions' faces that they had been thinking on this as well. "Morning Star will have our baby in a few moons or maybe less. She gave birth to Fox early and I missed his birth. I do not want that to happen again. Plus, I think often of my Puh and Ria and their new baby and wonder if the baby yet lives. I am worried for my family. I very much want to go home."

I felt selfish to be uttering these words given that my friends were so badly injured. Mino might be able to make the trek home relatively soon, but poor Bewok was still seriously wounded. Karno's face betrayed alarm at the thought that we might abandon him and his comrades.

"Karno understand how you feel," Karno said, taking pains to attempt to speak our language as best he could. He touched my arm with his fingertips to emphasize his sincerity and went on. "You have beautiful mate and child. Karno keep you away from your family for long time. You go home, but not go alone. Bear Wrestler Cousin go home, too. Tell Ru Karno return when he can. Tell her my heart is with her, always."

Karno took some time to utter these words as he struggled to form his sentences and pronounce the words with extreme care. I noted that he did not speak of Black Wolf going home, too. He must have assumed that Black Wolf was going to settle in with his other "mate" for a time before resuming his relationship with Little Fawn.

"Karno," I said, hesitating a moment as I tried to articulate my thoughts. "I do not want to desert you here. Perhaps we can arrange that I will come back after the baby is born."

"I will come back, too," Bror added. "I will go home with Tris, since it is much too dangerous to travel that distance alone. But I will come back with Tris and Lor and wait out your friends' convalescence with you."

Black Wolf had been listening to our conversation without comment, but I could see that he, too, was pondering the situation.

"No." Black Wolf shook his head, causing his many stiff braids to waggle. "There is no need for Tris and Bror to make the trip back. I will wait with Karno for his men to be restored to health and then I will lead them back to the family compound."

As Black Wolf spoke, he held my gaze, and then he turned to Bror and locked eyes with him as well. I am sure that Bror understood, as did I, that he was giving Bror an opening to spend time with Ru. That is, with Ru, but without Karno's constant attendance on Ru's attentions.

I quickly glanced at Karno to see if he had caught on to Black Wolf's real aims, but Karno's facial expression was one of simple joy and relief at the knowledge that he would not be left alone with comparative strangers.

"Many thanks, Black Wolf," I said to him. "If Bror is agreeable, we will leave first thing tomorrow morning."

"I am agreeable," Bror nodded.

* * *

We ate our nightly sup around the outdoor fire pit. As always, Willow Woman's repast was artfully prepared and served. I ate well, knowing that Bror and I would have to fuel our long walk home. I had stuffed myself with as much food as I could hold and was rising to my feet to take my leave when Willow Woman motioned me to her side.

I skirted the group of people who sat at the fireside and then obediently knelt by Willow Woman.

"Tris," she started, "I understand that you and your cousin are going home tomorrow."

"Yes," I answered, saying no more as I waited to hear the reason she wanted to speak with me.

"Your mate is with child and you are anxious to be with her again?" Willow Woman continued.

"Yes," I repeated. "I am eager to be with my son, too, and the rest of my family, as well."

"I see," Willow Woman paused briefly. "Black Wolf has told me much about you and your clan. I must confess, I knew little about Old Ones until he explained to me about your culture, your intelligence, and your devotion to family and friends. Prior to that all I knew was that you looked and talked differently from The People. But now that Black Wolf has praised his friends among the Old Ones so highly, and since I have become accustomed to your talk – after all, Black Wolf has spent so much of his life with you that he shares many of the Old One's pronunciations and speech patterns – now I can converse easily with you, and I have come to know that you are a very worthy people."

I nodded my thanks to her for her kind assessment.

"You do not often say much, do you?" Willow Woman smiled warmly at me.

"The falls are loud. I do not like to shout into your ear to be heard," I told her.

"Yes, the falls are loud. But their presence has the advantage of obscuring conversations that might be eavesdropped in other circumstances. Like now. I wish to ask you a few questions before you take your leave of us tomorrow. You have spent much time with these Wolf-men. Since they will be with us for some while, I would like to know your impressions of them. Karno may be a Great Man's son, but I do not I see him becoming a future leader of his people. However, he is young yet. Maybe he will mature into something other than a braggart and a hunter. What do you think of Karno and his men?"

"I know only that they have behaved honorably since we have met." I consciously left out such incidents as Karno seizing my sister by the buttocks and his sometimes boorish temperament – but really, other than that, they had been very good company.

"Black Wolf says that they are Bone Crunchers."

"That is one name for them," I concurred, "but they call themselves The People of the Wolves."

"I suppose that is a much nicer name." Willow Woman appeared to be thinking. She went on, "Will you tell me about Black Wolf's mate?"

This query took me by surprise.

"Um …" I stammered, "Her name is Little Fawn."

"She is little?"

"No," I replied. I did not want to have this conversation with Willow Woman. But I could not be rude to the person who not only was my host, but had in the past helped my people. I searched for a response that would satisfy her without divulging intimate details about Black Wolf's home life.

"She is not little?" Willow Woman sighed, "Tris, getting information out of you is like trying to pull an aurochs through a bird's hollow wing bone! Please tell me what she is like!"

"Little Fawn is a good mother and a she keeps a good home. She is very tall – taller than I am. She adores my son Fox. She comes to see him every day." I still felt guilty about revealing these things to Willow Woman. It was not my place to talk about Black Wolf's family to her.

"She is a good woman but he does not love her?"

"I cannot say," I muttered miserably, my gaze dropping to the floor.

When I lifted my eyes again, Willow Woman was looking at me, her face bearing a mixture of pity and understanding.

"That is enough, Tris," Willow Woman said, holding up her hand to stop me. "You look so tortured I cannot stand it. Thank you for describing Little Fawn to me. Black Wolf has told me about your family, so I did not think I would be breaking your societal protocol by asking you about his. Black Wolf has been very closed-mouthed about his mate and brood and I have been curious. Besides, I know you are an honest man and that if I asked anything of you, you would tell me the truth. I truly did not mean to pry. I am sorry if I made you uncomfortable."

Chapter Eight

I awoke early the next morning and soon joined the others for breakfast. Willow Woman knew that Bror and I would need to eat well to sustain ourselves during the arduous journey home, so she had arranged to have a veritable feast readied for our last meal at her house. This included eggs, cooked whole at the edge of the fire's coals, fish, several kinds of meat, such as our freshly smoked rhino, roasted fowl, and a variety of berries.

The sumptuous fare left my hands both greasy and sticky. Were I at home by our little creek, I would not have thought twice about washing my hands at that placid water source. But now I looked down at the frothing torrent and wondered yet again at Gran's Dream.

Just then Bror met me on the river's bank. He gave me a quick side glance and dropped to his knees to dip his hands in the wild rapids. I realized that it was ridiculous to just stand there. What harm could possibly come from ridding my hands of a little grime?

* * *

Later, Black Wolf found Bror and me sitting on the floor of our shared room, stowing food, water bags, and assorted gear into our packs.

"Are you almost ready?" Black Wolf asked.

Bror and I nodded in reply. I was still feeling remorseful over spilling details of Black Wolf's personal life to Willow Woman. I did not want my words to come back to haunt him.

"Black Wolf," I began, "I must tell you that Willow Woman was inquiring about Little Fawn."

Black Wolf smiled wryly.

"She was, was she?" Black Wolf did not seem startled or alarmed at this news. "I am not surprised. She has been hinting at her interest in Little Fawn and the children. Her inquisitive nature must have gotten the best of her. What did you say?"

"I told her that Little Fawn is a good mother. That she is tall. Maybe a few more things, too. Oh, yes … I said she loves Fox," I admitted. It was on the tip of my tongue to mention Willow Woman's query on whether or not Black Wolf loved Little Fawn, but all that came out was, "I am sorry, Black Wolf. I did not know how to evade her questioning. I tried not to say anything you would disapprove of."

"Do not fear, Tris," Black Wolf said as he laughed easily. "You did no wrong. Willow has been exceedingly curious about Little Fawn since – um – our initial involvement ... and, in fact, anything about my life when I am away from her. What scares me is the knowledge that one day she may appear at my door and meet Little Fawn face to face. But do not mind about that. Life is a funny thing. I sometimes wonder if I would have agreed to be paired with Little Fawn if I had met Willow first. But then I realized that it is through Little Fawn that my children came to be. And I cannot bear to think of my life without them. Besides, Willow claims that she does not want a mate with whom she would share her life. I think that part of her fears she may lose some of her power; that a mate might have designs on wresting the Head Eldership from her. But she enjoys my company. I enjoy hers. I care for her deeply. In many ways we are very alike. All the same, regardless of our personal circumstances, I do not believe we will ever be paired."

I nodded my thanks to Black Wolf for his kind words at the clumsy way I had handled the awkward chat with Willow Woman.

When at last Bror and I stood before the group that assembled to see us off, Willow Woman caught Bror and me off guard when she bestowed upon each of us a warm embrace. Then she wished us a fast and uneventful trek home. Black Wolf hugged us both as well.

"Be safe," Black Wolf said to us. Then, directing his comments toward me, he added, "Tell my family that I will be home before winter sets in. And take good care of Morning Star and my grandchildren."

"I will," I assured him, smiling at the pleasurable thought of being back with my loved ones once again.

Karno approached Bror and me. He, too, wrapped his arms around us. This almost as astonishing as Willow Woman's hug. I had never seen him hug anything other than a dog.

"Karno enjoy this hunt with you," Karno told us. "Send you home with message, too. Tell Ru Karno be back as soon as can. Karno miss her. Tell her that." Karno paused and then turned to Bror. "That lion almost kill Karno. Thank you, Bror, for killing lion before he kill Karno." He clasped Bror strongly for a long moment before releasing him, and then Karno thumped Bror's bulky shoulder as though to emphasize his gratitude.

Bror was temporarily rendered speechless.

"I am glad I was able to step in where needed," he said finally.

* * *

That farewell scene played itself out in my mind over and over again as Bror and I walked down the trail. I noted that Bror's countenance betrayed the fact that he, too, was lost in thought.

"What is it, Bror?" I queried.

"That was quite the embrace," Bror answered.

I felt my eyebrows rise up on my forehead.

"Karno?"

"No. Not Karno," Bror spoke in a definite tone. "Willow Woman. It was very soft. And she is so tall – I thought I might be smothered if it were to go on for any length of time. I had a moment in which to ponder that it would be a ridiculous way to meet my death."

I smiled at Bror's words, but I had to agree. Being pressed against Willow Woman's well-rounded physique provided a unique experience; after all, our mothers, mates, and anyone else who might have similarly come in such close contact were notably lean, so there was scant cushioning between two bodies. Embracing Willow Woman, however, was like embracing a very large, warm water bag.

"He called me by name," Bror then recalled.

"Karno?" I guessed again.

"Yes. That was the first time he has ever spoken my name. I did not know whether or not he even knew it. He has always referred to me as *Bear Wrestler Man* or *Cousin*." Bror shook his head. "Inasmuch as I do not like Karno's relationship with Ru, I cannot dislike him as a man. He may be self-important at times and a bit crude, but I cannot dislike a fellow so good-natured and goodhearted. I know he loves Ru, but I do not believe that she would be happy with him. Or is it jealousy that clouds my thoughts, Tris?"

"I agree, Cousin," I said, "I do not believe that Ru will put up with Karno's antics once the initial fervor has worn off. They are very different."

The Dreamer III – The People of the Wolves

"If I may say so, you and Morning Star are also very different."

I grinned sheepishly at this. It was true that Morning Star, with her silky black hair and dusky complexion, was a startling departure from my fiery curling hair and pale skin. One never knew when Morning Star might unleash her excitable disposition, while my nature was comparatively bland. Nevertheless, we both wanted the same things from life. We were fiercely united in caring for each other, our families, and our home.

"Yes and no. We might look and sometimes act in ways that may seem at odds, but we were raised much the same, and our families have been connected for generations. We both want our lives to revolve around our children and providing a good home for them. It is possible I do not fully appreciate Karno's qualities, but although I, too, like him very much, it seems to me he lives for adventure."

"Maybe Ru admires that in a man."

"Maybe," I said with a shrug, "but I think not."

* * *

Bror and I were advised to follow the river's southward course until we met the confluence of the White River and the River of the Bears. There would break away from those bodies of water and strike out across the broad expanse of land that was home to The People from the East's annual Gathering. The Gathering took place every fall, after most of the local population had finished its autumn foraging and hunts. The Gathering lasted one moon, and it gave the men of The People an opportunity to meet with one another to trade, to arrange pairings, to discuss who had the right to live or hunt at a particular place, or to bring grievances before the Head Elder. This being late summer, I expected that Willow Woman and her entourage would make their way to the Gathering site in a few moons and that Black Wolf, Karno, and the injured men would likely accompany her there. Assuming, that is, that Mino and Bewok were sufficiently healed to make the journey at that time.

In the meanwhile, Bror and I trudged along the stony path that ran roughly parallel to the river. Our feet were toughened from a lifetime of walking on all sorts of surfaces, but occasionally a sharp rock underfoot caused us to stifle a grunt of pain. The stones also had a tendency to roll and shift beneath our feet, making the hike all the more tedious. We began to seek out another trail that would still follow the waterway but get us off those rocks.

Despite the river's constant presence, I was not concerned for our safety. We soon found another pathway some short distance away, where the terrain was a little more forgiving on our poor feet. At this point, I was actually enjoying our journey. Puffy white clouds floated across the field of blue overhead. The firmament was often graced with flocks of migrating birds. At times, the flocks were so dense as to nearly blot out the sun. Noisy geese vigorously winged their way south, their honking clearly heard even over the roar of the nearby tumbling waters. This river, so named the White River because of its churning, foaming nature, flowed in the same direction as our travel and almost seemed to be accompanying us to our destination.

* * *

As evening fell, Bror and I set up a lean-to. We searched briefly for dry wood, but finding little, we did not build a fire. The air was cool, so we wrapped our cloaks around our naked torsos and huddled for warmth.

"Fall will soon be with us," Bror noted.

"Yes." I smiled. Any mention of fall made me think of Morning Star and our new baby. It was difficult to stop myself from wondering whether the child would be a boy or a girl. What would it look like? Would it resemble Morning Star, with her lovely dark coloring, or would it be like Fox and me, with red hair and freckled skin?

The light of day was quickly fading. As we ate a ration of smoked rhino meat washed down with water, the shadows overtook us. We spoke little. I had just lain down under our lean-to when I heard a flock of ducks pass overhead. They were so close that I could hear the flapping of their wings and their soft cries even over the river's constant burble. Bror heard them as well.

"The ducks are landing for the night," Bror said. "There must be a pond or lake nearby where they can rest and feed."

"Yes," I agreed drowsily.

The rush of the river soon lulled me to sleep.

* * *

Several mammoths sounded an unsettling rumble as they perceived our presence. There were many of them, cows and youngsters of all sizes. One of the mammoths bellowed a warning to the others in her herd and the cows began to drive the little ones toward the center of their group for protection. Then the herd's matriarch lifted her head and suddenly locked eyes with me ...

Bror did not have to shake me from this Dream. I awoke on my own accord, disconcerted by the mental picture of those huge hairy beasts and the attention I had garnered from the lead mammoth. I had not seen Bror in this Dream. I seemed to be alone. Maybe it was something that would happen in the future. On the other hand, Gran had spoken of ancient memories; I was not really sure what she meant by the term, but was this an ancient memory? Was this Dream a recollection of something that had occurred many generations ago?

The Dreamer III – The People of the Wolves

I arose and pulled my cloak more tightly around my shoulders. The air was damp and quite cold, nearly cold enough for a frost. The sun was only just beginning to rise above the horizon, filling the skies with vibrant color. Bror shifted a little in his sleep, no doubt roused by my movements around our camp. He then sat up and looked around for me.

"There you are," Bror said. "Did the chilly temperatures awaken you?"

"No," I replied, "it was another woolly mammoth Dream. But it is cold. I was just going to find a place to empty my bladder."

Bror studied my face, peering at me sympathetically. He knew that my Dreams sometimes showed me fearsome or disturbing images. However, he did not speak of them.

"I will go with you." Bror stood to join me and then collected his spear.

I carried my spear as well as we walked through wet clumps of low brush and yellowed grasses until we were just far enough away to leave the area around our lean-to unsullied. Our urine steamed in the low early morning light. We looked about us, constantly scanning for possible predators. There were none to be seen, but I did note several roe deer frolicking in the nearby misty meadow. As the rising sun crested the far-off treetops, its rays highlighted the dew-dappled bodies of the deer and caught in their large upright ears, making them appear to glow. The bigger deer such as the elk and the giant deer would have already started their rutting season. Smaller deer like these were still sparring playfully, practicing for the time when the bucks would begin to battle in earnest, gravely intent on winning or keeping a harem of does.

Feeling a tinge of regret, we watched the deer. Sadly, we could not linger here, and thus had no time to bring in fresh meat for our morning meal. We were eager not only to be home to be with our families, but to access articles of cold-weather clothing. Bror and I were still dressed only in our loincloths, and summer's mild days would soon be a thing of the past. We had our cloaks, of course, but they did not warm our bare legs and feet.

Bror and I paused just long enough to remove some smoked rhino meat from our packs, and then we resumed our hike homeward, gnawing on our breakfasts as we walked. As the sun continued to climb, so did the air's temperature. The winds were mercifully gentle, which made a frantically rocking treetop stand out easily amongst its calmer companions. Bror noticed the tree about the same time as I did. We continued to watch the spectacle for a few moments.

"It would take a very large bear to make a tree move like that," Bror said, stating the obvious.

"Perhaps we should take steps to avoid a confrontation with the animal," I suggested. Our current path would take us in the general direction of the tree, and I had no desire to find out whether the back-scratching bruin was a potentially cantankerous boar or a sow bear, possibly accompanied by cubs.

Bror nodded in agreement. We broke from the trail and began to make a wide circle around the small patch of woodland where the tree still danced. I was glad to see the tree's movement, since that assured us that the bear was still there, assuaging a persistent itch. But when the treetop became still, we watched the edge of the brush carefully, our ears attuned for the sounds of a heavy body pushing its way through the undergrowth. Our heartbeats drummed within our chests in anticipation. But no angry beast dashed out to meet us. Although most adult bears are much larger than a man, they often chose to avoid us. Either they did not hold our company in high regard or they did not like to engage our spears. Or, maybe, they simply had a notion to go elsewhere.

We maintained our course around the perimeter of the forest. The peaceful landscape created within me a happy carefree state. I began to enjoy the quiet of the day, broken only by the occasional cries from pair of hawks as they soared far above us.

While the day progressed, Bror and I were sufficiently warmed that we could now roll up our cloaks and drape them over our left shoulders. We stopped periodically to sip from our water bags and nibble on smoked meat. But mostly we walked without interruption. We were about to make our turn back to the river trail when we caught sight of a group of woolly mammoths and halted in our tracks.

It was a mixed herd of adults, juveniles, and babies. We did not want to catch their attention. We sought to blend in with the backdrop of trees behind us and thus elude the mammoths' notice by slipping into the wooded area that we had previously tried to avoid. As Bror and I hiked toward the sanctuary of the trees, we heard the low distant rumble that could come only from the throat of a huge woolly mammoth.

Bror and I hastened our pace. Another mammoth trumpeted. They were still beyond immediate threat, but we took no chances, especially in view of my recent Dreams. Bror and I finally reached the brush, and we quickly put as many bushes and tree trunks as we could between us and the agitated behemoths.

Bror and I looked over our shoulders now and then to be sure that the mammoths were not attempting to pursue us into the forest. We soon lost sight of them and no longer heard their urgent vocalizations, only their distant groans and husky squawks.

"Watch your step!" Bror exclaimed, pulling me toward him.

I was still so shaken up after seeing the mammoth herd that I was not thinking clearly.

"What?" I asked.

I looked about but saw no threat.

"Bear poop! And it is still fresh! You do not want to step in that!" Bror indicated the mound of bear excrement that would have been directly in my path had he not interceded.

"Oh! Many thanks, Bror."

We found ourselves in an interesting position. We had escaped the woolly mammoths, but now we were once again closer to the bear. As we walked, Bror and I inspected the ground for other signs of the creature. The bear appeared to be ambling around, going nowhere in particular. But one thing was for certain, this was a big boar bear.

Bror and I decided to make as direct a route to the river as we could. We would make no effort to hide our presence. Bears do not like to be surprised. Most often if they know you are in the area they will move off without engaging in a meeting.

"How I wish I could sing like Black Wolf!" Bror lamented.

"I was just thinking the same thing!" I agreed heartily. "No animals come near when Black Wolf sings."

"Do you know any of his songs?" Bror questioned hopefully.

"Only a few words here and there ... something about *the mighty hunter is bold and brave*; but my voice could not match his even if my life depended on it."

"Let us hope our lives do not depend on it," Bror said, removing his knife from its sheath. I did the same. We Old Ones might not sing, but we did have our own method of making noise to deter predators.

Bror and I walked quickly, hitting our deer antler knife handles against the shafts of our spears and calling out *Go away, bear! We are here, bear! Go away, bear! We are here, bear!* over and over again.

When we heard the faint sound of the river's surge, Bror and I felt relief. With luck, we had left both the mammoths and bear behind us. Bror and I hastened our pace, still striking knife handle to spear shaft and chanting as loudly as we could. But this bear must have been hard of hearing, or perchance it was simply curious to see what was causing all that commotion. When we came upon it, the bear immediately reared up on its hind legs and turned its head this way and that, as though it was an old man trying to fix his wavering gaze upon us.

Bror and I involuntarily froze. I hardly dared to breathe. I had never seen a bear so large. Bror ever so slightly elbowed me. He took a small step backward. So did I. Still tottering on two legs, the bear advanced a few steps in our direction. We retreated more steps. Thus far, the old boar did not seem aggressive. Its massive forepaws dangled peaceably in front of its belly, moving a bit as it adjusted its balance. Nonetheless, we did not wish to test the beast's benevolence. We continued to slowly back up, and the bear continued to advance upon us, its nostrils twitching curiously as it studied us.

Abruptly, the boar's mood changed and it tensed. Uttering a savage roar, it dropped down on all four feet and bounded the last steps toward us.

Bror and I poised our spears for what we were sure would be a crushing impact, but the beast surged past us. Within moments it collided with another bear, which must have also heard our supposed deterrents, only to be drawn to the puzzling sounds. But instead, it had met with one of its own kind.

Now, both bears were in full battle, grunting and growling at each other as they grappled. Although Bror and I could scarcely tear our eyes away from the horrifying sight, we forced ourselves to keep stepping backward.

The newcomer was a somewhat smaller, younger bear, and it was hard put to stave off the older boar's attack. The two ranged ferociously through the area, covering great stretches of ground. At times their large hairy bodies tumbled over fallen trees or crashed noisily through the brush. Every time the younger bear, now bloodied and tiring, tried to break off the fight and make an escape, the older bear followed and assaulted with renewed vigor.

It must have lasted only a few moments, but it felt as though it took us the better part of the day to at last put some distance between us and the bears.

When we could no longer hear their skirmish, Bror and I looked at each other.

"When that bear charged us, I thought we were dead," Bror said, hands trembling. "I believe that is the closest I have ever come to meeting my end."

I could still feel my heart thumping powerfully within my chest.

"It is times like this that I appreciate my Dreams," I told Bror.

"Why?" Bror inquired.

"Because my Dreams have shown me that I live to have many more children. I was scared, but I knew that I would survive," I replied.

"Yes, you survived," Bror began, "but what about me?"

"You did survive. Besides, it is unlikely that I could successfully reach home without you. Therefore, our fates, at least during this expedition, are unequivocally tied."

I grinned at Bror and he smiled back. We laughed soundlessly and set out down the trail once again.

* * *

"I can scarcely believe this," Bror said when we emerged from the forest and looked out across grasslands studded with low brush toward the White River.

The woolly mammoths had relocated to this spot, and they appeared to be traversing the river. The rapids were somewhat slower here, and the lumbering giants were carefully making their way through the runnels, encouraging the frightened infants to keep moving.

"We can wait until they have crossed and then we can go on," I suggested.

Bror nodded. There were not many options open to us. This one made the most sense. So Bror and I hunkered down on our haunches and decided to eat our evening meal while we were forced to temporarily delay our trek.

Many of the smaller mammoths did not care for this damp adventure. They balked and bawled, causing their mothers and assorted others to come to their aid. A few babies lost their footing, provoking concern for their safety even within Bror and me.

"Come on, little one!" Bror and I cheered them on, speaking under our breaths. "You can do it! You can do it!"

When the last woolly mammoth had completed its slog through the river, we repacked our foodstuffs and water bags and began to stride down the path. We could see that the mammoths were watching us from the other side of the river, but they did not seem inclined to worry about our presence. With the river between us, Bror and I also felt no need to worry about their proximity.

The body of water soon narrowed, causing the current to run more swiftly. Large boulders littered the waterway, confusing the torrent, which now splashed and frothed with increased intensity as it hit these obstacles. It would be almost impossible for even a woolly mammoth to cross here.

Our pathway became constricted by large rocks as well, forcing Bror and me to walk in single file between the stone formations. The sounds of the tumultuous waters filled our ears. The wild river broadcast a fine spray into the air that covered us with tiny droplets.

"It is slippery here," Bror noted as a misstep made him lurch to catch himself. "We came near here last winter, did we not? But I do not think we came up the trail this far." Bror had to shout to be heard over the raging waters.

"Yes, we did. Puh and I actually used this path when we were on our way to Ria's dwelling." This was before Puh and Ria had become paired. Willow Woman had sent us to find as many Old Ones as we could to testify whether or not any men of The People had been raiding their homes. We were supposed to recruit Ria's man Bakkae for the task, but when we arrived, we found that he was long gone and most likely dead.

"The rocks were not so slick at that time," I said. "The wind was strong that day; it must have blown the spray in the other direction."

The words had no sooner left my mouth when I, too, lost my footing. My spear fell clattering to the ground as I tried to grab onto the branch of a dead tree. The branch cracked under the sudden burden of my weight.   Before I knew what had happened, I was floundering in the rushing river.

The shock of the cold water made me gasp, which in turn caused me to swallow a mouthful of the frigid liquid and an errant blast of water went up my nose. We Old Ones are not built for swimming. We have heavy-boned, muscular bodies that do not float very well. My cloak washed away almost immediately. My pack was now saturated with water, and I found both its weight and its drag it effected to be most inconvenient.

I was mercilessly pushed by the powerful current, and most of the time I was completely submerged under water. I caught only flashes of my surroundings as I made my way downriver, now being dashed into a boulder, now being washed down a fall into yet another rock. This was a desperate state of affairs. My lungs and nasal passages burned. If in an instant I was able to gulp a breath of air, I choked on the water I also inhaled at the same time. My thoughts wandered to Morning Star, Fox, and the new baby. I had to find a way out of this river.

Abruptly, I came to a stop. I had been pinned against the hulk of a tree trunk, which lay partially across the river. I was chilled through and through. With numbed hands, I struggled to grasp the smooth wood against the force of the river, which still tugged at me relentlessly. Although my brain was addled from my tumble amidst that watery field of rocks, I had a brief moment in which to assess my situation. My vision was a little blurry, but all the same, I could see that blood was running down my face. I wiped at the blood with a clumsy hand to clear my eyes. I then realized that my pack was gone, probably battered off my back at some point. I felt for my knife, which was usually sheathed and tied at my right hip, but my hands were too numb to ascertain if it was still there.

Then I heard them. The mammoths must have made their way downriver, and I had found myself snagged on the tree exactly where they happened to be. The irate cows made ominous rumbles deep in their throats. My fingers were losing their grip on the tree trunk; I did not know whether to be alarmed or grateful that the current might again whisk me downstream. I wiped the blood from my face so I could see if the lower river continued to be treacherous, but my flopping hand did little more than smear the blood around. If I was sent hurtling down the river's flow once more, I did not know if I could keep myself afloat in my dazed and weakened condition. But the mammoths, after moving their young off to a safe distance to be monitored by other cows, were coming closer to determine the nature of the bloody being that clung to the tree at the edge of the water.

The river was indeed as turbulent downstream as the passage I had just endured. The herd matriarch was now near enough to catch my eye. Low rumbles issued from its throat. It stared at me purposefully, its brown eyes wide and comprehending. The mammoth brought its tremendous shaggy bulk closer and closer, its gaze never leaving my person.

I struggled to make my hands work, attempting to dig my fingernails into the wet wood, but all to no avail. My grip failed me, and the raging water tore me from the tree trunk and I was dragged beneath the river's surface.

I had not traveled but a short span when I was flung against something solid. But this time, it was not a rock or a tree. I began to wonder if I was losing my senses as I felt something warm and gentle wrap itself around my back. Suddenly, I was lifted from the river. To my utter astonishment, I found that the old matriarch had scooped me out of the water and was effortlessly transporting me to some new spot.

I had no notion whether or not it would throw me down on the ground and stamp out my life, but for the moment I did not care. I held onto its trunk and looked up at the face of this magnificent being. As one who must hunt to eat and must also take care that he not become something else's meal, I did not always appreciate the wondrous animals that shared our world with us; but right now, this cow mammoth was the most beautiful animal I had ever seen. Its late summer coat was somewhat shorter than it would be at the height of winter, but it was a lustrous brown. The cow had long lashes. I could see only one of its eyes from my position, but I returned its gaze, hoping to convey my gratitude. The mammoth might still dash me to pieces, but at least I was spared another torturous run down the sluice of rocks, which surely would have ended in my death.

I then noticed that a few of the other cows had joined in, creating a short procession back up the river. When we reached a calmer spot, the mammoths made a crossing. The water was still filled with rocks and quite hazardous, but they had chosen a place that widened to a comparatively sedate pool.

Now that I had been out of the cold waters for a time, I was beginning to feel a bit more like myself, but I was also in considerable pain. My head ached, and one of my shoulders seemed to be nearly wrenched from its socket. When the cow pulled itself from the clasp of the strong current, I saw that it had brought me to a broad, grassy bank. The rocks were fewer here, and the ground was largely flat. It was the perfect place to stomp on a puny human. The mammoth stood still and paused, giving the others a chance to catch up.

My hands were yet barely functioning, but I stroked the cow's upper trunk as I waited to see what would happen next. The other mammoths began to graze. The old matriarch just stood quietly, its truck continuing to cradle me.

"You are beautiful," I said softly to the animal. I did not know if it could hear me over the din of the river, but I said it anyway. "You are a lovely girl," I added.

Our one-sided conversation went on for a while. Then the cow's trunk slowly relaxed, and I was deposited with care on the grass. I shakily rose to my feet and looked up into its eye, so high above my head. The beast was completely calm. The mammoth blinked and then uttered a coo of sorts.

"Many thanks," I said. I no longer feared that I would be assaulted by this placid creature. My step was faltering, but I staggered to the mammoth's wet side and wrapped my arms around one of its forelegs. "Many thanks," I repeated, "many thanks, kind beautiful lady."

The mammoth seemed to understand me. Its trunk caressed my back for a stroke or two. But then it made a few short bursts of sound to its companions and the mammoths all turned and reentered the river. I was sorry to see them go.

 **Chapter Nine**

"Tris!" I recognized Bror's voice. "Tris!"

Bror came trotting breathlessly up the path. I was a little startled to see that tears were streaming down his cheeks. I was shivering and unable to stand for very long, so I reclined on the grass, watching the departing mammoths disappear into the distance. Bror dropped to the ground at my side and tightly embraced me.

"Tris! I was so frightened I would never see you again! When you fell in the water I feared that you had tempted fate's wrath by speaking of your surety that you would live to have many more children."

I was unable to formulate words. I did not know how to tell him all that had happened. I had been tumbled about so much I scarcely knew myself. The mammoth rescue was so improbable that I began to wonder if I had imagined it. But no, I could see the loose strands of mammoth fur that had adhered to my damp skin. It must have been real.

"Look at you," Bror went on. "You look as though that bear did get hold of you! Can you walk?"

"I think so," I finally answered. "I just need to warm up and dry myself. The wind is rising and now I am becoming cold."

"I will make a fire," Bror volunteered. "Take my cloak. We can camp here for the night and then see how you feel come morning."

The surrounding area did not boast much in the way of trees: the scant saplings in the vicinity were lifeless skeletons. However, the brittle wood, added to some dried twigs and grasses, were enough to allow Bror to spark a fire.

"Let me take a gander at you," Bror said as he knelt next to me once more.

Bror first examined my head, carefully pushing the sodden hair from my brow.

"You are going to be sporting quite a knot," he informed me. "Your nose is bloodied, too. Would you lower the cloak for just a moment?"

Trembling with cold, I obliged. Every move brought with it a fresh wave of pain.

"Your right shoulder took quite hit," Bror said, shaking his head; "also your elbows and parts of your back are scraped." Bror arranged his cloak around my torso once again and shifted to crouch in front of me as he checked my legs. "Your knees took a beating, too.

However, it does not seem as though anything is broken, except maybe your nose."

"I think I will be sick …" I suddenly gasped out.

"What?" Bror asked.

"*Sick!*" I said again.

I did not want to vomit in the middle of our camp, so I launched myself toward the line of small bushes behind us and promptly expelled the mostly liquid contents from my stomach – and possibly from my lungs as well – into the foliage. I retched repeatedly, until at last I had removed the last of the river from my innards.

Bror stood by me and then helped me to sit by the fire once more.

"Tris, you are a sight," he shook his head. "Do you want a drink of water?"

I looked at the river and thought on all the water I had drunk this day and had just vomited into the brush. Bror followed my train of thought.

"Perhaps not … I just remembered that when I have been sick that my throat was sore afterward and cool water relieved the burning," he said.

"Yes, you are right," I agreed, "I will take a sip of water."

Bror smiled and gave me his water bag.

"Something to eat, too?" he questioned.

I nodded.

"Many thanks, Bror."

Bror dug through his pack for a piece of smoked rhino meat for each of us, and then he prodded the fire while absently chewing on his portion.

"Hallo!" A new voice greeted us.

Bror and I glanced up in surprise to see my mother's brothers Inlee and Trae, and Inlee's mate's brother Sere, stride into our camp. They lived within several days' hike of this area; I guessed that they must be away from home on an extended hunt.

Bror and I rose to our feet as the men approached us.

"Tris! Look at you!" Inlee exclaimed. "And this is ... Bror? Do I remember his name correctly? What has happened?"

My uncles each put an arm around my shoulders, gazing at me with evident concern on their faces.

"We saw the smoke from your fire and came over to see who else was hunting in these parts. Are you two alone?" Trae inquired.

"Yes, we are alone. It is a long story," Bror started. And it was a long tale, but who better to tell it than the son of a Keeper of Stories? Bror, when asked, would retell the yarns and anecdotes his father had so often recited for us, but the description of our recent adventures seemed to rival any of our traditional lore.

Inlee, Sere, and Trae listened without interruption. When at last Bror concluded with my mishap at the river's edge, Bror looked to me. I had not yet explained what had taken place after I had fallen in the turbulent waters.

"So, Tris, you must pick up the tale from here." Bror wore a curious expression. He must have been as eager to hear how I had survived the river as were Sere and my uncles.

I took a moment to compose my thoughts. My brain was still somewhat muddled.

"As you probably know," I commenced, "I do not swim well, and I was quickly washed downstream, where I met with a number of rocks as I made my passage. I finally came to a stop when I fetched up against a downed tree. I tried to hold on, but the bark had long ago been stripped away, and the wet wood was too slippery to hold onto for long. As I hung there, I caught the attention of a herd of woolly mammoths. A few of them approached me, but then I lost my grip and was swept away again. Then, all of the sudden, I came to a stop once more, only this time, it was a mammoth that blocked my way. She picked me up with her trunk and carried me here. I know it sounds bizarre, but it is true. She and a few other cows stayed with me for a little while … until just before you arrived, Bror. Maybe they heard you coming up the path. All I know is that I am eternally grateful to that mammoth for saving my life … saving me from being pummeled to death on those rocks."

The men stared at me, temporarily struck silent.

"That is the most incredible luck!" Inlee declared.

"It is more than luck," Bror stated. "I believe she recognized that Tris is a gentle man and she felt his was a life worth saving."

"No," I said, shaking my head, "I do not think it had anything to do with me. I think it lies within the compassionate nature of these beasts. I was simply fortunate to benefit from it."

* * *

The men decided to camp with us for a few days. By that time, although my head throbbed more than ever and my aching eyes felt as though they might pop right out of their sockets, I was able to move about fairly well. I was a walking collection of abrasions and bruises, but I was eager to resume our journey home.

My uncles and Sere did not think it wise to let us go without their escort. I was thankful for that. Any nearby predators would surely catch the scent of my wounds and take note of the uneven cadence of my gait. While I was sure that Bror would try to protect me with his life – not because his father had done as much for mine, but because but any man would do it – we did not stand much of a chance against any large carnivores we might meet on our trek homeward.

This was my first opportunity to spend time with my mother's brothers. My Muh's parents had not approved of her relationship with Puh, and when they reluctantly agreed to let Muh and Puh be paired, my grandparents then cut them out of their lives. Therefore, I had had no contact with my Muh's family until we accidentally came upon their home last winter. My mother's parents were now deceased, but we were pleased to find that two of her older brothers still lived. Inlee and Trae were tall, like most of Muh's kin, and although they were now at an advanced age, their white hair still bore traces of the dark red that was also a family trait. I guessed that my uncles were well past forty winters old, but they were still strong and vigorous men. Sere was somewhat younger. He was of average height for an Old One, and he owned a stocky build, even more so than was normal for one of our people.

I had always heard that my mother's family members were rather unsociable, so I was happily surprised to find that Inlee and Trae were genial company indeed. Sere was also an affable man: he was very kind and always ready to laugh. I liked them all immensely. The pleasure I found in getting to know these men made the long trip home much easier to bear. I hobbled alongside them, listening as they told me all about the family of which I knew so little. It was bittersweet to hear them speak of my mother, who had been their youngest sister. They had never seen her again after she and Puh were paired, so they asked me many questions of her. I tried my best to accurately convey her serenity, her beauty, her grace, and, above all, her love of family. She had cared for us with a devotion that was unmatched. She had insisted that we were always clean and well-clothed. I am afraid that she would have been grieved to see how we looked now. We were not quite so clean, and our clothing might be a bit tattered. But then Muh's standards were hard to maintain.

Each day my step became surer, and despite the continued pain in my head, I no longer felt pressure behind my eyes. I was glad the days mild were enough that I did not miss my cloak. At night, we erected a large lean-to, combining my uncles' and Sere's lean-to with the one Bror and I shared. The men let me sleep toward the middle of the shelter so that their body heat would warm me. They also lay their cloaks so that one or more edges were atop me. As it turned out, at times I was too warm, but they were so good to me that I did not have the heart to ask them to move their cloaks aside.

* * *

We would soon need to hunt. The length of our trip and the fact that I had been toting most of our smoked and dried meat in my lost pack, while Bror had carried the lean-to tarpaulin in his, necessitated that we delay our journey to find fresh meat. My uncles and Sere had some food, but it was not enough to feed us all. The nearby countryside abounded with plenty of game animals, so we left the riverside trail and ventured off to the adjacent grasslands. There, the giant deer and elk were distracted with their annual mating rituals and would have made easy prey, but we did not need a creature so large. We needed only something the size of a goat or roe deer. Goats did not live in this place, but there were deer aplenty of all types. It seemed we could hardly go anywhere without stumbling upon one. For all that, every deer we encountered on this day were of the bigger species. We especially wished to avoid the rutting bucks, which would not tolerate challengers trespassing on their territory. These stags could be quite aggressive, and they did not always differentiate between potential two- and four-legged foes.

I was pleased that Bror had managed to recover my spear before he began his sprint down the riverside after me. That spear and the loincloth tied around my hips were the only things the river had not taken away. I disliked the need to depend on my kin for water, dried foods, even the use of a knife, but it was comforting to know that the situation was only temporary. After our return to the family compound I would once again have access to my own possessions. The only thing I would need to replace was my pack. For now, however, I could at least do my part in this hunt.

When we passed by a pond, we saw the remarkable spectacle of a young bull elk grazing at the pond's bottom. I had never seen an elk dive underwater before. The animal was oblivious to our presence and seemed quite content with its midday pastime. Elks are powerful swimmers, but I was curious why this bull was not caught up in the rut.

Maybe it knew it was too small and inexperienced to challenge the older stags and was willing to spend its day at this serene basin. It paddled around the water's surface until it found a promising spot, and then it plunged its entire body underwater. Moments later it reappeared, water cascading off its antlers. After a quick breath, down it went, over and over again.

This elk was so focused on this activity that we briefly considered pursuing the beast, but there was far too much meat on the hoof here. And besides, it seemed such a shame to intrude on its peaceful repast. We were not out of food yet; we simply wished to extend our dried rations. We could afford to be selective in our quarry.

* * *

As the day wore on, we enjoyed our trek under a bright sun. There was little breeze to disturb the air. We saw a pack of wolves in the distance as they loped across a section of open prairie. They looked our way, but they kept moving without breaking stride. They, too, were on a mission.

We walked without speaking, our eyes canvassing our surroundings for a potential victim. Just as we closed in on a clump of dense brush, a number of boars suddenly burst from their hiding places. Only moments before we had noted some churned-up earth, but otherwise had seen little sign of their existence. We did not expect to find them so soon and were taken off guard.

I reacted first. Maybe it was because I was the one who was not loaded down with a heavy pack and bulky cloak. I stepped forward to intercept one of the boars and lunged to thrust my spear into its body as it passed by, carefully avoiding the sharp tusks. The boar dropped to the ground, but it was still alive. One of its companions circled around and took a pass at us but chose not to make contact. It just kept running and trotted off to rejoin its fellows.

This boar was very modest in size, but it would provide us with a substantial meal. My comrades eagerly helped to finish the job. As we cleaned the carcass, we discussed our options.

"Shall we set up camp and roast this young boar?" Trae asked, "Or shall we go to the river? I can see the distant gleam of the sun off the water from here. It is a good hike, but it would be nice to have access to fresh water."

I nodded. I thought this was a good idea as well. One thing was for sure: we did not want to camp near the spot where we had heaped the boar's entrails and other miscellaneous body parts.

"Yes, let us make for the river," Bror agreed. "The only trouble is that there are no tree branches or saplings nearby from which we could suspend the boar to carry it," Inlee pointed out. "We could bundle a few spears together – that would handle its weight – but then we will be left partially defenseless without ready use of those spears. I do not like that thought, what with all the attention the dead boar might garner from predators."

"The alternative is to take turns carrying the boar's carcass over our shoulders," Sere suggested.

"Yes," I piped up. "I have no pack, so when I am not carrying the boar, I can wear the carrier's pack for him. That way at least some of the burden will be alleviated."

The others grinned. This would work. I hefted the boar onto my shoulders, stifling a groan of pain. I was still in the midst of recovery from my misadventure, but I was determined to take on my share of the load. In light of all the others had done on my behalf, I felt it was the least I could do.

* * *

We arrived at the river wearing a certain amount of the boar's blood on our bodies, but here we could easily wash it away. The boar's bristly fur had also chafed our skin somewhat, but we did not care. We had not eaten fresh meat in some while, and we eagerly anticipated consuming this animal's flesh.

Fortunately, we found a place where we could forage enough firewood to cook our feast. We were famished by the time it was ready to eat, tantalized as we were by the wonderful aromas that hung in the air.

"Oh!" Trae said as he picked up a slab of meat. "It is so hot it burns my fingers! But it smells so wonderful I cannot wait to get started!"

"I think the inside of my mouth is scalded as

well," Bror agreed after he swallowed a hefty bite of roasted boar, "but it tastes so good I do not mind."

It was a cheerful and thoroughly satisfying meal. By the time we were sated, our hands, faces, and beards were begrimed with the creature's grease, which we did our best to wash off at the river's edge.

That night as we settled down to sleep in our lean-to, I put my hands on my engorged stomach and rubbed it to ease the discomfort. I could hear the sounds of my neighbors' digestion processes, which like mine, were tackling the prodigious dinner with gusto. I was full. I was warm. And most important of all, I was in good company. Despite my ever-present headache, I slept very well.

* * *

Our detour through the grasslands actually shortened our trip. The river we were following did not flow in a straight line, but wandered in wide curves, much like the body of a gigantic snake. As planned, we cut across the prairie to the place where the White River and the River of the Bears intersected. This was also the location of The People from the East's annual Gathering, but that event was still some moons away. When we arrived at the spot, we were propelled by strong gusty winds at our backs. The clouds were dark and full of thunder.

"I think we have found the Gathering house at just the right time," Inlee said.

"Do you suppose The People would be angry if we took shelter in there?" Trae asked.

"The wind would blow away our lean-tos, and this area has been stripped of anything we could use to build something more substantial," Bror pointed out. "I believe we can risk their wrath. After all, we have just recently been hosted by Willow Woman, the Head Elder; I think we are safe."

It was true that many years of Gatherings, attended by hundreds of men, had left a rather barren landscape for almost as far as the eye could see in any direction.

"I guess if some of The People should come along and take exception to our use of this building, we can try bandying Willow Woman's name about, but they may not take our word for it." I did not like to have such a defeatist attitude, but I had seen how some of The People from the East despised us.

Lightening arced overhead, followed by sharp claps of thunder.

"Let us discuss this inside," Sere said, motioning toward the hide-covered entrance to the great structure.

We nodded with agreement and quickly passed through the doorway. The air inside the Gathering chamber was a tad stale, even though the roof's smoke holes and the loosely covered door opening admitted some fresh air. As we stood in almost total darkness in the huge main room, a bolt of lightning caused a shaft of blinding white light to stab through each chimney hole.

I walked to one of the several fire pits just as the skies released their sodden burden. Rain pelted into the fire pit, disturbing the ashes and stirring up the odors of many fires past. Another flash of lightning showed that someone had left enough tinder and wood to start a small fire by every hearth. While it was not cool enough to require a fire for warmth, the flames would help to illuminate at least a small part of the room.

"Look! We can make a fire," I announced.

My companions blundered their way through the murk to my side. One of my uncles bumped into me. I knew it had to be an uncle, because whoever it was, he was about my height. I heard another of my companions stumble against something.

"Ouch. I think I found the firewood," said Bror.

A well-timed flash of lightning lit up the area around the fire pit, allowing each of us to see the layout of the tinder and wood. We immediately set to work on producing flames. We had an unspoken understanding that these materials would be replaced before we departed for home. It would have been unforgivable to use these things without replenishing them.

It was fortunate that the room was so large and the ceiling so high, as it helped disperse the smoke from our fire. It took a little time for the fire to become hot enough to create a draft, which would enable it to rise straight up and out the chimney hole. Just the same, errant blasts of wind would occasionally blow the smoke back down at us, stinging our eyes and causing us to choke.

Our coughing was interrupted when we suddenly heard the voices of men.

"Well, look who has dropped by to make use of our Gathering hall," a man said.

We turned as one to see that we were joined by four men, belonging to The People from the East's tribe. We stood to meet them as they maintained their position by the doorway and talked softly amongst themselves. I could only catch parts of their conversation.

"Old Ones! Why are they here?"

"See the smoke; they cannot even build a fire!"

The men went silent as we approached them. My uncles and I were actually slightly taller than they, which I think took them by surprise. Most Old Ones are just under the average height of a man of The People. I could see that they were observing us as closely as they could in the dimly lighted conditions.

Inlee spoke up with quiet dignity. "We hope we are not intruding," he said. "We only wanted to take shelter from the storm ..." A crash of thunder drowned Inlee's words for a moment. He went on, "We will, of course, replace the tinder and wood we have burned."

The men seemed to be regarding us skeptically. Finally, one of them smiled.

"Well, three old men and two young ones, one looking as though he has been well-thrashed not too long ago. I would think The People can offer the hospitality of their hall to you in such conditions as these. We saw the storm coming and we abandoned our hunt to come here and escape the weather, as well."

"Do you have food?" one of the men inquired.

"We have a little dried and smoked meat, to which you are very welcome," Inlee said, continuing to speak for us. I could not help but notice what an impressive man Inlee was: tall, straight-backed, with a lean, muscular build. He was not a man to be trifled with. Trae was just a few winters younger and not quite as tall as his brother, but he, too, cut a splendid figure. I could only hope that I was as healthful when I reached their age. Sere and Bror were imposing men as well. I felt very self-conscious of my battered condition. It was not prudent to show any sign of weakness to strangers.

"We have a little dried meat too," a man chimed in. "Some aurochs and some venison. We were hoping to bring in some fresh deer meat during this outing."

The men, although not pleased at our presence, at least seemed willing to accept us for the time being. They found a few torches and set them up so we would have more light. Then we all settled around the fire.

The Dreamer III – The People of the Wolves

In the meantime, the thunder and lightning raged all around the structure. The driving winds shook the building and occasionally bathed us with smoke each time a gust forced it to belch back down the chimney hole.

"It will be hard to sleep with the weather so chaotic," another of the men observed.

"Perhaps we should introduce ourselves," Inlee suggested. "I am Inlee, this is my brother Trae, our friend Sere, my nephew Tris, and his cousin Bror."

"*Tris?!*" one of the men repeated, "the Tris who beat Snow Leopard?!"

"Yes," I replied, nodding. I cringed inwardly, wondering if they were friends of Snow Leopard's. Not only had I beaten him in the Challenge Circle to win Morning Star, I had also killed him after he abducted her away from our pairing ceremony. But there was no changing facts. I did what I had had to do.

"He is paired with Black Wolf's daughter," a man whispered to his comrades.

This seemed to give them pause. The men had forgotten we Old Ones have much sharper hearing than they. But they were quickly reminded when they glanced up and saw the knowing looks on our faces.

"If Black Wolf let you pair with his daughter, you must be a man of some importance." This remark was directed toward me. "I am Spotted Buck, and this is my brother Swimming Otter. These are our friends,

Reindeer and Little Horse. You seem to be recovering from some nasty wounds. What happened? Did you have another bout in the Challenge Circle?"

Challenge Circle competitions usually ended when one of the opponents was dead or incapacitated, so I could understand why he asked.

"No," I answered. "I fell into the White River."

"I see." Spotted Buck nodded. "The White River is full of sharp rocks. You are extremely lucky to survive that mishap."

"Indeed," I concurred.

"Do you know Black Wolf?" Bror inquired.

"Only by reputation," Spotted Buck replied. "He is well-known. Black Wolf is said to be the tallest man of The People. Also, he is rumored to be the confidant and paramour of Willow Woman. Some People wonder if Willow Woman will persuade Black Wolf to leave his family and share the role of Head Elder with her."

"There was some other gossip about bears …," Little Horse piped up, "but maybe the less said about that, the better."

We did not respond to these statements.

"Um … so, Tris: as I recall, Black Wolf's daughter was very beautiful. Do you have any children yet?" Spotted Buck broke the awkward pause in conversation.

"Yes." I smiled involuntarily. "Morning Star is lovely. We have a fine boy named Fox. Morning Star is due to give birth to our second child in a moon or two."

The others smiled, too. Babies were always happy news.

I hoped to hear some clues about whether or not these men were Snow Leopard's associates, but our talk wandered to other subjects: hunting, family, and when winter might arrive. We chatted and chewed on our dried and smoked meats companionably, listening to the winds pull at the great hall as the tempest ran amok over the landscape.

We were tired, but the storm's rampage went on without letup. The torches had already gone out. We lay wearily on the floor of the main room, watching the shimmering red glow from the dying embers.

"A story would be nice," Swimming Otter said wistfully.

"Yes," agreed Spotted Buck. "Do any of you know stories?"

"Well," Bror began. "My father was a Keeper of Stories. I can recount a story or two if you would like."

"Oh, yes!" The men of The People readily accepted his offer, sounding somewhat surprised and very happy that their wish would be fulfilled.

Bror took a sip of water and then began to speak.

"Many generations ago lived a man who wanted to build his home in a tree…"

When that story was completed, the men begged for more. Bror grinned as he started again.

"Old Ones do not swim well. But there came a day when one of the men decided to test his aquatic skills in a very fast-moving river. Much to his woe, he found that the rapids quickly carried him off. The fish had to hurriedly move aside to get out of his way as he hurtled downstream. The man did not think he would be able to pull himself from the water until he was borne all the way down to the great sea beyond the forest, but then he came to an unexpected stop. The current had carried him into the path of a woolly mammoth. The mammoth was a cow who had recently lost her baby, so she was looking for something else to mother. She saw this waterlogged man and thought to herself that here was a being that needed her! She carried him on her trunk as a human mother would carry an infant and took him back to her herd. There she intended to blow warm air on him with her trunk until he was dry …"

"Come now!" Reindeer cried out with a laugh, "that is the most preposterous story I have ever heard!"

The others laughed, too.

"But it was most amusing!" Spotted Buck agreed as he chuckled appreciatively.

I had been almost asleep when Bror commenced his narrative, but now I was wide awake. Bror had taken certain liberties with my recent experiences, but I knew he was telling my tale. It took me some while to relax sufficiently to drift off to sleep. Images of woolly mammoths marched continuously through my thoughts. I believe that all the others were snoring soundly by the time my eyes finally closed.

Chapter Ten

The smell of burning wood permeated the air and smoke wafted all around me. Panicked animals of all kinds ran past as though I was not there. Particles of ash rained down from the sky. Fire was everywhere.

I awoke to see slanting rays of sunlight shining through the chimney holes in the roof. The stillness of the room made me think back on how different it had been when I was here last autumn, when this vast chamber was filled with throngs of noisy men. Now that the new day's sun-laden skies were rousing us from our night's rest, the only sounds were those of our yawns and low sleepy mumbles.

I sat up and rubbed my eyes, which still stung from the smoke they had been subjected to during the previous evening. I expected I might Dream of mammoths, but instead I had Dreamt of fire and a blackened world so desolate that nothing had been left alive. Considering that the aroma of yesterday's fire still hung heavily in the air, it was little wonder I should have such a Dream.

We ate a breakfast of dried and smoked meats and drank a little water as we sat around the empty fire pit. The light emitted through the chimney holes allowed us to see one another clearly, and it seemed to me that the men of The People were regarding us thoughtfully as they ate.

"What will you do today?" Swimming Otter questioned us.

"First we will forage for enough wood to replace what was burned last night, and then we will continue our journey homeward," Bror replied.

"It will require a long walk just to find the wood," Spotted Buck noted.

"That is true," Inlee nodded with a grin, "but if there is one good thing about the storm, it should have shaken any deadwood out of the trees to where it can be conveniently picked up from the ground."

"I think it almost shook the hall down around our heads," Spotted Buck agreed.

"And you? What will you do today?" Inlee asked the men.

The Dreamer III ~ The People of the Wolves

"We shall do the same as you," said Spotted Buck, "collect wood and go home. But maybe we will find some game while we are going in that direction."

* * *

Shortly thereafter we all filed out the door into the cold morning's air. The scant breezes were just enough to move the tattered hide that covered the structure's entryway. We walked as a group over to the nearest section of forested land. This was also the spot where we Old Ones had camped while we attended last year's Gathering. The men of The People had set up their shelters just outside the huge building that housed the Gathering, but we had not felt welcome to do the same, therefore we erected our huts on this little wooded knoll at the edge of the forest. Our small sapling and pine-bough constructions had held up fairly well despite the passage of time. The remaining pine boughs were dry and losing their browned needles, but the sapling frames were intact. All that was needed to set them to rights was a fresh layer of pine branches.

As we ambled about in the chilly air piling wood and kindling on our arms, I saw that Spotted Buck and the others were collecting theirs a short distance from us. The men looked over at us from time to time as they spoke in whispers to one another.

We soon had plenty of wood and tinder to replace everything that had been burned, and more besides. The men rejoined us for the trek back to the Gathering site.

"I – um – we wanted to tell you fellows that ..." Spotted Buck began, "well, you Old Ones were not what we expected. We have not met any of your people before. Of course, we saw Tris and Bror and a few additional Old Ones when Black Wolf brought them to the last Gathering, but we did not have any interaction with you. At that time, there was much speculation about the Old Ones. I am sorry to say some saw you as brutish louts. But now we know that it certainly is not true."

"Thank you for your kind assessment," Inlee responded quietly.

"Yes," Reindeer added, "we will tell others of our meeting with you. You have been very pleasant companions with whom to wait out a storm. Bror's stories were the most entertaining tales I have ever heard!"

When it came time to depart and go our separate ways, the men did us the honor of grasping our forearms in farewell. We did the same. I was thoroughly pleased to have made new friends. They said they would stop by our family compound when they were in the area, and they invited us to their homes as well. I had only a vague notion of where they resided, but in any case, it was good to know we were welcome.

* * *

The day continued to be sunny and as before, the wind was still at our backs. This made for pleasant hiking. I was excited to finally be on the last leg of our long excursion. If we pushed hard, we should reach our destination within four days. Unless we stopped to hunt for more meat, we would be completely out of food by the time we reached home. Therefore, hoping to move forward with as little delay as possible, we decided to carefully ration our stores.

I was elated at the thought of seeing Morning Star and Fox soon. I missed the rest of my family as well, but I missed my mate and son so badly it produced an ache deep within my chest.

But despite my happiness at our anticipated homecoming, something in the air was not quite right. I could not decide what was amiss, but I thought the others sensed it as well. I could see by the way they looked and listened with more attention than was usual that they, too, were searching for the source of some enigmatic threat.

The sun was setting when a sow bear and her two plump cubs burst out from the brush and ran past us in terror, the roly-poly little ones struggling to keep up with their mother. We had been somewhat alarmed at the sight of the big sow running at us, especially a big sow with cubs in tow. But it all happened so fast that the bears were gone just as quickly as they had appeared and we had scarcely time to react.

"That was odd," Sere commented.

"Indeed," Bror said, looking after the departed bears.

"It makes me ponder what is ahead to make them run so," I spoke up.

"Maybe we should make camp here for the night and let whatever lies up the trail move on before we, too, venture that way," Inlee suggested.

We all agreed that this was a prudent course of action. We made a fire and once again set up our lean-tos. After we ate our evening meal, we bedded down for a night's rest.

As before, I was given the spot at the center of the lean-to where I could be kept warm. The day had been cool and the night was colder still. From my vantage point within our shelter, if I craned my neck slightly, I could gaze up through the tree branches overhead to see the starry field of black. The moon was just a sliver and the firmament was free of clouds. I watched in wonder as shooting stars crossed the skies. There was a very old legend about a night such as this when a star fell to Earth and set the woodlands on fire. The mere thought of such an occurrence was unsettling.

* * *

The next day brought more cold clear weather. I was glad to have spent the night at the center of our lodgings. Even in that prime location, I could not say that I was exactly comfortable. I had again Dreamt of fire, but it was my painfully chilled feet that stirred me to wakefulness. We poked the coals from last night's fire to bring them back to life. The flames were fed just enough fuel to warm ourselves as we consumed our morning repast before embarking on our travels.

By midday we found that it was not a living thing that had frightened the bears; it was something much more ominous. First we came across multitudes of dead birds. Their feathers were seared. Then we saw bodies of animals: deer, rabbits, martins, a young bear, and more, all showing horrific burns. It seemed to me that they must have come in contact with fire and lived long enough to escape, but then succumbed to their injuries.

We had not gone too much farther when we reached the fringe of scorched terrain left in the fire's wake. A huge tree was near the edge of the devastated area, its blackened trunk appearing violently splintered and broken, with many of its branches and sections of its charred bark lying scattered about on the ground.

"Lightning has struck this tree!" Sere cried out.

"Yes," Inlee concurred, "and the wind blew most of the fire this way." He indicated the direction ahead of us. "It must have been a very strong fire to survive the rain."

Bror and I exchanged anxious glances. The fire would be headed directly toward my family compound, which was still two days' trek away from where we stood.

"We must get home; we must hurry," I urged the others.

My uncles and Sere instantly grasped my meaning.

My headache and other pains were forgotten as we trotted through the ravaged countryside. The ground was blanketed with soot, now kicked up by our footfalls, and we were soon covered with a fine, gray powder. There was no sign of life, no leaves to shade us from the sun. Even though we each sported summer tans under our coating of soot, our skin was yet unaccustomed to such extended exposure to full sunlight. I could tell I was acquiring a sunburn, but I did not care. I had no thought for anything other than the safety of my family and friends.

I rationalized that surely they would have sense enough to get out of the way of the oncoming fire. But where would they go? Would we be able to track them across a wasted habitat? Every time we came across the corpse of another dead animal, I forced down a growing sense of dread about the fate of my loved ones.

That night we made our camp at the edge of a small swampy pond. We did not wish to sleep on the blackened banks of the pond, so using our hands we brushed away the top layer of loose soil until we found clean earth, just a finger's depth underneath. We were almost unrecognizable, our faces and bodies thoroughly dirtied, except where we had tried to rid the irritating dust from our eyes or otherwise rubbed or scratched a spot clean. My companions and I then took the time to wash away the dark filth from our persons. We ate and fell into an exhausted sleep, our rest often racked by coughing from the dust we had inhaled during the day.

* * *

Morning dawned cold, damp, and gray. Although I was chilled to the bone as we started to jog toward home, I was glad when it began to rain. The steady drizzle would keep the soot anchored to the ground, making the air much cleaner for us to breathe. And our continuous exercise would soon warm us. The trail's coating of ash tended to adhere to our feet, and now that it was wet, it was slippery underfoot. Nonetheless, we moved onward without stopping.

I was amazed at my elderly uncles' endurance. We were not running quickly; we hardly moved faster than a very brisk walk. But my uncles easily kept pace with Sere, Bror, and me. Again, I found myself hoping that I would manage to age as well as they had.

The rain was just letting up when a flash of color caught my eye.

"Look, a bird!" I pointed at the first life we had seen in almost two days.

We all watched as the delicate creature alighted on a charred twig, which promptly gave way under its weight. The bird flew off. We grinned at one another. This was a good sign. We must be near the far perimeter of the fire.

As the day wore on, we saw more and more living birds and animals. Although the landscape had been significantly altered by the flames, I thought I could discern familiar features indicating we were nearing my family compound. I was beside myself with anxiety to reach home and discover how my loved ones had fared.

Late in the day we arrived at the ancient burial ground that covered a broad expanse of open meadow near the compound. I was grieved to see that it had burned. Each person interred here was marked with a pile of stones, one stone for every year of life he or she had lived. Now the formerly grassy area was completely barren except for the blackened rocks. I paused at my mother's gravesite in the semidarkness and put a hand on her cairn. The stones were cold, so the fire must have been out for some time. I felt a wave of grief overcome me as though the ugliness brought to my mother's resting place had done her an injury. I took a moment to compose myself while my comrades waited respectfully for me to stand and rejoin them.

There was barely enough light to see as we made our way through the heaps of rocks to what I hoped was the path entryway leading to the compound. However, even though dusk had set in and shadows were obscuring all around us, I could smell the fragrance of pine and thought I could hear the rustle of the wind rushing through trees. The enormous pine trees that flanked each side of the trail had survived the fire unscathed! This was almost beyond belief. Pine trees are full of resin and extremely flammable. I did not understand this incredible stroke of luck, but I was immensely relieved at the good news it foretold.

My family and the remaining Wolf-men were assembled around the outdoor hearth at the center of the compound. My eyes sought out Morning Star, who was busily tending food over the fire. Suddenly, all my weariness evaporated.

"Morning Star!" I called out as I ran the last few steps to her.

Morning Star gaped at me in astonishment and dropped the spit of meat she had been readying.

Then she was in my arms and my mouth was on hers. It seemed I could not kiss her enough.

"Oh, Morning Star, my sweet Morning Star! I am so glad to be home," I murmured into her ear and then resumed kissing her once more.

Morning Star was struck mute by the surprise of my sudden appearance. Tears streamed down her cheeks as she returned my kisses and held me tightly.

"Oh Tris, oh Tris," she finally spoke. "I have been so ... I ... I am so happy to see you!"

Bror was also joyously greeted by his mother and siblings. Even Ru was swept up in the moment, and before she realized what she had done, she hugged Bror and kissed his cheek. Sadly, it was just a momentary lapse. Ru then looked abashed and went back to her mealtime chores. But Bror was plainly thrilled at Ru's show of affection.

I soon noted that Little Fawn was hovering at our sides, toting Fox. Fox was jabbering with great animation, arms outstretched to me. I kept an arm around Morning Star's waist and tenderly took my baby from Little Fawn. I covered his face with kisses until he squirmed in rebellion. Fox caught my beard in his fingers and yanked the somewhat sooty whiskers.

"All right, little Fox, I can take a hint. I will stop kissing you," I told him.

While I held Fox, Morning Star had taken a few moments to assess my condition.

"Oh, Tris," she said again, "look at you! What happened?"

"Ask Bror. He tells the story much better than I do," I said, smiling at her.

Bror overheard us and laughed at my words.

It was a merry homecoming for most of us.

"Where is Black Wolf?" Little Fawn asked, taking this opportunity to break in on our conversation.

I noted poor Little Fawn's haggard and fearful expression.

"He has decided to stay with Karno, Mino, and Bewok until they are healed enough to make the journey back here," I replied.

"How long will that be?" she asked.

"I am sorry, Little Fawn, I do not know," I told her. "He said he would return before winter."

The Dreamer III ~ The People of the Wolves

The Wolf-men had gathered around us and they, too, were eager to hear reports of their leader and fallen friends.

"What news?" inquired one of the men. "Karno always strong, but we fear for Mino and Bewok. How did you leave them?"

"They were mending," I assured them. "Mino's leg is nearly well. I hope that Bewok continues to recover and that he will ..." I was at a loss at how to explain Bewok's perplexing condition. "... that he will soon be himself again."

The Wolf-men were not sure how to take my statement. They were pleased about Mino but somewhat confused about Bewok. I could hear them conferring amongst themselves, sometimes in their own language, sometimes in ours. *If Bewok was not himself, who was he?* I felt it was a good question. I wish I knew the answer.

Little Fawn was understandably unhappy that Black Wolf had not accompanied us home.

"But why did not Black Wolf come back with you? Could not someone else escort the Wolf-men here? He has been away for a long time," she said forlornly.

"He was the only other person there who knows the way," I replied.

Puh presented himself at my side. I released Morning Star long enough to give Puh a one-armed hug, careful not to crush Fox between us.

"Welcome back to your home," Puh said. "I am glad you are here but sorry to see you return to us looking so battered. Are you well?"

"I am fine," I informed Puh, "I fell in the White River and hit a few rocks on my way downstream. Luckily, I was not too hurt."

"*Not too hurt!*" Morning Star echoed. "Tris, you are a mess!"

"How is the new baby?" I asked Puh, speaking of his latest child.

"He is growing. Ria will no doubt bring him to see you when she is done feeding him." Puh said with a grin, "She is always feeding him. Little Mror had a precarious start to life, but he has been doted on and fussed over. He seems to be determined to thrive."

"That is wonderful, Puh." I patted Puh's shoulder as I spoke. "I have been worried."

"We were, too," Puh admitted. "We are thankful he seems strong."

As if on cue, Ria, holding her precious infant, emerged from the group of people surrounding us. Baby Mror was swaddled tightly in an assortment of fur blankets, and he appeared to be sleeping soundly. He was still just a mite of a thing, but Ria displayed him proudly. I thought I had never seen her so happy.

"Let me see my youngest son." Puh held out his hands for the baby.

Ria obligingly settled him into his father's arms. Puh's hands looked enormous as they cradled the small being. I was startled to see that the cracks in Puh's rough hands and his fingernails were stained black.

"Puh," I began, "what have you been doing?" I pointed to Puh's hands.

Puh hesitated before he replied.

"I will tell you about it later," he said.

Just then, Morning Star's younger brothers Hawk and Swift River darted by, chasing one another as they often did. They had raggedly lopped off their hair in our absence, in imitation of the Wolf-men. Morning Star saw my stunned countenance and laughed.

"Those boys even added water to ground charcoal and ocher to paint pretend tattoos on themselves," she explained. "Mama was so angry with them for using up almost all of her ocher. Now she will need to find something to trade for more when next she goes to the Village."

Before we all sat down to eat, my uncles and Sere were introduced all around. They seemed especially pleased to meet the rest of their sister's children.

I should have been more interested in my meal, but I was so affected by being back with my family and glad for their apparent safety that I wolfed down my food only mechanically, hardly aware of what I was putting in my mouth.

After our evening repast was completed, Gran came over and sat next to me. I had had the chance to greet her but briefly, what with everyone trying to talk to the new arrivals all at once. Now that things had quieted down, we were at last able to speak.

"I heard from your Puh that you found a river after all," Gran said.

"Yes," I nodded, "your Dream was accurate. But ... did you see any woolly mammoths in your Dream?"

"No." Gran shook her head. "Am I to assume they were there?"

"Indeed." I leaned closer to Gran and spoke in a low voice: "That is the only reason I am here today. A cow mammoth rescued me from the river. She was so gentle. She and a few other mammoths stayed by me until Bror caught up after my impromptu swim downstream. I will never look at mammoths in the same way again."

Great Gran smiled. I imagine that she was picturing the unlikely scene in her mind's eye.

"Neither will I," stated Gran as she affectionately squeezed my hand.

* * *

Morning Star and I said our goodnights not long after Bror related the tale of our adventures, including my mishap at the river. He embellished this story even more than he had before, much to everyone's delight. Almost everyone, that is. Puh and Great Gran appeared thoughtful and subdued, and Morning Star listened with growing horror evident on her face.

The Dreamer III – The People of the Wolves

We climbed the hill to our cozy abode and tucked a sleeping Fox into his bedding, snug and warm in his little nook off the main room of our home.

"Oh, Tris!" Morning Star said, whispering so she would not awaken Fox. "Was Bror's story true?"

"Partly," I acknowledged. "I did fall in the river."

"I can see that by the new gash on your brow and the cuts and bruises that cover the rest of you!" Morning Star was carefully examining my now naked body. "Your knees! Your elbows! Even your ankle bones are scraped! Oh, and you're sunburned, too!" She shook her head ruefully. "That gash is going to leave quite a mark on your brow!"

Morning Star was speaking of the newly acquired notch over my left eye. It was next to the scar I had received from Snow Leopard in the Challenge Circle. But I was aware only that her hands were on me as she examined my wounds. I brought her round to stand in front of me and embraced her.

"Never mind all that. I am healing," I said, kissing her face and her lips, one arm around her and one hand resting on her swollen belly where I could feel the faint movements of our baby. "You are well?"

"Of course I am." Morning Star started to remove her clothing.

I adjusted the fire one last time and then we both lay down in our bed. It seemed so long since we had last lain here together. I held her close and kissed her lips long and deeply. As I leaned Morning Star onto her back, she abruptly broke off our kiss.

"Tris, I cannot lie like this. The baby is too heavy. I cannot breathe," she stated a little breathlessly.

I shifted Morning Star back onto her side.

"Is that better?" I asked.

"Yes," she nodded.

"I want to make love to you, but I do not want to hurt you," I said, nuzzling her neck.

"I was thinking the same thing," Morning Star told me. "I mean, I do not want you to hurt, either." Morning Star then pushed me onto my back and straddled my hips. "I love you, my dear Tris," she said, stroking my hair away from my face.

"And I love you, my sweet."

* * *

The fire had burned down to embers when we succumbed to exhaustion and lay peacefully in each other's arms. I felt a contentedness that was beyond description. I could just see Fox through the dim light in his tiny bed chamber. Before long we would have a second baby in our little home. As I drifted off to sleep, it occurred to me that soon I would need to create another room to accommodate our growing family.

* * *

The next day, Morning Star, Fox, and I enjoyed some time to ourselves rather than go down the hill to join the others at the family compound. We ate a leisurely breakfast and then, after Fox was laid down for a nap, Morning Star began to dress my wounds. She wanted to ply them with poultices, but I became too distracted and we then found ourselves in bed once again. Later, as I enjoyed being snuggled up with my mate, Morning Star became serious.

"Where did you bring the injured men after the rhino hunt?" she questioned.

"We brought them to the Head Elder's summer house," I said. "That was the nearest place in which we could procure the services of a healer."

"And that is where Da is staying?" she went on.

"Yes."

"He stayed with the Head Elder at the Gathering too, did he not?"

"Yes."

"Why?" Morning Star seemed to sense that there was more to the story.

I searched for words that would not worry or wound her.

"Why do you not answer?" Morning Star persisted.

"It is difficult to speak of," I responded.

"Tris, I know you would protect my father the same way you would protect Fox and me. Is it a woman? Is that why you do not want to talk about it?"

"I would not cause you pain if I could help it," I said, stroking the lines of her face. "I also do not want to say anything that would damage your father in your eyes. He loves you very much."

"I know that, Tris. But Da's dalliances with other women are nothing new. Mama knows about them as well. But those were just brief flirtations. Da has never stayed away for so long. He is not leaving us?"

"No," I stated, "he has never spoken of giving up his family and home."

"But yet, he keeps house with her?"

"The woman in question is the Head Elder. At first she more or less demanded his attentions, but now they truly care for each other. She is a most unusual woman."

Morning Star seemed thoughtful.

"Is she beautiful?"

"No. At least not to me. But she is different."

"How so?"

I wished Morning Star was not so curious.

"She is ... *big*. She wears tattoos all over her skin. She keeps her hair in braids, coiled around her head like a hat. But she is also strikingly intelligent. She is a warm and generous person. She is pregnant with your half-sibling."

Morning Star gasped. Maybe I should have led up to that last announcement a little more gradually.

"So that is why Da stays with her!" Morning Star cried out, clearly upset. She paused as she composed herself. "When is the baby due?"

"Almost any time now, if she has not had it already. Do you think your mother suspects?"

"I think she is beginning to speculate on why Da is willing to be away for so long." Morning Star sighed. Then Fox started to awaken, hungry once again. "I must arise and feed little Fox," Morning Star said, kissing my cheek as she reached for her clothing. "Thank you for telling me, Tris. I know it is not easy to speak of such things, least of all when they regard family or a friend. In this case, for you, both."

* * *

It was midday before I wandered downhill to the main family compound, where I found Puh speaking with my uncles.

"Pleasant day to you, Tris," Puh said, greeting me with a smile.

I smiled in return and nodded my reply. The sun was evaporating the last of yesterday's rain puddles, and it felt good to soak up its warming rays. I was finally dressed appropriately for the weather. Now that the days and nights were distinctly cooler, I donned light leggings and a tunic over my loincloth. I was also glad that these articles hid most of my cuts and bruises. I hoped this meant I attracted fewer stares.

"Your father was just recounting their narrow escape from the wildfire," Inlee told me. "It was a stroke of genius to set the burying ground ablaze to burn up all the fire's fuel before it could reach their homes."

"It was the only course of action I could think of," Puh said, looking aggrieved. "I hated to desecrate the graves of our family in such a way, but I did not know what else to do. We could see the smoke in the distance, and we knew the prevailing winds would blow the fire right to us. Your cousins Dor and Lor and the Wolf-men helped me to make sure that just the grasses and weeds burned. We shoveled dirt on or stomped out any errant flames. It was frightening to watch the fire come closer and closer, driving all the wildlife before it, some unharmed, some not. Even though our burned-out area kept most of the fire at bay, we still had to be vigilant against flying sparks causing flare-ups amongst the big pine trees that border the burying grounds. I am thankful the rain came when it did. It snuffed out the last of the fire."

Dor had stopped to listen in on our conversation.

"Yes," he added, "and I am also thankful the fire that continued to burn to the east of us eventually came to a stop at the great bend in the river. Lor and I walked out that way this morning and found that the fire must have consumed all in its path, and once it reached the end of the promontory, it died there, since there were no combustibles left to keep it going."

Now Bror joined us.

"It has been a very dry summer," he said. "I am so happy that your family, friends, and homes were spared; but we saw a good many dead creatures on our way here. I fear that a significant number of prey animals have been lost."

"Yes, that is so," Puh agreed soberly. "If it were not for the efforts of our Wolf-men guests to contribute to our winter stores, I would be concerned. At first, I worried that they would kill every living beast in the vicinity, and now I am glad that they are such proficient hunters. It is better to harvest the meat, hides, and other useful parts than to have them needlessly consumed by fire. But I do worry what will happen when our supplies run low. We can only hope that the wildlife will return by then."

I then noticed that Bror had stepped away. Ru and my Aunt Vee were adding foraged wood to the fire pit, which was now just a bed of dying coals. Bror looked as though he wanted to approach Ru, but he was unsure how to do it without inviting a possible rebuff. My youngest sisters, Saree and Mi, intercepted Bror and pulled him down to sit with them and their dolls. Hork was now accompanied by another doll, this one made of sticks and dressed in scraps of deerskin.

Bror complied with their wishes, patiently listening to the little girls' piping chatter.

"Bror," Saree began, "when I am grown, I will be paired with a big strong man like you."

"Is that so? Will you name your first baby Hork?" Bror asked with a twinkle in his eyes.

"I guess so." Saree held up Hork and examined the thoroughly bedraggled doll. "Or maybe *Garkle.*"

"*Garkle?* That is quite a name," Bror responded.

"I just like that name," Saree told him.

"I see," said Bror.

"I can make lots of good names," Saree stated.

"You most certainly can," Bror agreed.

Mi climbed into Bror's lap and gazed up into his face adoringly.

"*Brah!*" she said to him. "Nice *Brah!*"

"Silly, it is *Bror!* Not *Brah!*" Saree said, correcting Mi.

Sere was also watching this exchange.

"Such lovely children," he said wistfully. "Before my mate Asha passed, she and I had three boys, and they are men now. I would have enjoyed having a daughter or two."

Sere then left us, and he too took a seat on the matting by the fire pit to become better acquainted with Saree and Mi. They took to him as easily, as they did Bror.

At that moment, I felt a heavy weight on my foot, upon which our family's old dog Rooph had placed one of his paws. He was panting and looking up at me bleary-eyed. I knelt and put an arm around his substantial furry body as I patted him.

"Rooph, old boy," I crooned to him, "good dog. How I have missed you." I kissed the top of his noble head, feeling sadness at the state of my aged childhood playmate and loyal friend. If my dog Raena had been here, she would have jealously wormed her way in, hoping to receive her share of attention. But for now Rooph had me to himself and leaned against me as I stroked him, and he burrowed his sizable muzzle between my arm and my body. Rooph sagged more and more until he was on the ground, and then he rolled onto his back so I could rub his stomach. Ru left the fire and stooped to pet Rooph, too. As the oldest daughter, Ru was often left at home to tend her younger siblings, prepare food, work hides, sew clothing, and attend to other innumerable chores. Therefore, especially now that the dog was too lame to travel far, she and Rooph were constant companions and she loved him dearly.

"That is a very old dog," Inlee observed to Puh.

"Yes," Puh concurred. "I brought him home when Tris was about six winters old. He has been with us many years now."

Rooph soon sat up and I gazed into his face, now almost completely white. He took advantage of my closeness and began to lick my cheeks and nose with his wet tongue. I laughed silently, as we Old Ones do, and hugged him tighter.

The Wolf-men were avid dog lovers, and they too laughed at the sight.

"That a good old dog," one of the men said. "Handsome dog."

Some of the men patted Rooph briefly. But Rooph just panted and stared at me, nudging me with his nose if he felt my attention was waning.

"You were always Rooph's favorite," Ru told me. "He has stayed around the compound with me since he could no longer follow you everywhere, but I could tell that his heart was not in it. Rooph wanted to be off on an adventure with his boy, even if his boy has now grown to be a man."

Rooph began to droop once more until he was again lying on the ground. I cradled his head in my lap as snores emitted from his large snout. His eyes moved behind his eyelids and his feet paddled the air.

"Dream, my old friend," I said to him, "dream of the days when the world was ours and you and I ran through the forest, unfettered by any cares or woes."

Chapter Eleven

My daughter was born shortly before Black Wolf, Karno, Mino, and Bewok returned. I did not expect them until later in the fall, but as it turned out, they marched triumphantly into the family compound less than a moon after my homecoming. My uncles and Sere had already left within a few days of our arrival. When Black Wolf and the others appeared, the rest of us were congregated at the center of the compound, where we were occupied with our various chores.

The Wolf-men greeted their leader and friends joyously, speaking to one another rapidly in their own tongue. Karno soon broke away from his comrades and strode over to Ru, the woolly rhino's giant forehorn in his grasp. Ru beamed at Karno. Obviously she had lost none of the fervor she felt for him. Karno took one hand from the horn and placed it at Ru's waist, pulling her to him.

"I am so thrilled to see you again," Ru told Karno as she put her arms around his neck.

Karno grinned at her words and then lowered his forehead until it was resting against hers. After a moment, Ru stretched up to kiss him, but Karno dodged the buss and instead thrust the rhino horn at her.

"Here! Karno bring gift!"

The horn was so large that Ru needed both hands to clasp it. She looked at him, perplexed. She tried to work up a grateful smile.

"Many thanks, Karno …"

But Karno was already walking away. My cousin Dor was at my side, and he looked nearly as confounded as Ru.

"Is it me," Dor began, "or does the presentation of a huge horn to a nubile woman imply some sort of questionable underlying message?"

"It is not you," Black Wolf said, "and I am not sure I would call it an *underlying message*. It seems rather blatant to me. However, I do not know if Karno has the subtlety to understand the potential nuances of such an offering."

Black Wolf was elated to be back. His children swarmed round him, excitedly asking questions about his journey. But he did not receive a kindly welcome from Little Fawn. She stood back and folded her long arms across her chest.

"So you finally found your way home," she said to Black Wolf. Then she promptly spun on her heel and disappeared inside their house.

"Ack!" Black Wolf lamented, looking after Little Fawn. "She does not seem glad to see me. Maybe I should have stayed away."

"No, Black Wolf," I assured him, "your family has missed you. And, you have a new granddaughter to meet."

"Morning Star had the baby?" Black Wolf exclaimed. "I must go to her!"

Black Wolf immediately set off down the short trail to the little home I shared with Morning Star. I quickly followed him, eager to show off my cherished infant. When she had been born, I was pleased to see that she was raven-haired. I hoped she would also grow up to have Morning Star's lovely dark eyes and bright smile. We named the baby Pony. At one time Morning Star and I had considered calling her Awna, for my mother, but then I realized that it would have been hard for Puh to hear the name spoken; it would only bring poignant memories of the mate he had loved and lost. So Morning Star and I opted for another name that we hoped would embody her beauty and spirit.

As with all things, Morning Star handled the baby's birth with a minimum of fuss and complaint. She was reluctant to have me present during the process, and even Gran suggested that I might wish to be elsewhere; but, especially after having seen my half-brother Mror's entrance into the world, I very much wanted to see my own child's delivery. Ria also had had her baby without much ado, but her baby was born was a full two moons early. So I was somewhat surprised in witnessing the birth of my daughter, for, though she may have come just a little before her time, she was a good-sized infant, and it required a great deal of work to push her out. It grieved me terribly to see my beloved mate suffer so. I was unprepared for the grueling nature of the business, and if I had not truly appreciated Morning Star's fortitude and endurance, I surely did now.

When Black Wolf and I came through the doorway, Morning Star stood to embrace her father and then offered him something to eat and drink.

"Never mind that! I am just so happy to see you!" Black Wolf said to Morning Star, hugging her warmly. "You look so well!"

"I am happy to see you, too, Da," Morning Star told him; "sit down and I will let you hold our new baby. Her name is Pony. She was born eight days ago. She still sleeps most of the day, but she is so sweet. Fox just loves his new sister."

Black Wolf took a seat on the matting. Fox was crawling easily now, sometimes pulling himself up on anything he could reach and "walking" from one hand hold to the next. At this time, he pulled himself up on his grandfather's arm and stood, wobbling slightly and drooling copiously. Morning Star placed Pony in Black Wolf's giant hands.

"So tiny!" Black Wolf marveled. "So tiny!" he said again. "And so pretty! She reminds me of you when you were a baby," Black Wolf said to Morning Star.

Fox gurgled and made random noises at his grandfather. At least the noises seemed random to me.

"What do you think, Fox?" Black Wolf held the baby so Fox could see her. "Do you like your little sister?"

"Gah!" Fox replied.

"*Gah?*" Black Wolf repeated. "He has been listening to those Wolf-men too much!"

"I think that is just his word for yes," I said with a grin.

"Hmmm!" Black Wolf sounded skeptical. "The Wolf-men are good fellows, but I was aghast to see what my own sons have done to themselves in their efforts to look more like them."

"Oh, Da!" Morning Star giggled. "Swift River and Hawk are just children. They only play at being Wolf-men. The paint will wash off and their hair will grow back."

"I hope so," he responded, "Those two imps should have half the sense you have."

"You have a new suit of clothing, Da," Morning Star observed, her voice more serious.

"Oh, yes." Black Wolf and the Wolf-men had come back to us wearing well-made clothes, all obviously freshly constructed. "It was courtesy of my host. Most generous."

"Hmmm," Morning Star uttered. She could be much like her father at times.

* * *

A little while later I accompanied Black Wolf as he walked back down the hill.

"You may congratulate me on a birth, as well," Black Wolf said quietly.

"Congratulations, Black Wolf."

"Willow had a fine big boy. She is pleased beyond measure. And, honestly, so am I. I stayed a little while after the baby came, and then, since Mino was well and Bewok suddenly made a startling recovery, we decided to leave for home." Black Wolf paused. "But what sights we saw! The last few days of our trek were through burned forest. We did not know what we would find when we arrived here. I was so relieved to see that all is well. Well, except maybe Little Fawn. She was as sour as a green apple. Does she know?"

"I have no notion." I shrugged. I had taken pains to never be alone with Little Fawn so she would not have the opportunity to ask questions about Black Wolf's guest accommodations while he was away.

"She is not happy. I am not happy. Do you know she has not let me touch her in almost a year?" I was surprised at this revelation. Black Wolf continued, "There was a point in our lives when we were able to get through the hard times and we found periods of happiness, but now I do not even know if she still loves me. I can only hope that will change and we will one day have good times again, and forget all that has passed between us. I have been thinking about this a lot. We have the children to think of. I do not know what to do, but I do know that I must stand by my family, and I must make sure that my offspring – all of them – are well provided for. Ack. I am torn between two families."

I nodded with sympathy.

"What did you name the baby?" I suddenly thought to ask.

"Black Oak. Willow wanted to name him Standing Oak for her father, but then, after an epiphany, she decided on Black Oak, after his father and grandfather." Black Wolf smiled, showing a set of strong teeth. "I am so pleased with this child. We call him Oak, for short. He is an exceedingly robust infant. He will be a force in the world, much like his mother." Black Wolf paused to sigh wistfully. "I have to keep reminding myself that she is not mine. That she does not require ..." Black Wolf's words trailed off. "She is a remarkable woman." He finished simply, but his expression was that of a man in torment.

* * *

When we returned to the compound, we found that Karno, Bewok, and Mino were sitting near the fire pit, where Ru was serving food and drink to them. Morning Star's younger brothers also joined the assemblage, taking care to sit with exactly the same posture as the Wolf-men and hanging on their every word.

"Ho, Tris!" Karno hailed me with a wave of his arm. "Karno guess you not think to see him so soon! Look at Bewok! Strong again! One day he awake ... truly awake. Lion bite much better! And Mino, too; leg heal like new!"

I noticed that Karno had gone back to speaking in chopped sentences.

"I am very glad," I said. I was somewhat confused about Bewok's unexpected *awakening*, but there was no doubt that whatever had ailed Bewok, he was past it now.

"My men take good care of Ru when we gone," Karno went on. "Karno tell them, you do what Ru say! You bring meat! You bring wood! You watch children! You work hides! You do anything Ru say!"

"Yes, we are most grateful for all their hard work," I agreed.

It was true. The Wolf-men had done everything they could to see to the welfare of our families. I thought back on when we had first made their acquaintance and how strange they had seemed. While they were still different from us in appearance and in some of their habits, they were pleasant men and most conscientious in their work.

Karno left his men and took me aside.

"I think we leave soon," Karno announced. "Karno speak with your Puh, speak with Ru. Bring Ru to Karno home."

"You have not spoken with Ru yet?" I was surprised to hear this.

"No," Karno said shaking his head. "Man must bring woman great gift to show his feeling for her before he talk. Most important! Most important Great Man's daughter be approach in correct way!"

"*Great Man's daughter*?" I repeated incredulously. "Do you mean Ru?"

"Of course Karno mean Ru!" Karno said indignantly.

"It is just that ... Ru is not a Great Man's daughter."

"Tor not Great Man?" Karno asked, obviously taken aback.

"No. We have no Elder ... no Great Man. Why did you think my father is our Great Man?" I queried.

Karno seemed to ponder this carefully.

"Karno not understand. No Great Man? Karno thought you and he have much in common; Tris and Karno about same age, and we both Great Man son. Karno have special liking for you, Tris, because of that." Karno looked up at me sheepishly. "Karno still have special liking for you. And still want Ru. Even if

Tor is not Great Man. Karno think Tor Great Man because everyone go to him for answer. He quiet man, but wise. Very like Great Man."

"When will you talk to Puh?" I questioned, changing the subject.

"Soon," Karno shrugged. "Karno wait for right time. Want talk to Tor alone."

I could understand why he would want to speak with Puh at a time when they could converse confidentially. This was not the sort of thing most suitors would want to discuss in public.

"You are funny people," Karno noted, as he often had in the past. "Karno meet other Star People, now Karno think on it they not have Great Man, too."

"*Star People*? Who are the Star People?" I asked. Karno had never mentioned this clan before.

"That what we call you," Karno informed me.

"But we are Old Ones," I said. "Where does the name *Star People* come from?"

"Karno know you are Old One, but that name sound so ... *old*. Karno not want to bring mate home and say *this my woman, she is Old One*. So Karno look at all dot on your skin; many dot like star in sky. So call you Star People. Also, not all Old One like you. Some Karno meet have no dots. No fire hair. Those Old One can be Old One."

I had never heard of members of my people who did not have our light freckled skin and red hair.

"Are you sure they were Old Ones?"

"Oh, yes. They have darker hair and skin, and hair no go in circle," Karno motioned with his finger to draw a spiral in the air. It took me a moment to realize that he was referring to our curls. "Beside that, they look like you."

I had to concede *Star People* did sound more impressive than *Old Ones*. Yet the awe-inspiring night sky seemed almost too grand to be in any way associated with mere humans.

Just then, Bewok approached.

"Karno," Bewok said, "I would like to say something to you."

Bewok nodded to acknowledge me. "Pleasant day to you, Tris."

"Pleasant day to you," I returned. "It is good to see you looking so well."

Bewok only reply was to grin broadly and then he and Karno moved a short distance away.

I decided to seek out Bror and convey the information that Karno had just relayed to me. If Bror was to have any chance with Ru at all, he must do something soon. Since our arrival at the family compound Bror had made no progress with her. Bror did not attempt to ingratiate himself with Ru; he only maintained his placid and kind demeanor. I believe that Bror chose to display his good qualities by his actions, and not by flattery or overt romancing.

I searched for Bror by following the sounds of an axe striking a tree trunk. Bror and his brothers were in the process of producing firewood. The Wolf-men had hewn trees while we were away, but they had yet to chop and split them into manageable sections that could be burned in our fire pits and fireplaces.

There was no time for formalities.

"Bror," I started urgently. "Karno intends to ask Puh for Ru in the very near future. And after that, he will speak to Ru."

"He has not asked for her yet?" Bror said, appearing both startled and saddened at the revelation.

"No. Apparently, in his culture, a man does not ask until bestowing his future mate with an extraordinary present to show his great esteem," I answered.

"I did not think the horn exactly delivered that message," Dor said with a smirk.

"I do not think my sister sees the horn in the same light as do you," I countered.

"I am sure she does not," Bror agreed, "although she did seem befuddled by the gift." Bror paused. "Many thanks for bringing me this news, but I do not know what I can do to gain Ru's affections. She seems to care only for Karno."

"Maybe you will think of something," I said hopefully. "You have much to offer, too."

"Anything I can give her will seem paltry in comparison to that horn." Bror hung his head dejectedly. "But I will think on it. Perhaps I can devise a way to make Ru want me."

"Yes, do think on it," I encouraged him.

"We will help you, big brother," Lor and Dor chimed in. "We will think on it, too."

A thought abruptly came to my mind.

"What if …" I began … "What if Puh were to go hunting? If Puh went away for a while, Karno could not ask him for Ru until Puh comes back."

"That is true," Bror said, seeming somewhat heartened. "I am not sure the delay would be much help, but at least it would give us a little more time to put off what may be the inevitable."

"Your Puh would have to go away without revealing his intentions. If Karno knew Tor planned to go hunting, he would surely want to go with him," Dor pointed out.

"We could keep Karno busy while Tor and whoever goes with him make their departure," Lor suggested.

This plot was a bit more involved that my original scheme to arrange for Puh to simply go hunting, but I had to acknowledge that their ideas made sense.

* * *

"Puh, are you expecting to go hunting any time soon?" I asked him later that afternoon. It had been a little tricky to find him at a time when he was not surrounded by my littlest siblings, who surely would broadcast the topic of our discussion to all within hearing.

Puh looked somewhat surprised at my question.

"I have been thinking on it," Puh replied. "Maybe in a few days or so. Why? Are you hoping to go out soon, too?"

"I wish to know because Karno has told me that he wants to ask you for Ru soon. I ... I thought that if you were not here, he could not ask," I admitted.

Puh's expression turned grim.

"I see." Puh appeared deep in thought. "I do not like to do anything that would interfere in Ru's personal life. If she truly loves Karno, as much as I would hate to see her go away with him, I cannot stop her."

"Do you believe that she truly loves Karno?" I questioned.

"I believe she is thoroughly enamored with him. And he is equally besotted with her."

"And Bror? Will you give him a chance – give him those few days – to change Ru's mind before it is too late?"

Puh appeared to be caught on the horns of a dilemma.

"I will speak to Ria and Black Wolf about leaving first thing tomorrow morning. I am sure they will want to come," Puh finally said.

"Ria, too?" I was surprised at this.

"Oh yes, she would not miss a hunt. She has said that she will carry the baby, snuggly against her chest in a sling under her clothing. She has promised not to run with him, just walk, so he will not be jostled. Her skill with bow and arrow will not be impaired, and she will keep him fed and warm. And Black Wolf, he is most eager to get away."

I nodded. After Black Wolf's recent confession regarding the rift between himself and little Fawn, and today's news from Morning Star's that her mother was still not speaking to Black Wolf, I could well imagine that he would be willing to accompany Puh and Ria on an excursion. The small hunting party was probably a good idea, too. The smaller the group, the fewer people to know about it until after they were gone.

"Many thanks, Puh. I will tell Bror to be ready to spill his heart to Ru, or whatever it is he intends to do. He will not have much time to make an impression."

* * *

That night the Wolf-men played their music for the first time in many moons. Now that they were all together again they were in fine form, and we all enjoyed their delightful performance. I noted that Puh and Ria slipped away early in the evening. Black Wolf also made a premature departure, begging weariness after his long trek homeward.

Ru sat next to Karno, as she always did, nestling up to him in between songs. At times, their faces were quite close together. But though those occasions might have been the perfect moment to indulge in a kiss, Karno managed to avoid actually pressing lips together.

"Why does he not kiss her?" Morning Star said, noticing this lapse as well. It was so obvious to all present that it was not even necessary to point out which people she meant.

"The Wolf-men do not kiss. They think it is unclean," I whispered into Morning Star's ear. She looked at me disbelievingly.

"*Unclean*? Compared to what? I have seen that they have no qualms against being elbow-deep in offal."

I shrugged. This was undoubtedly true. Morning Star shook her head as she stared at Ru pityingly.

* * *

I was a little groggy the next morning when Karno came up the hill to see me. Morning Star and I had not slept much the previous night. Our new daughter was restless, and she made sure that everyone in the household knew about it. Pony now required frequent feedings and endless walking sessions. I could not help with the feedings, but I could take a turn at pacing with her back and forth across the floor.

Karno grinned widely when he met me at the doorway to my home, oblivious to my bleary-eyed and muddled condition.

"Ho, Tris!" Karno greeted me cheerfully. "I not find Tor. I need talk to him."

"Pleasant day to you, Karno," I mumbled, consciously striving to think coherently. "You wish to speak with Puh about Ru?"

"Um ... no. Karno speak with Tor about Bewok."

"*Bewok?*" Did my ears deceive me? "I do not understand. Bewok is well, is he not?"

"Oh, yes. Bewok not sick. Bewok say to Karno he want no want to go home. Bewok want stay here," Karno stated, now becoming forlorn. "This make Karno very sad. Bewok very old friend. Karno no want leave Bewok here. But Bewok want stay and Karno must ask Tor if friend live here. Stay here always."

"Why does Bewok wish to remain here after you leave?" I was trying to wrap my thoughts around this mysterious concept.

"Three reason." Karno held up two fingers. "Bewok not sure he make long trip. And, Bewok feel Karno take Ru away, he stay here and do Ru's work. You not miss Ru so much. Work get done." Droplets of moisture appeared in the corners of Karno's eyes. "This make Karno very sad," he said again.

I looked over at Morning Star, who had just finished nursing Pony. The baby was nearly dozing, and I thought if perchance we left them, both Morning Star and Pony might get some much-needed rest.

"Let us talk outside," I suggested. "Come Fox, come with your Puh-Puh." I lifted Fox from the spot where he was quietly amusing himself on the floor mat, and I caught Morning Star's eyes. I gave her a wan grin. Morning Star gratefully received my unspoken message. As I ushered Karno out the door, I saw her lie down with the baby on our bed. I hoped she would get a good, long sleep.

"I have not seen Puh today," I said, feigning ignorance. "Did you ask Ru if she knows where he is? Puh usually tells Ru if he is going somewhere."

"No," Karno responded. "Ru busy. Ru say dog sick. She worry."

"Which dog is sick?" I asked with alarm, afraid I already knew the answer.

"Old dog. Too bad. He very good dog. Dog special to my people. Honored as much as a man. Like wolf, dog value family and friend. Dog loyal."

I picked up the pace of my step, holding onto Fox tightly to be sure he wasn't bounced out of my arms as I jogged downhill. Fox laughed merrily at his bumpy ride. My younger sisters Twie, Saree, and Mi were playing outside my ancestral home, so I set Fox down with them.

"Will you girls watch over Fox for me? Just for a little while?" I asked them.

The children were overjoyed to take on the task.

"Oh, yes, Tris! We love to play with Fox!" Twie replied, holding out her hands for him.

"Many thanks," I said to them as I left Fox in Twie's waiting arms. Then I quickly entered the domicile.

Ru was kneeling on the floor with Rooph, who was lying still and strangely quiet.

"Is he still ... still alive?" I queried, dreading her response.

Ru petted Rooph's magnificent old head, struggling to speak.

"Yes," she said, "he just collapsed moments ago. I sent the children outside to play."

"That was good thinking," I told Ru. "They do not seem aware of what has happened to Rooph. They are busy amusing Fox."

"They know that Rooph has fallen several times lately, so they are not yet concerned," Ru told me. "But I fear that this time he will not get up."

Karno had accompanied me indoors, but he abruptly left us without saying a word.

"Oh, Tris," Ru sobbed soundlessly. "I cannot bear to lose Rooph."

"I know," I told her gently. "I do not want to lose him, either."

I knelt on the other side of Rooph, running my hands through his fur and talking to him softly. I was annoyed at Karno for deserting Ru in her anguish, but I put those feelings aside and concentrated on Rooph.

"Good boy, Rooph," I said to him. "You have always been a good boy." Tears rolled down my cheeks and dripped off the end of my nose as I spoke. Ru was too broken up to talk. I kept telling Rooph that he was a good dog until he heaved a great sigh as the life took flight from his body.

Bror and Lor happened by at that moment. They must have assessed the situation immediately. Bror promptly got down on his knees behind Ru and placed his arms around her. She turned and leaned into him, weeping brokenheartedly. Bror caressed Ru's hair and kissed her face repeatedly.

"Oh, Ru," Bror murmured to her. "Oh, Ru, I am so sorry about Rooph!"

Ru held onto Bror tightly, desperately soaking up the comfort he provided. However, unlike Karno, when her lips were near, Bror had no compunction against putting his mouth on hers. He kissed Ru until she was breathless.

I happened to glance over at Lor as he too watched his older brother and Ru. His mouth was agape and his eyebrows had risen way up high on his forehead. Then realized that I was likely wearing a similar expression. It was not until Ru had regained her composure that Bror released her, but she still clung to him, her head lying on his shoulder. Bror continued to touch her soothingly, stroking her hair and her back.

At last, Ru wiped her eyes and she put her hands on either side of Bror's face as she gazed up at him. Ru did not speak, but after a brief pause, she kissed him tenderly on the lips and then rose to her feet. Ru soon returned with an armload of assorted fur pelts.

I was still kneeling at Rooph's side, absently fondling his ears, as I often did when he was living. My countenance was tear-streaked, and Ru's weeping renewed as she began to place the furs around Rooph.

"He must be buried properly," Ru said, sniffling.

Bror put an arm around Ru's shoulders, using one hand to help Ru adjust the pelts.

"Yes," Bror agreed. "I will dig the hole wherever you would like. Just tell me where."

Karno then reappeared with Mino, carrying a litter between them.

"Karno and Mino take dog," Karno said. "We put dog in ground. Dog get big ceremony."

"Not yet, Karno," Ru said, speaking gently but firmly.

I searched Ru's face for some sign that the recent events with Bror had changed things for her. But I saw nothing to make me think that she thought any less of Karno or any more of Bror.

* * *

Rooph was interred in the family burial grounds near Muh, my brother Dak, and my two infant siblings who had not survived their first winter. Rooph was granted a pile of thirteen stones to mark his years. Bror and I excavated his grave. It was a two-step process, since we had to stop digging once we hit the layer of permafrost. Then it was necessary to build a large fire and wait for the earth to thaw before we could complete the task. It was a dirty operation, given that the burial grounds had recently been burned to thwart the progress of the wildfire. Bror and I were blackened with soot by the time the job was complete. We washed before presenting ourselves to carry Rooph to his final resting place.

Ru seemed drained, but she was sedate when we arrived. Karno's litter, now covered with fur blankets, still lay on the floor by Rooph, awaiting his body. When we stooped to lift Rooph onto the litter, Ru held up her hand to stop us, and she bent to kiss Rooph's cheek. She touched his fur lovingly, a few tears dropping from her eyes. Then she nodded to us, unable to speak. I, too, choked on words unuttered. Bror and I placed Rooph on the litter, and Ru tucked the pelts around him.

We emerged from the house, Bror and I carrying Rooph between us. Our family and friends gathered around us, ready to proceed to the burial grounds. Karno seemed concerned about Ru. She thanked Karno for providing the litter, but she did not otherwise speak to him.

When it was over, Morning Star and I brought our children back home.

"Oh, Tris," Morning Star said. "I am so sorry that you have lost Rooph. I loved him, too. I know how much he meant to your family."

"Many thanks, my sweet," I replied. "He was a wonderful dog. Poor Ru is grief-stricken. Puh, too, will be unhappy at the news when he returns home."

"Ru seems different," Morning Star noted.

"She does?" I questioned. "How so?"

"I do not know," Morning Star said. "I cannot exactly say what it is. Perhaps it is that I perceive a new serenity within her. Or perhaps she is simply exhausted by grief."

 **Chapter Twelve**

It is a cold night. A wolf laments at the moonlit sky. There are no answering cries. The wolf howls and howls. It is a lonely and desolate sound.

It may have been my sadness at the loss of Rooph that made me experience such a bleak Dream. We grieved for him as we would a family member. Puh, Ria, and Black Wolf returned in two days, bearing a young red deer doe. The fire had driven most game animals so far away that the hunting party had had to travel for more than a day before they found that fine specimen of a deer. Fortunately the cool temperatures had kept the meat fresh during the journey home.

I did not like to interrupt the joyous homecoming with bad news, so I held off telling Puh about Rooph. Yet when we all sat down for our evening meal and

Rooph did not present himself for his share of the food, Puh arose from his seat and went to seek out our faithful dog.

I followed Puh into the main house. I knew he would look for Rooph at his usual spot by the hearth. Puh stopped just inside the entryway and stared at the empty place where Rooph should have been.

"Puh," I began. "I did not want to tell you and spoil your return from a successful hunting trip, but Rooph passed while you were away."

Puh's breath left him in a slow gasp.

"I am sorry, Puh," I went on. "We buried him by Muh, Dak, and the babies."

"Did he go quietly?" Puh asked after a pause.

"Yes," I answered. "It was a very peaceful death. Poor Ru was devastated."

Puh simply nodded. Tears coursed down his lean, scarred face. He wiped them away. Puh cleared his throat, reaching for the water bag so he could pour some of the liquid into a gourd cup. Puh quickly drank the liquid down.

"Is there anything else I should know about?" Puh asked.

"I do not know."

"*You do not know?*" Puh echoed. "What do you mean?"

"I mean, something happened between Ru and Bror. Bror kissed her and she let him. But I do not know if … if … if Ru feels any differently about either Bror or Karno."

Puh studied my face for a long moment, as though he might somehow discern additional information from reading my expression. He must have decided that there was nothing more to be found there. He merely refilled the cup and once more swallowed its contents in one gulp.

"Well," Puh started, "if anything has changed, I am sure we will soon find out."

We then rejoined the others and sat down to a somewhat subdued repast. Morning Star and I were both still very tired from our nighttime activities with baby Pony, so we excused ourselves early and went home to bed. Fox had never demanded of us the sort of attention Pony now required. While I did not begrudge our little one the attention, I did worry that perhaps she was unwell. Sometimes infants did not live long. I did not know how I could stand another loss so soon after Rooph.

* * *

I awakened in the middle of the night to the sounds of a wolf howling. At first I thought the mournful cries were part of another Dream, but then I realized these were real. I roused myself from the comfort of our warm bed and went outdoors, accompanied by Raena. We went to the border of the family compound, where we typically deposited our urine. I looked up into the starlit night sky. A falling star streaked through the heavens. I thought about Karno's name for us. *Star People*. I wondered if The People from the East who did not like Old Ones would think better of us if we were instead called Star People. So far as I knew, the original moniker was arrived at because we Old Ones had been on these lands since before anyone could remember. I had been too busy and too tired before now to consider Karno's explanation about not wishing to return to his home and introduce his new mate as an Old One. He did not think the name was good enough. But I did not think *old* had a negative connotation. To be old was to be learned and venerated. Surely that was a good thing.

Another howl rent the air. The sound sent shivers up and down my spine. Raena was alert, sniffing and looking about. There was little to see in our darkened surroundings, yet she gave the impression of being able to sense exactly what was out there beyond my ken.

"Let us go in now, girl," I said to her.

Raena's tail wagged in response, and she followed me indoors.

Soon I was sound asleep once again. And for at least this one night, Morning Star and I were granted a peaceful night's repose.

* * *

I arose the next morning feeling much refreshed. After we broke our fast, I again took Fox down the hill so that Morning Star would have to tend to one only child at a time. The family compound seemed almost abandoned. Puh and Ria were busily slicing deer meat into strips for the smoking racks, and the younger children of my family were entertaining themselves nearby. No one else was to be seen.

My little sisters requested that Fox be set down in their midst so that they could play with him, so I placed Fox down on the matting as he squealed with delight.

"Where is everyone?" I asked Puh and Ria.

"Ru, your cousins, and Vee have gone out to pick apples. Gran, Ty, and Black Wolf's offspring are foraging for root vegetables. I have not yet seen Black Wolf and Little Fawn, nor any of the Wolf-men," Puh replied.

"It is strange to find things so quiet," I said.

"Yes. It is almost as it used to be, when it was just our little family," Puh said with a smile, but I thought I saw a tinge of regret in that smile.

"It was very odd that Wolf-men were not here this morning. I wonder if they went hunting," Ria pondered aloud.

"That is possible," Puh granted. He then looked a little more closely at me. "You seem a bit more perky today. Did the baby let you sleep last night?"

"At least for most of the night, and we are grateful for that," I said happily. "Morning Star and I have been concerned for Pony. I hope she is past whatever was ailing her."

"Gran has told me not to eat onions," Ria told me. "The onions get into the mother's milk and upset the baby's stomach. Does Morning Star eat onions?"

I was startled to hear that the mother's dietary habits could affect the infant, but then I realized that very often our game could take on the flavor of the foods they had been eating. For example, deer fed on acorns often tasted like those bitter nuts. So it was quite possible that Morning Star's food was also tainting her milk.

"Sometimes she does," I answered. "Many thanks, Ria. I will tell her about the onions."

"Watch Fox walk!" Twie called out to us. She and Saree had Fox by the hands, and they were helping him to take steps across the clearing. Fox was now eleven moons old, and he could walk easily when assisted. Mi trotted along after them, giggling softly. Mi was at an age when she could begin to control the sounds of her laughter and weeping. In a few more years she would express both her happiness and her sadness in silence, like all Old Ones.

Raena, ever the devoted mother dog, stayed home with Morning Star and Pony; but the many dogs of my cousins and Black Wolf were present. Some napped, some followed the children as they ranged all over the clearing. It was not long, however, before the dogs started to bark. Fox did not like the ruckus and began to cry. His little aunts attempted to console him, but I swiftly retrieved my son and brought the girls to stand closer to Puh, Ria, and me.

The Wolf-men entered the compound, dressed in full regalia, including their wolfskin cloaks. Black Wolf and Little Fawn also presented themselves as they exited their home, eager to see what had set the dogs off.

"Ho," Karno said to us. "We have been in meeting. Karno come to talk."

Karno seemed stiff and formal. I wondered if he had decided to ask Puh for a private conference and wished to appear before him as a proper Great Man's son should. I had never known a Great Man's son, so I was not sure of the correct protocol.

"Tris," Karno continued. "Karno want speak to you."

I was startled at this request.

"Of course," I said, nodding. "Do you wish to talk here or elsewhere?"

"Karno not know *elsewhere*, but here no good." One of Karno's men whispered in his ear. "Oh! *Elsewhere!* Ha-ha. Yes, go elsewhere." Karno motioned for me to follow him. Still toting Fox, I walked a short way into the pine forest before Karno turned to face me. He hesitated before he spoke, evidently trying to articulate his thoughts.

"Tris," Karno said, breaking the awkward pause in conversation. "We go soon."

"Yes?" I encouraged him to continue. This was not news, but I wondered if he had already spoken to Puh and Ru without my knowing.

Karno fingered a pendant that hung around his neck, and I then noticed that it was the necklace he had given Ru. Karno swallowed hard and seemed to be fighting to maintain a calm countenance.

"Ru give Karno back gifts. Ru no go home with me."

Karno's grief was extreme. Tears poured from his eyes, but he quickly brushed them away. I put my arm around his shoulders and Karno succumbed to weeping.

"I am sorry you are so unhappy," I uttered. The words seemed familiar. Had I said them to Bror as well? "I did not know you had approached Puh and Ru, yet. I am sorry it did not go as you hoped." I meant to be comforting, but my sentiments felt so unequal to the depth of Karno's sorrow. Fox did not like to see anyone cry, and he began to wail loudly in accompaniment.

"Karno make baby sad!" Karno observed, breaking off his sobbing. "No cry, Fox." Karno gently patted Fox's back. "No cry. Karno better now, see?"

Karno made a heroic effort to smile and he again wiped his eyes. Fox was not completely convinced that all was well. He looked at Karno and me unsurely.

"It is all right, my little Fox," I said, kissing him and stroking his curly head.

"Gah! Even smoosh face to baby!" Karno winced. "You funny people, Tris. But I come to tell you we leave in one day, maybe two." Given that Karno did not have a clear understanding of our numbers. *One day, maybe two* might mean anything. "Bewok come, too. Bewok see Karno sad and not stay and make Karno more sad. Tell Bewok no worry, Karno take care him. No lions get him."

"We will be sorry to see you leave," I told Karno. It was true; we had come to like these young men. They had brought a lively sense of fun and adventure with them, the likes of which we had never known before. They had also taught us much.

"Karno sorry to go, Tris. Karno like being here. Like your family. Like Black Wolf, he good man. Especially like Ru ..." Karno trailed off. "Karno cannot believe that Ru give back presents before Karno talk to Tor or ask Ru to be my mate. She say she cannot ... she ... she find love. She find love with Bear Wrestler Man." Karno became agitated. "Bear Wrestler Man Ru's cousin! Cousins not mate!"

"But sometimes they do," I said to him, "at least amongst our people. Sometimes a cousin is the only other person available to take as a mate."

"But Tris not take cousin," Karno pointed out.

"No, I did not. Morning Star is the only woman I have ever loved, and I could not love any but her. And besides ... all my cousins are male."

Karno frowned and was silent for a moment.

"That lucky for you sisters." Karno paused again. "Cousins! Gah! You funny people, Tris. You funny people." He sighed. "Karno not know what do. Karno love Ru. Not want leave her. But cannot stay to see her paired with Bear Wrestler Man. If he not save my life, Karno kill Bear Wrestler Man to get Ru. But Karno not do that ... owe him Karno's life."

I shook my head. I not only had serious doubts about Karno's ability to slay Bror, but I also thought it unlikely that Ru would willingly agree to be paired with Karno if he killed or even tried to hurt Bror.

"Ru would not like it if you were to kill someone – anyone, not just Bror – just to remove your competitor. She would not accept you if you were to do that."

Karno stared at his feet.

"Karno not bear to make Ru hate me," he snorted and wiped his nose on his arm. "Karno go now."

I did not know if he meant that he was returning to wherever he had been with his men or leaving us forever.

"Will you be back?" I asked Karno's retreating figure.

Karno simply shrugged in response.

* * *

The Wolf-men's absence made our existence at the family compound seem dull and spiritless. But while Karno was away, Ru and Bror were finally able to be together without fear of further injuring Karno's feelings. I often saw them sitting with each other, holding hands and chatting amicably. I was amazed at the transformation that had come over Ru. She seemed older, more mature.

Everyone was so pleased to see that Ru and Bror had at last found a mutual happiness in each other. Bror had spoken to Puh about Ru several years ago and received Puh's permission to court her. All the same, Bror asked again to make sure that Puh had not changed his mind. Naturally, Puh had not. Only Ru had changed her mind. They began to make plans to be paired on the day of the upcoming full moon. A full moon was supposed to bring luck to a newly paired couple.

* * *

We were surprised when the Wolf-men returned a few days later. As before, they were still dressed in their full complement of clothing, only they were slightly grimier. I wondered at their arrival. Did they come in peace to say goodbye, or did they come as abductors to take Ru away with them?

I scanned the faces of the men, but it was hard to see them with the protruding wolf-head cloaks overshadowing their features. However, the men's stances were relaxed, and I took that to be a good sign. Just the same, I was glad that Ru and Bror were not at the family compound.

We invited them to sit and eat with us. Karno shook his head in response.

"Karno come to bring message," he said, "message for Ru."

"Do you wish for someone to retrieve her?" Hawk queried.

"No," Karno said, holding out his hand to stop him. "Just tell Ru Karno give this back." Karno lowered his wolfskin hood and removed the pendant from his neck. He turned to me and placed it in my hand. "Karno want Ru have this. Ru use it as sign. If she need Karno, she make someone leave it near mountain to north. Big rock by trail have green water flow down. You know rock?"

I did not. I shook my head.

"I know it," Puh replied.

"Tell Ru I come if she make someone leave necklace at rock. Hang where seen." Karno replaced his wolf-head hood. "Karno always come for Ru if need me."

"I will tell her," I promised.

"Good," Karno gave me a strained smile. "Tris, Karno never forget friend. You friend."

"I will never forget either," I assured him.

"And never forget Ru." Karno added, "Maybe Ru find she want or need me. Karno come back for her."

I very much doubted this would come to pass, but I wondered if Karno's love for Ru was so great that he would wait for a signal and hurry back to get her. It was an unlikely but not impossible scenario. If it took the Wolf-men two years to journey all the way here from their home, it would take at least as many years for such a message to be received and responded to. I was impressed that Karno's fervor for Ru was so strong that he would propose such a thing.

"I am sure that Ru will appreciate the gesture," I stated.

"Karno wait for message. Wait until day he die," Karno said solemnly.

"You would wait your whole life for Ru?" Black Wolf asked.

"Yes," Karno nodded earnestly. "Karno always love her. Never stop."

I laid a hand on Karno's shoulder, touched by his devotion to Ru.

"You would stay unpaired your whole life as you wait for her?" Little Fawn spoke up.

"Oh, no," Karno waved the question aside as if it were ridiculous. "The men of my people take many mate. Ru was to be Karno's first. Very big honor to be Great Man's first woman."

A stunned silence fell over the family compound.

"How many mates do you take?" Dor asked.

Karno did not know how the correct word, so he held up eight fingers.

I was sure Ru was not aware of this aspect of the Wolf-men's social practices. She would have been outraged at the very idea if she had known. I then realized how lucky Ru was. Not only because she and Bror had found bliss together, but in that she had not endured a long, arduous journey to a strange land, populated with strange people, only to find herself trapped in a relationship with a man that eventually included up to seven other women. And who knows how many children there would have been to care for?

Karno must have noticed our startled visages.

"Maybe some men in other clan take more women, but this …" Karno held up eight fingers again "… this plenty."

"I should say so," Puh said as he approached Karno. His outward demeanor had not changed much, but I could see that he was definitely irate. In fact, he was fuming to know that Karno had almost lured his daughter into such a completely unacceptable pairing. "Karno, I would like to wish you and your men a pleasant trip back to your homelands. We will be certain to give Ru your message."

I could tell that Puh was not so much saying farewell as inviting them to leave.

The Wolf-men stayed just long enough to talk briefly with us before they left. They spoke of how they would fondly remember their time here. For the most part, we felt the same way about them. Bewok then approached me and put something in my hand.

"This is for your new baby," Bewok said to me. It was a carved pony.

"Many thanks, Bewok." I was genuinely affected. "It is an exquisite gift!"

Bewok smiled gently and nodded.

"I consider you to be my friend, too," he said. "I will never forget the time I have spent here and how good you all were to us. Black Wolf was loyal indeed to stay so far from home while Mino and I recuperated from our wounds. I have felt happy here. I would remain, if allowed, but Karno wishes me to stay with him, so I will go home, too."

"I am sad that you are to leave us," I told Bewok. "I feel you are my friend, too."

"You know, Tris, I do not look forward to this trip. I see that lion every night in my sleep; during my waking hours, it crouches behind every bush. It is all in my mind, of course. I can only hope that those fears will fade." Bewok fingered the neckline of his tunic as he spoke, where vivid scars from the lion's bite were still plainly visible. "When the lion seized onto my shoulder, I fell into a deep dream-world. I have been fighting to come back from that, but sometimes I wonder if it was not easier to live in that world where nothing was real and everything was safe. It is more difficult to be wide awake. Before that time, my friends and I had been adventuring for over two years, and nothing too terrible had occurred. It gave us a feeling of invincibility. Now I know we are not. But never mind. I see my comrades are readying to leave.

Farewell, Tris." Bewok touched my forearm with his fingertips in parting.

"Farewell, Bewok," I said to him, laying my hand on his arm as well. I sympathized with his plight. "May your journey homeward be free from incident, and may you be free from harm. I will keep you and your friends in my thoughts. And when Pony is old enough to understand I will tell her of the kind man who made this gift for her."

Bewok rejoined the rest of Karno's men. Karno spoke a few words to them. And then the Wolf-men were gone.

* * *

Ru and Bror came back from their outing later in the day, looking as enthralled with each other as two people in love could be. When Ru heard the story of the Wolf-men's return and all that Karno had divulged, she was at first awed that Karno so loved her that he would wait for her signal to come for her. Bror stood by her side as she received this news, looking pained that he might again seem lacking in comparison with Karno.

"In light of this, I feel badly to have hurt him," Ru said. "But I realize now that we would not have been happy together."

"It is probably just as well," Little Fawn started, "because, as it turns out, the Wolf-men have the habit of taking as many as eight mates."

"That is impossible!" Ru gasped out the words. "Surely you are joking."

Little Fawn just shook her head.

"It seems excessive to me," I chimed in.

Ru's face went red with anger and showed that she still was capable of displaying a fiery temperament.

"The audacity!" Ru exclaimed, throwing the pendant away from her.

"Do not think on it, Pretty One" Bror said as he touched Ru soothingly. "It is not worth being so angry."

Ru stopped fuming and she relented, giving Bror a slight smile.

"Yes, you are right," she agreed, "but if I never see that man again it will be too soon!"

* * *

One evening as Morning Star and I readied for bed, we were chatting quietly. The little ones were soundly asleep and we were enjoying a rare moment of peace and quiet.

"I believe our family will grow soon," Morning Star announced.

"What?" I was not sure I had heard her correctly. I had been kneeling by the fire, adding wood to the flames, and I was deeply lost in thought about the Wolf-men. They had a very long trek home ahead of them. The nights were much colder now, and I hoped that they would be all right. Sometimes we awakened to a heavy frost on the ground, and I expected that we might receive snow any day now. But they were from a place far north of our lands, and I knew that they must be used to coping with extreme conditions. I wished them well and I wondered if we would ever see them again.

"I said, I believe our family will grow soon," Morning Star repeated.

I spun around to look at her and noted her impish grin.

"Another baby?" I asked incredulously. Even if she was pregnant again, how could she know so soon?

"Not me! Not so far as I know, anyway," Morning Star said lightheartedly. "But have you looked at your dog lately?"

"Raena? You think she is with pups?"

Morning Star nodded.

Raena was lying in her usual place near Fox and Pony's bed chamber. She raised her head and perked up her ears when we spoke her name.

"Raena, come here girl," I called to her.

As Raena rose to her feet, I saw that she had indeed thickened through her belly. I ran my hands along her sides and felt what could be developing puppies.

"Puh was just saying he would like another dog."

"I predict that soon he will have several from which to choose," Morning Star spoke with a laugh as she stroked Raena's head. "Good girl, Raena. So many pups in there … for myself, I am glad myself to have only one at a time!"

"Me, too!" I said as Morning Star and I lay down on our bed. I pulled Morning Star into my arms and kissed her long and lovingly. "I am so happy with our babies," I went on, thinking of our occasional sleepless nights with Pony, "but I can only take so much of that kind of happiness at once."

* * *

The day of the full moon dawned cold and bright. Occasional light snow filtered down from the sky. I saw this only from the doorway of our home, since Morning Star had left early in the morning to help Ru prepare for her pairing day and I was tending our babies while she was away. I only hoped that she would return before Pony wanted to be fed.

Fox was climbing on me and Pony was just beginning to squall when Morning Star popped through our hide-covered doorway, accompanied by a blast of cold air and a few flakes of snow. I could see empathy on her face as she took the baby from me.

"Poor Tris," Morning Star said, baring a breast for the infant. "I hope the babies were good for you!"

"They were fine," I told her. "Is everything almost ready at the main house?"

"Yes, almost. I just have time to feed Pony and get myself cleaned and dressed."

I, too, needed to wash off the various liquids and miscellaneous biological matter that a parent accumulates during the care of his young children and to don my best clothing. Ru and Bror's pairing ceremony was to be held outdoors, so we would need to dress warmly.

I gave Fox a piece of dried meat to gnaw on, in hopes that it would keep him occupied long enough for Morning Star and I to pull ourselves together. By the time Pony's stomach was sufficiently filled, I was ready to resume holding her. Morning Star quickly changed into the only gown she owned that was suitable for this event. It was the same dress she had worn during our pairing ceremony. It was made of tanned deerskin, and the neckline was trimmed with the fur of a marten. The garment had suffered during her abduction, but it had been carefully cleaned and restored so that it appeared almost as good as new. Morning Star wore the dress with pride; she instinctively knew that it suited her well. She glowed with contentedness and good health. I still thought my mate was the most beautiful woman I had ever seen.

"You are lovely," I said as I kissed Morning Star's cheek.

"Thank you, Tris," she smiled at me, "so are you. How lucky am I to have such a good man! Just so long as you do not entertain the idea of adding seven more women to this pairing." Morning Star giggled as she spoke.

"I am not a Wolf-man," I reminded her, "and I am very pleased with things the way they are." I held

Pony slightly to the side so I could embrace Morning Star. "I am the lucky one."

Lastly, Fox was wiped down and stuffed into a different outfit. The poor little boy looked confused at all the sudden activity. This was not something that happened during his usual day. His whole expression asked *what is all the fuss about?*

* * *

Our families were gathering at the center of the homestead, where a considerable feast had been laid out in readiness for the post-pairing celebration. Thankfully, the sun was melting away what little snow had fallen. The still air hung heavily over the family compound, filled with delicious aromas.

Bror and his kin stood expectantly by the fire pit, eagerly waiting for Ru and Puh to emerge from the main house. They did not have long to wait.

I had never seen Ru look so radiant. She was clad in spectacular attire: a dress of carefully fitted and stitched deerskin, with a collar made from the pelt of a lynx. The shoulders and sleeves were also decorated with spotted lynx fur. We did not often hunt animals strictly for their pelts. Puh and I had found this lynx already dead. It had shown signs of having been recently slain by another predator, possibly a cave lion. Smaller predators often suffered attacks from larger animals that wish to steal its kill, leaving the victim to slink off and die of its injuries. Now the beautiful fur of the unfortunate animal adorned my sister's pairing gown.

Snow started to fall once again, floating down from low gray clouds overhead. The flakes settled on Ru's dark red hair, which was coiled and twisted into a mass that was affixed to the back of her head. This was the everyday fashion for a woman of the Old Ones, but the delicate bits of wintery fluff gave the mundane hairstyle an enchanting appearance.

Puh smiled at Ru and Bror as he took both their hands. Then, placing Ru's hand in Bror's, he began to speak the age-old rites.

"Bror, son of Mror, I give you my daughter Ru. I could not have hoped for a better match for my daughter, who, like all my children, has been one of the lights of my life from the time she was born. If only Awna could have lived to see this day. She so wanted this for both of you. May you each have all the love and happiness you so deserve."

"Many thanks, Tor," Bror began. "I gladly accept Ru; I have waited for this moment for almost as long as I can remember."

Ru gazed at Puh open-mouthed.

"Muh-Muh wanted this?" Ru asked Puh, "Why did you not tell me?"

"We did not want to influence your decisions."

Ru seemed to be struck dumb at this statement, but tears dampened her eyes. She stared at Puh for a moment, as he reached out to stroke her cheek.

"We wanted you to choose the man you truly loved," Puh went on.

"Yes," Ru finally smiled, "I have."

Our family and friends crowded around the newly paired couple, embracing and kissing them, and bestowing their good wishes and best hopes for long and happy lives together. This scene made me recall the day when Morning Star and I were paired; we were so shy when we received congratulations from our loved ones. In contrast, Ru and Bror accepted the bounteous verbal offerings with great aplomb.

It was not long before we hungrily set to eating the ceremonial feast. Morning Star, our little ones, and I sat with Black Wolf and Little Fawn, who were eager to dote on their grandchildren while Morning Star and I attempted to feed ourselves.

"What a happy pairing!" Black Wolf gushed. Black Wolf was not only pleased for Bror and Ru, but he was excited at the prospect of attending The People's autumn Gathering, which had begun today. Black Wolf had delayed his departure just long enough to be present at Ru and Bror's ceremony. He was expecting a few men from the Village to stop by tomorrow and together, they would make the trip out to the annual Gathering where Willow Woman and his new son awaited him. "This is a very happy day!" Black Wolf added.

"Oh yes," Morning Star agreed. "While I liked Karno, I must say that I am delighted that Bror and Ru finally worked things out. I wonder what made Ru change her mind. Did she at last see Karno for the goodhearted but at times rather graceless man that he was, or was it Bror's stalwart love and fine qualities that won her over?"

Personally, I thought it was Bror's kisses that had reversed Karno's fortunes. I know I would not want to face a future that did not include kissing my mate. If Karno was determined to withhold that affection from Ru, I could well understand her decision.

"It all turned out for the best," Black Wolf observed. "If any man had treated my daughter so offhandedly, enticing her into a pairing and only later announcing that his people took up to eight mates, I would have been tempted to pummel him into oblivion."

"Yes, Puh was furious," I said. "When Karno spoke of the additional mates, I did not think I had ever seen Puh so angry."

"When that bit of information was disclosed, I wonder that our men did not desert us in droves and follow the Wolf-men to their homeland," Little Fawn pondered out loud.

"Oh, Mama!" Morning Star laughed. "Do not think such unflattering thoughts of our men!"

"*Gah!* Eight mates!" Morning Star's brother Swift River said with apparent revulsion in his voice. "I used to think that I wanted to be a Wolf-man, but not if it means having to live with all those women!"

"Yes," agreed Hawk. "Girls! Gah! Those Wolf-men must be mad!"

"I am not even sure I want one mate, except for that someone will have to do my cooking and sewing," Swift River went on. "I wonder how long it will take to grow my hair out again?"

"Hmmm. Well, you may change your mind as you become older," Black Wolf said, chuckling.

The late-fall days were much shorter now. After the food was consumed, it was then time to help Ru and Bror settle into their home while we still had a little sunlight left. They were to be moved into Puh and Ria's house. Puh and Ria lived in a small earthen dwelling carved into the hillside, just like the one Morning Star and I inhabited, but now they were giving up their home to the newly paired twosome. Since Muh's death, Puh had been too grieved to reside at the main family domicile, despite that it was the only home he had known throughout his life. But now enough time had passed that Puh could once again take up residence in his ancestral homestead. It was somewhat crowded these days. Besides Gran and my younger siblings, Aunt Vee and my cousins were also sheltering there. Puh, Ria, and Baby Mror's belongings were shifted to the bed chamber that Puh and Muh had shared, and Bror and Ru's things were toted next door to the cozy haven that awaited them.

As I assisted with the transfer, I was pleased to see that Ria and Puh had taken pains to make the tiny household comfortable and well-stocked. A lively fire blazed in the hearth, and an inviting bed piled with lush fur blankets was arranged with care.

When I had a moment to get in a word with Bror, I stopped to converse with him.

"Did you have a chance to make a pairing gift for Ru?" I asked.

"I did. I am afraid it is a very modest gift. But when I gave it to her this morning she seemed quite pleased," Bror replied.

"That is good! What did you give her?" I expected that I might see Ru wearing some new ornament, but if she was, I had not noticed it.

"I made wooden rods to hold her upswept hair in place," Bror said. "I knew your father had made ivory rods for your mother when they were paired and thought that would be something that I could make, too. Only I did not have any ivory. So I chose the best wood I could find: the branches were close-grained and very straight, and I cut and smoothed them to the right size. I hope to replace these rods with new ones of ivory some day; Ru deserves ivory, not plain old wood. She was very sweet and very gracious when I gave them to her, but I cannot help but think that my gift is unworthy of her."

I could understand Bror's sentiment.

"I, too, felt that way when Morning Star and I were paired and I gave a shell necklace," I admitted. "I looked at the dazzling beauty I had won, the love of my life, and the necklace seemed so clumsily made. But she still wears it all the time. She never takes it off. I can only surmise that she must see not the necklace, but all the love that went into making it." I put a hand on Bror's shoulder. "I will hazard a guess that Ru sees the same thing."

"Many thanks, Tris," Bror said as he smiled broadly. "I hope you are right."

* * *

That night Morning Star and I were lying peacefully in our bed, still blissfully tangled up together. This had been an auspicious day. I felt full. Full of love for the woman I adored and my darling babies. Full of affection for my family and friends. Full of food and drink. Full with the goodness of life. I absently touched Morning Star's face tenderly as I drifted off to sleep.

* * *

It is summer, and Morning Star stands on a hillside cradling a baby in her arms. I do not recognize this place. A pair of vultures sweep lazy circles against a clear blue sky. Numerous children and dogs engage in a spirited chase through the tall grasses. I wonder: Where are we? And is it possible that all these children and all these dogs belong to me?

~ finis ~

Author's Note

As usual, we have the obligatory disclaimer: All characters in this novel are fictional, and any resemblances to persons either living or dead are purely coincidental. I have been asked whether these portrayals are based on anyone I know. I can only say that there is a bit of myself, however minute, in each character.

* * *

Although considerable effort was put into making this work as historically accurate as possible, the constant influx of new discoveries and ever-changing theories makes it impossible to ensure that the novel's details will hold up to the test of time. Each book in this series is written with the best information I have at hand.

Until recently science has looked to fossils, stone tools, and other hard evidence to build hypotheses about early man (such as the Cro-Magnon,

Neanderthal, etc.), but some studies are now beginning to look at the conditions survived by early peoples to extrapolate new theories about these enigmatic times. Exploration and archaeological digs at the Denisova Cave in Siberia have brought to light fascinating artifacts dating back at least 125,000 – 180,000 years. The cave's frigid year-round temperature has preserved many items that would have been destroyed under other conditions. These finds have shown that some early peoples used technologies far beyond what had been considered available during that period. The fortuitous discovery of this site has provided us with a mere glimpse into the lives of prehistoric humans. There is so much that we can only guess at, and so much yet to be revealed.

New genetic research has brought forth more interesting data. It had been assumed that Neanderthal families were closely related to one another, but recent testing has found that some were not. The number of Neanderthal individuals whose DNA has been analyzed are still very few and we must be careful not to draw definite conclusions about an entire people based on such a small quantity of samples.

Fossilized Neanderthal remains are also bringing new information to light. Recently scientists have been studying tartar buildup on Neanderthal teeth, from which it can be determined what they ate and what they are assumed to have ingested for medicinal purposes. The teeth and tartar also provide clues to whether they had adequate nutrition and what was in their saliva (more on that below).

Some scientists are now revising their opinions of the number of Neanderthals who inhabited the earth at any one time. The new figures are projected to be slightly higher than originally estimated. Although in some areas Neanderthals struggled and were on the wane, in others their populations seem to have thrived – and in fact appear to have survived for thousands of years after the demise of their fellow Neanderthals in other parts of Eurasia.

* * *

While the Cro-Magnon and the Neanderthal and Denisovan peoples differed physically from one another, it may be helpful to remember that although their individual cultures may have accounted for slightly different styles of traditional clothing, coiffeurs, ornamentations, etc., they were still limited to animal skin or plant fiber-based clothing. In the absence of shaving methods, adult men probably wore beards, which would have hidden many minor variations in their facial features. Early modern humans in general were three or four inches taller than most Neanderthals, and Neanderthals (and probably Denisovans) had a heavier build than early modern humans; but I don't think that under an Ice Age wardrobe of tanned hides and thick furs the differences in build would have been terribly noticeable. In other words, to our eyes, there wouldn't have been a great disparity in their appearances.

In addition, as the millennia passed, the Neanderthal people's appearance began to change. Later fossils show that some were beginning to lose their brow ridges and others were starting to develop a definite chin. It is not known today whether this was a result of evolution or admixture with early modern humans, or both.

* * *

I would also like to address the various ways different cultures have viewed kissing throughout history. Some see kissing as a rather recent addition to human behavior. The hard evidence, such as what is depicted in ancient art, shows that the practice dates back approximately 3,500 years. Yet, recent analysis of Neanderthal dental plaque revealed that they shared a particular bacterium (*Methanobrevibacter oralis*) with early modern humans that could have occurred only through an exchange of saliva. It is hard to imagine another way this could have happened unless the two populations engaged in kissing. We can speculate on other possible explanations, but I generally go with the Occam's razor theory: *"Other things being equal, simpler explanations are generally better than more complex ones."*

I was born into an affectionate family, so when doing research for this book I was startled to discover that (according to different sources) anywhere between 10 percent and 40 percent of cultures do not kiss.

Most Western peoples embrace kissing, and some Eastern peoples do not. Within some cultures it is considered to be a vile and very unsanitary practice. In others it is acceptable only in certain social situations or in absolute privacy. I do not mean the story to be either pro- or anti-kissing. I simply hope to portray the situation for what it is.

* * *

It also may be of interest to note that in times past, some cultures did believe that their long hair gave them a sensory boost when it came to hunting, tracking, and interacting with nature. Back in the mid-1800's the United States Army is reported to have done a study on this very topic when they noticed that their aboriginal scouts were less effective after their hair was shorn in compliance with Army regulations; the findings supposedly confirmed that the scouts' sensory perception was lessened after a haircut – though whether this was psychosomatic or a true physical change that came over the men is still up for debate. Internet myth also holds that similar research was done during the Vietnam War, but that claim has since been refuted.

* * *

This book series has brought me on a fascinating journey. I have been interested in history, nature, and paleoanthropology for as long as I can remember, so it is with rapt attention and eagerness that I delve into these topics for my research. Although the story originates in my mind, when I am writing it is very real to me. I block out the world and I am transported to ancient times. It is almost as though I am reporting events as witnessed by me, as opposed to creating a plot line and developing characters. I hope my readers enjoy my work as much as I enjoy its production.

* * *

The fourth book in this ongoing saga of Tris's life, *The Dreamer IV ~ The Cave of Bones,* is due to be released in the summer of 2019.

Finally, I would like to extend my love and gratitude to all my family and friends who have steadfastly shown their support for my literary endeavors.

With warmest regards,
E. A. Meigs

Index of European Ice Age Animals

Antelope (Saiga Antelope) These small antelope (24 to 36 inches tall at the shoulder weighing approximately 80 to 140 pounds) ranged over a good part of the northern hemisphere. They are exceptional in appearance due to their unusual muzzles, which feature a long, flexible snout that looks much like a truncated elephant's nose.

Aurochs (Extinct) Predecessor of domesticated cattle. Size varied between 61 to 71 inches at the shoulder, with weights of 1500 to 3300 pounds. Their horns could reach up to 31 inches in length. Sometimes aurochs is spelled "auroch", but from

my readings, I am lead to believe that but the "s" is often included even when the animal is referred to in singular form because it is an alternative form of spelling "ox" and isn't intended to indicate plurality.

Boar Wild boars are the plows of the animal world. They are built for digging. Their heads and massive

shoulders make up a good part of their bodies and their large, sharp tusks, which continue to grow throughout the life of the animal, are very effective at turning over soil. The largest adult male boars can reach weights of nearly 800 pounds and attain a shoulder height of 49 inches. Sows (females) are much smaller and they lack the mane and thick shoulder/back "shield" of the boars. Their tusks are also of a more modest size. The coloring of their coats varies from anything between white and black, but most tend to run towards darker shades.

Brown Bear

(Eurasian Brown Bear) Although this bear is called a "brown bear" its color can range from black to a tawny light brown. Males average 550 to 650 pounds but very large specimens can exceed

1000 pounds. Females weigh 330 to 550 pounds. During pre-history, the brown bear did consume some plant matter, but it was generally carnivorous.

Cave Bear (Extinct) This was a very large, stout bear. The average male weighed in at 880 to 1100 pounds.

Females averaged a little over half that (495 to 550 pounds). Despite their size, bone analysis and other indicators suggest that cave bears were primarily herbivores.

Cave Lion (Extinct) (European Cave Lion) These efficient feline predators were some of the largest known cats in animal history. Based on skeletal

remains, it is speculated that the males may have reached 11 ½ feet in length from nose to tip of the tail, and weighed over 880 pounds.

Chamois A medium-sized goat/antelope. They are 28-31 inches tall at the shoulder and range in weight from 55-132 pounds. Besides being a fine source of meat, their hides were used to make garments.

Crow (Carrion Crow) A large black bird, approximately 18 to 21 inches in length with a large, heavy beak that is well adapted to catching and eating small prey such as mice, frogs, insects, etc., and scavenging off the kills of other animals.

Elk (Eurasian Elk) ("moose" in North America) A medium-sized elk/moose, now extinct in many parts of Europe. They average from just over 600 to just over 1000 pounds, with shoulder heights at 5.6 - 6.9 feet.

Fallow Deer A medium-sized deer, about 30 to 37

inches at shoulder height and weighing 66 pounds (small doe) to 220 pounds (large buck), although unusually large bucks may tip the scales at 330 pounds. Their winter coats are brown, but they are freckled with white dots on their backs and sides during the summer.

Giant Deer (extinct) (Irish Elk) The giant deer was

one of the largest deer ever to walk the earth. Commonly, it has mistakenly been called an Irish elk, although it was neither exclusive to Ireland nor an elk.

This huge deer averaged nearly 7 feet in height at the shoulder and carried antlers with a spread that could span 12 feet. They are estimated to have weighed nearly 1200 to just over 1300 pounds but larger individuals could have reached upwards of 1500 pounds.

Horse   The Eurasian Ice Age horse came in many

different varieties. They were more than likely the size of modern ponies and appeared in all colors, spots and stripes. They may have resembled the Przewalski's horse that still exist today or the now-extinct Tarpan horse.

Ibex (Alpine Ibex)   A moderate-sized, dun-colored mountain goat. The bucks' horns sometimes reach 39 inches in length. The does' horns may grow to a length of nearly 14 inches. Similarly, bucks achieve a much larger body size (35 to 40 inches at the withers and weighing from 150 to over 250 pounds) than the does (29 to 33 inches at the withers and 37 to just over 70 pounds).

Lynx (Eurasian Lynx) The biggest of all species of lynx. Approximately 24 to 30 inches at the shoulder, and including its short tail, it may be 31 to 51 inches in body length. The largest males weighed nearly 100 pounds, but the typical lynx will run between 18 (very small female)  and 66 pounds (good-sized male).

Marten (European Pine Marten) A small, weasel-like animal with dark brown fur, often with blond markings or a blond bib on its chest.  At a little less than 3 ½ pounds and about 21 inches in length, the marten was hunted for its beautiful, silky fur.

Mink (European Mink) A small mink,

even the largest is just under 20 inches in length and only about 1¾ pounds. They have been prized for their dense, luxurious winter coats.

Porcupine (Old World Porcupine) This rodent wears an impressive coat of quills, some of which may be up to 14 inches in length (Crested Porcupine). These species of porcupines come in a variety of sizes: the smallest adults run from 11inches to 34 inches long, and may weigh between 3.3 to 60 pounds.

Red Deer (European Red Deer) Another very large species of deer. The buck weighs in at 350 to 550 pounds (48 inches at the shoulder) and does run 260 to 370 pounds (45 inches at the shoulder). These deer, unsurprisingly, are known for their reddish coats. During autumn, the males often have a short mane on the backs of their necks.

Red Fox The biggest of the fox species, the adult ranges from 14 to 20 inches tall at the shoulder and weigh from 5 to nearly 40 pounds. These animals were often harvested for their fine fur.

Reindeer (Also known as caribou) This important game animal consists of several different subspecies and varied in size from 120 to 550 pounds. Color varied as well, but all subspecies shared many of the same basic characteristics, such as a fairly

impressive set of antlers (in most reindeer, both the bucks and the does grow antlers) and a two-layered coat of fur, featuring a woolly undercoat that thickens dramatically each winter and an overcoat of longer, coarse, hollow hairs.

Roe Deer (Western Roe Deer)   This small deer averages just over two feet to two feet, 6 inches at the withers, and a mere 33 to 77 pounds. Nonetheless, they were an important source of meat for prehistoric humans.

Sheep   The actual breed(s) of ancient sheep that roamed

Ice-Age Europe are unknown, but it is recognized that sheep were hunted and eaten by early man. It is possible that the Mouflon (shown in image) is the modern day link to prehistoric sheep. The Mouflon have a shoulder height of less than 3 feet and weigh from 75 to 110 pounds.

Snow Leopard This beautiful cat is well adapted to life in a cold, mountainous habitat. It has a stout build and long, dense fur that varies in color from white to pale gray, with dark gray to black spotted markings. It is about 24 inches at the shoulder with a weight of 60 to 120

pounds, although larger males have been noted at 165 pounds. Their fur was considered to be very desirable and they have long been hunted for their pelts.

Vulture (Eurasian Griffin Vulture) This large scavenging bird may have a wingspan of over 9 feet and weigh as much as 33 pounds, although most individuals range from 14 to 25 pounds. It is known that early men consumed the meat of vultures.

Wisent (European Bison) An impressive animal, the

wisent is the heaviest land animal that still resides in modern day Europe. Fully grown specimens range from 5 to 6 ½ feet at the shoulder and weigh 660 (small female) to more than 2000 pounds (large male). The wisent was an important source of food and hides for prehistoric humans.

Wolf (Eurasian Wolf) These are the largest of the

European or Asian wolves. Their sizes vary greatly from 70 to 212 pounds. Although their coats could be black, white, or even reddish, by far the most common color was a grey/buff and white combination of medium length, dense fur.

Wood Grouse (Western Capercaillie) This Eurasian bird is the largest of the grouse species, weighing as much as 15 pounds. The cocks have an average weight of 9 pounds and a wingspan of 36 to 48 inches. The hen is considerably more modest in size, with a weight of

approximately 4 pounds and a wingspan of 28 inches.

Woolly Mammoth (Extinct) This large mammal lived in Eurasia and North America, and was similar in size to today's African Elephants, but with considerably longer tusks, a shorter tail, and much smaller

ears. The males of this huge species could attain heights of up to 11 feet at the withers and weigh over 12,000 pounds. Females were somewhat smaller, although still impressive in size at up to 9½ feet at the shoulder and weights up to nearly 9000 pounds. Their hairy hides came in a wide range of colors that could be anything from blond to quite dark. They were protected from the extreme Ice Age weather conditions by a double fur coat that consisted of a short, dense, woolly undercoat and strands of long outer guard hairs.

Woolly Rhinoceros (Extinct) Looking much like a

modern rhinoceros in a heavy fur coat, the woolly rhinoceros sported two horns on its long snout and carried its thick body on short, stout legs. This animal averaged about 4000 to 6000 pounds, with a shoulder height of about 6½ feet. The larger front horn that grew from the woolly rhinoceros' nose could reach lengths of 24 inches.

About the Author
E.A. Meigs

I was raised on Cape Cod (Brewster, Massachusetts, USA) at a time when the Cape was still a rural area made up of woodlands, marshes, beaches, streams, and ponds. There, my life was divided between the land and sea. My father was a commercial fisherman, backyard boat builder, and an outdoorsman; so I had an early introduction to boats, working in the commercial fishing industry and spending lots of time in the local fields and forests. When I wasn't on a boat or roaming around the great outdoors, chances are I was reading or writing. I have been a compulsive writer literally since I could first put words on paper, producing my first full length novel at ten years old. Even at that age, my goal in life was to someday find a way to combine my love of nature, the outdoors, and writing.

After raising a family and embarking on a long and varied career that included many years working on and around boats and in the commercial fishing industry; a stint with Florida Fish & Wildlife in a small field office; and other jobs that actually allowed me to use my writing skills, I awoke one day with *The Dreamer* in my head. I began writing the novel with the intention of producing just one book, but as the story progressed it became apparent that the plot would require much more than one volume to tell the tale.

I have two wonderful adult daughters and eight delightful grandchildren. I am an avid camper and I strive to get out hiking as often as possible, daily, when my schedule allows.